LADY OF VISION

AMANDA LABONTÉ

Published in Canada by Engen Books, St. John's, NL.

Library and Archives Canada Cataloguing in Publication

Title: Lady of vision / Amanda Labonté.
Names: Labonté, Amanda, author.
Description: Series statement: Daughters of aether ; 1
Identifiers: Canadiana (print) 20200350137 | Canadiana (ebook) 20200350161 |
ISBN 9781989473863
   (softcover) | ISBN 9781989473870 (PDF)
Classification: LCC PS8623.A255 L33 2020 | DDC C813/.6—dc23

Distributed by:
Engen Books
www.engenbooks.com
submissions@engenbooks.com

First mass market paperback printing: January 2021

Cover Design: Ellen Curtis
Cover Image: DepositPhotos.com

LADY OF VISION

DAUGHTERS OF AETHER BOOK 1

ENGEN
BOOKS

To Laura and Gabby.
The best, most supportive of friends.

CHAPTER ONE

Hazel ducked behind a wooden crate and pushed a curl up under her cap. She wished she'd been able to do a proper braid before heading out before dawn, but there hadn't been any time to waste.

She was grateful that the clear night meant there was no need to worry about the air. A sliver of moon was visible with just the slightest haze of red like a lens over it's brightness. The dank smell of the Thames filled her nostrils, replacing the usual tinny smell of aether dust that filled the London streets during the day. As she took in the dockyard in the early morning light, the tall ships with their lowered sails flapped in the breeze like ragged ghosts.

But that wasn't what she'd come to see.

An airship was moored further down, its large white balloon looming over a schooner. From the looks of its narrow width, Hazel figured it was a merchant ship used for coastal runs. She might have gone for a closer look under other circumstances; right now she had other plans.

Under her booted foot was a dampened copy of the *London Daily*. She glanced at the headline: "Princess' birthday celebrations waste of money." If everything went as expected this morning, her next story would be a front page headline, rather than be buried on the society pages.

She scanned the docks again. They were mostly empty, at least they were until she gazed upon the *Florentina*, where a dozen men and boys were unloading crates.

"Gotcha," Hazel muttered as she stepped fully into view and sauntered down the dock. It was so much easier to move about in trousers than it was in her skirts.

Perhaps she would try to start a new fashion. Young ladies wearing trousers.

Her maid would quit on the spot.

"You there, boy!" A man's voice boomed from the deck of the ship. "Quit lazing and get up here."

Hazel hid her grin and hurried up the gangplank. This was the opportunity she'd been hoping for. She stopped in front of a bearded man with a scar down one side of his face.

Probably from a knife fight.

Or so Hazel imagined.

"Sorry, sir," she said in what she hoped was a passable young male voice. "Where do you want me?"

"Get below."

Hazel climbed down the ladder, into the hull of the ship. If the strong smell of mildew and the splintered deck boards were anything to go by, the *Florentina* had seen better days. Her feet landed in a shallow greenish puddle that was illuminated by a lamp hanging off a rusted hook in the wall. There were three boys already in the cargo area, none over seventeen or eighteen, but one wearing a navy blue cap stood apart, clearly taking charge.

"What am I supposed to do with a scrawny thing like you?" He asked, looking Hazel up and down.

"The man up on the deck told me to come down here," Hazel said. "The one with the scar on his face."

As she'd expected, Blue Cap didn't appear to want to cross the bearded man.

"Fine." He pointed at the stack of barrels. "See if you can get some of those down. Harry and Georgie, you hand the barrels up on deck."

The barrels were stacked three high, making the tallest just barely within Hazel's reach. She joined the others and stood on her tiptoes and pulled one down.

"What's in these anyway?" She asked the boy called Georgie. He was a few inches taller than her but even skinnier. Hazel couldn't be sure in the low light, but she thought he was probably of African descent.

"Not for us to know."

Hazel examined the top of one of the barrels. There was no spout and no easy way to open it.

"Hell's bells," she muttered to herself.

"You wanna get a move on?" Blue Cap called from two stacks over. "We don't want to be here all day."

Hazel reached up, ready to get another barrel when the tingling in her temple started.

She gave her head a quick shake and took a deep breath. She hadn't had an episode in ages, no way was she having one now. Not here.

As the tingling persisted, Hazel reached out, grabbing onto something for support as she waited for the feeling to pass. She could feel the darkness pulling at her, but her brain fought back.

"What are you doing?" Georgie's question dragged her back to the present just in time to feel the barrel she was leaning against tip forward with a thud, splintering apart and spilling its acidic contents on the wooden decking, mixing into murky green puddle water.

"You ignorant foozler," the blue capped boy shouted. "That'll come out of your wages."

But Hazel didn't pay any attention to him. She was watching the contents of the barrel spread across the floor, her brows drawn together in a frown.

"Vinegar," Hazel said to her maid as she stripped off the button-down shirt. "They were barrels of vinegar."

"Yes," Penny said, picking up the discarded items and wrinkling her nose. "I can smell it."

"What I want to know," Hazel said, removing a red, leather-bound diary from the waistband of her breeches and tossing it onto the bed, "is why anyone would bother bringing in a shipment of black market vinegar? It's one thing that there's an adequate supply of."

Penny dropped the clothes into a pile near the door. Though not much older than Hazel, she'd been working for the Winchesters long enough to know the quirks of all the family members.

Hazel took off her cap and tried to run a hand through her curly red hair but it was a mass of tangles. Penny swiped at her hands and led Hazel to the seat in front of the vanity.

"Perhaps someone is doing a great deal of pickling," Penny said, picking through the curls in an effort to separate and pin them. She hit a snarl and Hazel hissed, but Penny continued her pining.

"Or maybe there was something else on that boat and I missed it."

"How do you know you aren't on some fool's errand?" Penny asked. "You're sneaking about before dawn on gossip you overheard in the print room."

"There must be something to it." Hazel stood up and took off her breeches. Penny held out a chemise for her to pull over her head. "And, anyway, why bother unloading before dawn? If all is above board, why not wait until sunup?"

"Because the air quality is better at night," Penny said, helping Hazel shimmy into a corset. "Most of the factories have their smokestacks shutdown and it's faster work if everyone doesn't have to wear an airmask."

"Of course you're right," Hazel said, her body jerking as Penny pulled on the strings. "It's still quite disappointing. I thought I'd gotten a big break."

"Deep breath," Penny said, leaning back and giving one last tug. "And why do you need to chase down a black market story? What's wrong with your column? There's always a ball or a luncheon to cover."

Hazel pursed her lips. "Being Lady Hazel can be quite dull sometimes."

"Says the first ever lady who was given permission to write for a daily newspaper."

"It's something," Hazel said, trying to take a deep breath. "Can you loosen the stays? Just a little?"

"Half an inch," Penny said. "That's it."

"You're a gem."

Penny loosened the corset and helped Hazel into one of the proper gray dresses she wore to work. She then sat Hazel down and fixed her hair into a respectable chignon.

Hazel glanced at the clock on her dressing table as Penny adjusted her lace collar. She needed to get moving.

"How do I look?" She asked, standing up.

"Like a proper lady headed to work."

"Proper ladies don't go to work."

"Fine. An improper lady then."

Hazel grinned. "Do you have my reticule?"

Penny handed over the beaded blue purse. Hazel picked up the red journal off the bed and dropped it inside.

"You'll also need this." Penny picked up the cotton satchel that contained her aether mask, securing it to the strap of the reticule. "It's a cloudy day, you'll need it."

"Thanks."

"And don't forget your mother's visiting hours this afternoon."

"Is it Tuesday already?"

"You know it is. And with the start of the season right around the corner—"

"I know. I'll be there."

"Before you go, is there anything you need picked up at the markets before tomorrow?"

Hazel frowned. There were still two days before the start of the season. "What's tomorrow?"

"The Day of Mourning," Penny said.

"Of course," Hazel said, a sense of impending dread

washing through her. "I hadn't realized it was that time of year already."

"Your mother gave the cook a list and we're all preparing for a quiet day."

"Yes, Mama always finds the afternoon hard. Thank you."

Penny nodded and picked up the trousers and cotton shirt on her way to Hazel's dressing room. "I'll do my best to get the smell out, but I'm not making any promises."

"You're an angel," Hazel said, pausing for one last glance in the mirror before heading off to work.

Someone was beating on his door.

Duncan Walters put his pillow over his head and rolled over. He underestimated the size of the bunk he'd passed out on the night before and hit the floor with a thunk.

"Mr. Walters!" The door crashed open and his valet, Myers, rushed in. "Are you all right?"

"I'm fine." Duncan sat up, squinting as Myers pulled back the curtain on the porthole. Light poured into the small cabin. "What time is it?"

"Just gone seven."

Duncan stood up, rubbed his shoulder where it had hit the floor, and flopped back on the bed. "I told you to leave me until at least noon."

"Yes but—"

"You remember what time I went to bed last night?"

"Yes but—"

"Close the door behind you."

"It's your mother."

Duncan threw the pillow onto the floor, sat up again, and looked at his valet. Myers was two years his junior, but acted like an anxious old man, complete with mustache and thinning hairline.

At least he was starting to get some color back in his pasty complexion. Myers had spent most of their time aboard suffering from sea sickness.

"What about my mother?"

"She sent a telegram."

Duncan's head throbbed. "Myers?"

"Yes, sir?"

"Where are we?"

"On a boat, sir."

Duncan closed his eyes and rubbed the bridge of his nose. "And where's that boat?"

"About a three days voyage to the Shetlands, sir."

Duncan cleared his throat. "So how did my mother get a telegram here?"

"She sent a naval airship, sir."

"Of course she did." Duncan scratched the three day's worth of stubble on his chin. Shaving had not been a priority. He took in the mess of clothing around him. They'd taken on a rather large shipment of salted herring from Iceland that would do well in the Scottish markets and a much smaller shipment of unsweetened schnapps that needed to be consumed before reaching British soil.

"I believe the captain of the airship is awaiting your reply."

"Pack my trunks, Myers."

"Are we leaving?"

Duncan stood up, the floor rocking beneath his feet,

either from the boat or his hangover, he wasn't sure.

"Yes."

"But we don't know what the telegram says."

Duncan got his bearings and headed for the wash-stand. He leaned over the basin and poured the contents of the jug over his head.

"My mother sent the navy to bring me a message," Duncan said, toweling himself off with a shirt he picked up off the floor. His dark hair had become unruly. He couldn't remember the last time he'd had it cut. "Do you really think we can stay?"

"You have a point sir."

The valet turned to the door, but Duncan called him back. "Before you start with my trunk get me something for my head."

"It's already being prepared in the galley, sir."

"You're a saint and a scholar."

"Yes sir. I'll just leave the telegram here on the desk."

Myers took an armload of discarded clothing and headed into the small dressing room attached to Duncan's sleeping compartment.

Once he was alone, Duncan picked up the envelope and ripped it open. There were four words typed across the middle of the page.

Your father needs you.

CHAPTER TWO

The smell of hot ink hit Hazel's nostrils as soon as she entered the *London Daily's* offices. She took a deep breath before heading to her desk.

"What's the story, gigglemug?" William, the elderly copy editor asked as she passed his office.

"Same as always," Hazel paused outside his door. "I left my journal here and I wanted to grab it before heading out to cover the Ladies' League public talk."

"Better you than me."

"That's why I'm the highest paid female columnist in London."

William smiled, his blue eyes crinkling at the corners. "And I'm sure that would still be true even if you weren't the only one."

"You're enough to make a lady's head turn," Hazel laughed. "Have you had time to consider my request to take on some of the editing duties?"

"If it were up to me, I'd have you on the editorial staff in a heartbeat. But I have to get confirmation from the big man himself."

Hazel glanced at the editor's empty office. "Is there

any word on Mr. Walters?"

William's smile disappeared. "Nothing yet."

Hazel gave a quick nod. "I'd best get going."

"Before you do, I have a special assignment for you."

"Not a luncheon?"

"No. I said this one is special."

William held out an invitation printed on white card-stock with a naval crest featured prominently front and center.

"What's this?"

"An invitation to tour the *HMA Triumph* before it's de-commissioned."

Hazel reached for the card. "You're giving me the assignment?"

"You're more than ready for it."

"You won't be disappointed."

"Don't I know it?"

Hazel smiled as she headed to her desk. She stopped on her way to pick up a fresh-off-the-press copy of the morning's paper. The front page had the headline: "Remembering the Rain." Hazel skimmed through the opening paragraph.

On the twenty-first anniversary of the event known to all Londoners as 'The Day of Mourning' the country continues to rebuild. The horrific event, marked by poisonous aether rains, brought about the treaty that ended the Great Sea War. In a statement from the palace, a representative for Her Majesty Queen Catherine...

Hazel put down the paper and opened the drawer in

her desk, taking out the plain brown journal she used for ordinary events and placing her red one back inside. She locked the drawer and put the key in her reticule next to her best fountain pen, her pillbox, pocket watch and her press pass, which was really just her photograph on a card with the London Daily's address and the publisher's signature on the back. She glanced at the pocketwatch. She was fairly certain she could make it on foot and be, more or less, on time.

Just before stepping outside, she pulled the brass and leather aether mask out of its pouch and secured it around her mouth and nose. The mask covered the lower half of her face, with valves on each side to purify the air.

Hazel emerged into the London streets. A blanket of rusty fog hung about the city on overcast days. A combination of the heavy aether smoke from the factories and the low cloud cover left behind a reddish mist. Without a mask, the air had a metallic taste that coated the tongue.

She rounded a corner and dodged a steam carriage as she crossed the street to the Royal Stuart Hall. Eleven flags from countries throughout Europe and Africa hung off the front of the brown stone building. The Hall was where the Alliance of Nations had first been formed almost thirty years before at the Peace Summit of 1842.

Which was an ironic name, as the United Kingdom was still very much at war.

She flashed her press pass to the doorman who barely glanced at her before waving her in. She paused in the marble tiled entry hall to both take off her mask and take in the mural on the history of flight that dominated the ceiling thirty feet above. From a ship at sea, to a ship in the sky, the mural was a tribute to the discovery of the aether engines that had given the United Kingdom the necessary advantage to force a treaty with the Americas.

Knowing she couldn't put it off any longer, Hazel went toward one of three sets of blue and gold double doors that led into the five-hundred seat auditorium.

The stage was already set with Lady Ashburn at the podium, looking out at the crowd from beneath a wide-brimmed hat with no less than a dozen handsewn silk flowers as its centerpiece. Though there were several empty rows, Hazel was surprised at the turnout.

The audience was mainly female and skewed toward her mother's peers, but there were still more younger women than Hazel would have expected.

"First of all, I would like to start with a moment of silence so that we may remember the casualties of the Day of Mourning," Lady Ashburn began. She tilted her head to look out at her audience and for a fraction of a second it appeared as though her hat would succumb to gravity and slide right off her head. But even hats feared Lady Ashburn and the flowered concoction stayed firmly in place.

Hazel bent her head, waiting until Lady Ashburn began speaking again before unscrewing the cap of her pen and taking out her notebook.

Her readers would be less interested in the content of the speech and more interested in who was there and what they were wearing. The front rows were occupied by the exclusive league members—those ladies of society who had both title and enough wealth to be able to afford the exorbitant league subscriptions. The middle was taken up by women like herself, titled but lacking a family fortune. The final rows were the curious onlookers.

"I stand before you this afternoon to promote the good works being done by the League of Ladies," Lady Ashburn continued. "Most recently we raised the funds necessary to open a new wing at the London Home for Children where the most vulnerable in our society can receive treatment for the aether lung disease. It is our most precious duty as the League to ensure that the noble class continues to thrive during these most challenging times so that we can reach out to those in need."

Hazel skimmed the front row, taking down the names of the prominent attendees. Even with their backs to her, she could still recognize the society women. It was a talent that had been honed from years of covering such events.

"The contribution to charitable endeavors, to running the great British estates, to keeping the very culture alive, must not be overlooked."

None of the League Ladies worked outside the home. It was a requirement of membership. All families were required to send a child either into the workforce or into the navy for service.

Unless, of course, you could afford to pay the Idle Tax.

"In our haste to reassert the dominance of the British Empire, we must not lose sight of our values," Lady Ashburn said, returning to a popular theme. "Many noble women have been subjected to toiling outside the home like tradesmen. Many of our sons have been conscripted to aid the Royal Navy in protecting Europe from the threat of the Americas. We have not forgotten you."

"No, so long as you are highly born and white," Matilda Martin, the *Daily's* only female photographer, whispered as she sat down next to Hazel, her wooden photobox with lenses sticking out of one end at the ready.

"You know she was one of us, don't you?" Hazel said as Matilda tucked her mask in a courier style leather bag.

"Who?" Matilda brushed a dark curl back from her face and looked up at the lectern then back to Hazel. "No!"

"Lady Ashburn was a nurse before Lord Ashburn came along."

"No wonder she wants to liberate us all." Matilda shook her head. "That sounds like awful work."

"Unlike the news business," Hazel said. Then she nodded at the stranger seated at the end of the front row. "Do you know who that lady is? I've never seen her before."

"But I'm sure you've heard of her," Matilda said. "That's the Duchess of Roscommon."

"Really?" Hazel quirked an eyebrow. "What's she doing in London?"

"Apparently the Duke has taken up temporary residence here."

"Why do I feel like there's more to the story?"

Matilda leaned in close. "The word around London is that it's no longer safe for the Queen's representatives near the West-Irish border."

Hazel bit her bottom lip. "You think they've sided with the Americas?"

Matilda shrugged. "Who really knows what goes on in the colonies?"

At the front of the room, Lady Ashburn concluded her

talk and invited the attendees to partake in tea and cakes.

"Who should I get a photo of?" Matilda asked, rising to her feet.

"We haven't gotten Lady Ashburn in ages," Hazel said. "I suppose she'll boycott the *Daily* if we don't put her picture with the column."

As Matilda walked away in search of her model, Hazel's gaze followed the Duchess of Roscommon. She made her way through the crowd to the front of the room where the ladies had formed small groups and located the duchess standing near the tea table speaking to Lady Carmella Barton. Hazel hoped her feelings didn't show on her face.

Though she was barely two years Hazel's senior, Lady Carmella had been married for almost five years and had never let the other ladies of her acquaintance forget it. She may have the delicate features and golden hair of a china doll, but Hazel knew she could pounce on unsuspecting prey like a cat.

It wouldn't have been Hazel's first choice for an introduction, but it would have to do.

"Lady Carmella," Hazel said. "How are you?"

The lady sighed and laid a hand on Hazel's shoulder. "I'd be ever so much better if you'd get yourself married to a good man so you could stop going to work."

"I do it for the benefit of the Commonwealth," Hazel said with her most solemn expression.

"I suppose you'll want an introduction to the duchess?" Lady Carmella said, nodding to a very well-preserved lady of petite stature and fine-boned features wearing a deep blue, narrow skirted dress that was the very latest fashion. Hazel knew because her sister had insisted on dragging her to the dressmakers just last week.

"That would be lovely."

Hazel allowed Carmella to link arms and lead her to the duchess as though they were the very best of friends.

"Your Grace, may I present Lady Hazel Winchester, second daughter to the Earl of Winchester.

The duchess gave her a nod.

"I did wonder if your grace would give a quote to the *London Daily*?" Hazel asked. "We'd like to highlight to our readers the illustrious company in attendance at the League's event."

"Of course," the duchess said. "Though I do find it strange to be interviewed by a peer of the realm."

"Wait until you go to the dressmaker's and find the designer is the daughter of a count," Carmella cut in. "Or the marquess' daughter serving you in a bookstore."

"With so many sons of England conscripted to the navy I suppose we must all do our part," the duchess said. "I, for one, am more than a little curious to see this London with so many women at work."

"I won't quote you on that," Hazel said, catching the shocked look on Carmella's face out of the corner of her eye.

"That would be for the best," The duchess agreed. "Instead you may say that I was more than pleased by the showing at the League's lecture and am gratified by the efforts to return to the traditional values that made this country great."

"Thank you for your time, your grace," Hazel said as she finished jotting down the quote.

"I suppose I will see you at Lady Germaine's ball?" Carmella asked before Hazel could escape.

"You will," Hazel said and made a split-second decision to try to get into Lady Carmella's good graces. At least for the duration of the Season. "Before I go, was there anything you wanted to add to the column?"

Lady Carmella brightened. "Well, I suppose I could give you a quote or two."

CHAPTER THREE

Duncan climbed up on the deck of his ship, clean shaven and dressed for travel in a fitted brown jacket that hugged his wide shoulders. He'd even allowed Myers to trim his hair.

Though the sky was a clear blue, something was blocking the sun. He looked up and saw one of the Royal Navy's finest vessels hovering above and his headache returned full force.

"I've already had your trunks sent up," Myers said as he came to stand at Duncan's side.

"Then all that's left is for us to climb on up and join them."

"Yes," Myers said, looking up with a lack of enthusiasm.

"I'll be sorry to see you go," said Captain Ballo, coming to join them. He was a middle-aged man who'd originally migrated from South Africa. Aside from his imposing height, his most distinguishing feature was the impressive gray sideburns that came almost to his chin. "We all will."

"I won't say that I haven't enjoyed being on board,"

Duncan said. "I don't suppose I could convince you to take a position closer to London? I'd love to have you take over some of our local runs."

Ballo gave him a grim smile. "I won't say I'm not tempted, but I know things are different closer to land. Out here I'm a captain. My men don't care where my family came from."

"But it's different in London?"

"You know it is."

Duncan couldn't argue. He held his hand out to the captain. "Till next time."

"Godspeed," Ballo said with a firm handshake. He then looked up and made a broad gesture to the pilot of the airship and a rope ladder swung down, stopping two feet from the deck boards.

"Shall we?" Duncan glanced over at Myers.

"If we must," the valet agreed.

Duncan climbed up with ease while Myers followed more slowly. As Duncan emerged through the trap door of the airship he was greeted by a grinning Captain Merritt Lancaster.

"I should have known you'd be the one to fly out for me," Duncan said, getting to his feet and reaching down to help Myers up.

"How could I resist?" Meri said, adjusting his hat on his dark blond head while a cadet and first lieutenant pulled up the rope ladder and closed the trapdoor. As the officers finished their work and stood, waiting for orders, Meri nodded at one of them. "Lieutenant, let the wheelhouse know we are good to go."

"Yes captain," the young officer answered and headed

for a spiral staircase at the end of the cargo area.

"Can someone show me to our rooms?" Myers asked. "I'd like to see to our trunks."

"Yes sir." The cadet stepped forward. "Right this way."

As Myers followed the officer up the stairs, Meri gave his friend a once over. "You look like you could use a drink."

Duncan glanced at his pocket watch. "It's barely past nine."

"Doesn't change how you look."

"Lead the way."

Duncan followed Meri up a wooden staircase, lined on both sides by paneled walls. They emerged into a viewing area with floor to ceiling windows that looked out over the horizon. There were a few seating areas with tables which they passed on their way to the small bar at the back of the viewing deck. A large window behind the mahogany bar allowed for a clear view of the vast ocean below. Duncan went to the window to see if he could spy his ship but he was looking from the wrong angle.

Meri reached behind the bar and pulled out a bottle of brandy and two glasses. Duncan looked around, taking in the common area as he took a seat on a stool next to Meri. He guessed the airship probably housed a dozen or so officers and cadets when it was at full capacity. Not a large ship, but then that was hardly needed for the occasion.

"Have I told you that being captain is a good look for you?" Duncan asked.

"It's not as glamorous as it seems," Meri said. "I spend most of my time ferrying diplomats into countries that don't want anything to do with the United Kingdom."

"Still, it's quite a promotion, jumping three ranks. You really are the golden boy now."

It was a nickname Duncan and their friend Lord Fletcher had given Meri based on his dark blond hair, light brown eyes and pleasant demeanor. But after his heroic actions several months back it suited him now more than ever.

"That's hardly the case." Meri poured a generous serving into each glass and handed one to his friend.

"You're basically a national hero."

"The attempted highjacking of the *Triumph* is not common knowledge," Meri sipped his drink. "You're the one who helped keep it out of the papers."

"When one's father is a press baron, one does have some sway," Duncan said. "Even with the smaller independent outlets. Still, the right people know what happened."

"And they know it wasn't all my doing, I assure you."

"Your mother and sisters must be pleased. The promotion would mean a lot to them."

Meri stood up, replacing the brandy bottle behind the bar. He was taller, a couple of inches over Duncan, but not as broad.

"They are indeed. And how about your family? I assume that's why you're being called home."

"That's a fair guess."

"Not a guess. I know you well. You wouldn't leave without a good reason. Not given the work you were doing for the Bureau."

"It's my father." Duncan swirled the amber liquid in his glass. "Am I a terrible son for not wanting to go back?"

"You'd only be terrible if you refused."

"Honor and duty," Duncan said, holding up his glass. Meri clinked his own against it. Duncan took a healthy swallow. The brandy melted a path down his throat, warming him from the inside out.

"Can I ask if you discovered anything during your travels?" Meri asked. "Anything of interest to the other agents?"

"Only that there doesn't appear to be anything amiss in Iceland."

Meri tapped his fingers against his glass. "Then the Amer-Irish Guard must have been acting on its own when they attempted to take down the *Triumph*."

Three months earlier, during what should have been a three hour pleasure cruise, a rebel group calling themselves the Amer-Irish Guard had attempted to take out a naval airship. Fortunately, Duncan had been there to assist his friend in foiling the terrorist plot.

"Well, that's good news, isn't it?"

"It is," Meri agreed.

Duncan finished his drink and rested his empty glass on the bar with a thunk and turned back to his friend. "Given the attempts by the Guard to go after British aristocracy, is it wise to continue with the public party for the princess' twenty-first birthday?"

"The queen won't hear otherwise. She says it's an opportunity to show the people we've moved past the war years. Besides, it's still some months away."

"I suppose the event will sell papers, so that's something."

Meri laughed. "You're ready to take over the family business then?"

"I've been running the shipping side of things for the past four years."

"I was talking about the paper."

"I know," Duncan sighed. "That'll be a bit more tedious."

"Can't be that hard," Meri said. "You'll just be a figurehead."

"I'm more worried about not enough to do than too much."

"I'm sure Lord Fletcher can find something to keep you occupied," Meri said, leaning an elbow on the bar. It was often a source of fascination to Duncan how his friend could go from standing at attention to a relaxed slouch and back in a split second.

Probably came with the training.

"When was the last time you saw Fletcher?" Meri asked.

"We've corresponded, of course, but in person it's been over a year."

"He'll keep you busy. There's always work to be done in London and as you've said, with the birthday celebrations coming up we've all got to be on our toes."

"That's true."

"Not to mention your dear mama," Meri continued, making an attempt to hide his smile behind his drink. "I'm sure she will keep you busy, parading you in front of all the eligible misses. Isn't the Season about to start?

What timing you have."

Duncan glared at his friend. "Don't even suggest it."

"You're an excellent catch." Meri punched him in the arm. "Wealthy, worldly, some might even say attractive."

"I don't want a wife."

Meri shrugged. "Doesn't mean you can't have fun in the meantime. All those balls with their garden paths. Lots of nooks to get lost in with the right lady."

"I wasn't good enough to grace the ballrooms of the aristocracy before I left, so why should I be good enough now?"

"Because you're a wealthy heir."

"I'm still the son of a merchant."

"A wealthy merchant, if the rumors are to believed you've more than tripled the family fortune since taking on the shipping business. You'll be sought after by every single lady under forty."

Duncan drained his glass. "That's what I'm afraid of."

The walk back home at the end of the day was much more hectic than at the start. The sidewalks were nearly impassable with the servants from every fine house in Mayfair running around doing last minute errands before the shops closed.

The low hum of an airship had Hazel looking up to the sky. It was hard to see through the fog, but she could just make out the bow of a patrol ship. She supposed even the Royal Navy was jittery this close to the Day of Mourning.

Hazel passed a line-up at the bakery, and a longer one

at the grocer. The factories at the edge of the city were going full tilt and along with the oppressive cloud cover, were making the aether fog completely unbearable.

All this because tomorrow was the Day of Mourning. What would people do if the city shut down for longer than a day?

Hazel was grateful for her breathing mask that at least made the air bearable, and was relieved to see most of the servants she passed also wearing them, but there were still many people with nothing but handkerchiefs and swaths of cloth up to their faces. Masks were an expense that many still couldn't afford.

Rounding the corner toward Mayfair, some of the crowd died off making the sidewalks more passable, though the streets were busier as the well-to-do went about in steam carriages. Hazel rubbed her forehead with her gloved hand. It took her a moment to realize her temple was tingling. She took a deep breath and pushed on.

She made it almost a block before her vision began to blur. She stepped around a manservant in blue velvet and grabbed onto the wrought iron fence in front of a blue gray townhouse right before her world shifted.

Within seconds the vision descended on her.

Hurrying down the sidewalk, the tinny taste of aether crept through her ill fitting mask. Two children came barreling toward her, bumping her basket and nearly sending the loaves of French bread flying. She stopped long enough to set her wares straight. Foremost in her mind was getting back to the kitchen. She couldn't be late.

Hurry. She had to hurry…

Hazel opened her eyes. A lanky man with a dirty cloth

under his nose had stopped beside her.

"Are you all right, Miss?" He asked in a muffled voice.

Hazel nodded, unable to speak through her mask. The man gave her a nod and continued on his way. He was probably running an errand for a wife and family. Belatedly, Hazel realized she should have offered him a coin for stopping.

She breathed as deeply as the mask would allow. There was a slight tremor in her fingers, but she was close to home. Glancing down the street, she saw a young maid with a basket on her arm heading in the opposite direction.

A shiver started down her back. There were baguettes sticking out of one end of the basket and the maid was clearly in a rush.

No doubt she had seen the maid in passing and her mind had concocted a daydream around it. It wasn't the first time she'd gotten caught in a vision, but it hadn't happened in several years. She mustn't be taking her medications properly. What with trying to chase down a story on the black market at all hours, it was no wonder.

She continued the rest of the way home, keeping to a sedate pace. When she reached the wrought iron gate of her family's town home she could have cried with relief. She climbed the stone steps, examining the ivy trellis that she hoped hid the worst of the peeling paint. Or, at least it did in the spring and summer when the plant was in full bloom.

The clock in the foyer was striking half-past three when Hazel opened the front door. She was immediately greeted by their butler and only man servant, an older man who'd worked for the family since her father had been a boy.

"How are you, Mason?" Hazel asked as she removed the mask from her face and pulled the gloves off her still shaking hands.

Before the butler could answer, Penny pushed past him, half out of breath. That's when Hazel remembered: Her mother's at-home day.

"You forgot," Penny said, her lips compressed in a thin line of disapproval.

"Are there many in attendance?" Hazel asked. Mason and Penny exchanged a look.

"It's a full drawing room, Miss," Mason answered.

Hazel glanced at the hall clock. She was already half an hour late. She shrugged out of her cloak and gave it to Mason.

"I'll have to go in wearing my work dress," Hazel said. "There's no time for a change."

She climbed the stairs two at a time, forgetting about her corset until it dug into her ribs at the top step. Dressing as a boy was much more freeing. She took a moment to catch her breath before smoothing her skirts with the palms of her hands and heading into the drawing room.

As she paused in the doorway, the conversation came to an abrupt halt as a dozen sets of eyes belonging to the posh ladies of her mother's most intimate circle turned her way. The most piercing gaze belonged to her mother, Lady Winchester, whose face froze in a forced smile as she took in the gray-clad appearance of her youngest daughter.

"Mama," Hazel hurried to her mother's side and leaned down to kiss her cheek. "Sorry I'm late. I was finishing my column—"

"Never mind dear," her mother cut her off. "Have a seat next to your sister."

Hazel took the empty seat next to her sister Lilith, who pulled in the skirts of her violet-blue day dress as though Hazel were covered in chimney ashes.

"Couldn't spare a moment to fix your hair?" Lilith said in a low voice.

Hazel gave her sister a bright smile as she accepted a cup of tea from Molly, who served as both parlour and kitchen maid. "Some of us wear many hats."

"Still," Lilith whispered. "One would think you'd have time to wash off the stench of the presses before coming home. Is that ink on your fingers?"

Hazel looked down and saw that there was indeed black ink on her right index finger. She curled it around the handle of her cup and was about to point out that her sister had no problem spending the money her filthy press job brought in, but her attention was taken by Lady Germaine, a formidable woman who'd managed to marry off all her own children and now liked nothing more than to pair off those of her extensive acquaintance.

"Are you fully prepared for the Season, Lady Hazel?" Lady Germaine asked.

Hazel laid her cup down on her saucer with a delicate clink. Her stomach rumbled and she eyed the poundcake on the silver platter next to her mother. A side effect of her episodes was how hungry she was left afterward.

"Yes, my lady, I believe so."

"This is your fourth season, is it not?"

"As always, you are correct."

"High time you made a match," Lady Germaine said with a sniff. "You wouldn't want to enter your fifth with nothing to show for it."

Hazel felt Lilith stiffen next to her on the settee and was grateful when the conversation turned.

"Have you seen what's happening in Hyde Park?" Miss Julia Bannister asked, she leaned forward in her seat. "We drove by Friday past, and they're already setting up for the birthday celebrations."

"A waste of time and money." Lady Germaine set down her teacup with another dramatic sniff. "Are we meant to forget what happened the last time we had such a public event?"

Hazel watched as her mother's cup teetered on its saucer before she stilled her hand.

"I heard there was a run on sugar at the market today," Mrs. Bannister, mother to Julia and close friend to Lady Winchester, cut in. "I assume everyone's cook is taking tomorrow to get a head start on the Season."

"I don't get my sugar from the market anymore," Lady Germaine waved a dismissive hand. "My housekeeper has a source."

Hazel sat up straight. "You're referring to the black market?"

"Of course. It's much better quality than what the merchants are selling and costs less too."

Hazel was about to point out that this was because the blackmarket dealers didn't collect taxes, but her mother shot her a narrow-eyed look that shut her up.

"Would anyone care for more refreshments?" Lady Winchester nodded at the maid. Despite her annoyance, Hazel reached for a square of the heavy yellow cake as the platter passed in front of her. The conversation moved on to talk of dresses and fabric patterns and Hazel found that if she nodded her head at the right moments, she could eat her cake in relative peace.

The ladies left about half an hour later.

"I hate Lady Germaine," Lilith said, flopping inelegantly onto the chair that had been vacated when their mother had retired to her rooms. "She only pointed out that it was your fourth season to remind everyone that it's my seventh."

"I'm more annoyed that she's contributing to black market sales," Hazel said, slathering butter on a slice of bread before the maid could carry away the remnants of the tea tray. "Especially when she can well afford to go to the shops."

"You and your fair market lectures," Lilith blew out a frustrated breath. "And did you hear her crack about not wanting to go into your fifth season without a match? It is the outside of enough."

"Ladies who've managed to marry off their daughters during these trying times feel they have useful advice to give. I'm sure she didn't mean anything by it and even if she did, it's not like we're the only young women who've been left without a match after several seasons. In fact, we're in the firm majority."

Lilith glared at her sister. "You haven't even tried to find a husband."

"It would hardly be the thing if I were to marry before

you."

Lilith made a strangled noise in the back of her throat. "It doesn't help you know. Having a sister in the trades."

Hazel rolled her eyes. "I'm hardly in the trades. I write a column."

"It's paid work."

Hazel stood up and dusted the breadcrumbs off the front of her dress. She'd long ago grown immune to her sister's rants. "You know the law. One of us has to work."

"If you'd let Papa pay the tax—"

"With what funds, Lilith? You know as well as I do we haven't the money."

Hazel turned on her heel and left the drawing room before her sister could reply. She regretted letting Lilith get under her skin. It's not like her sister's disdain took away from how much she enjoyed her work. Sometimes it even added to it.

No, she was more bothered by her sister's insistence that she give up her job like the League Ladies—a terrifying thought indeed.

Hazel's foot was on the bottom stair when she heard her father's voice calling from his study. "Hazel? Is that you?"

With a smile, she headed into the small room at the base of the stairs. She was immediately hit by the smell of old books and tobacco.

"Hello Papa," she called and waited for him to emerge from behind a bookshelf, his hair sticking out at all angles in a way that would cause her mother a coronary. "You're home early."

"We cut our counsel short on account of this being the

eve of the Day of Mourning," Lord Winchester said, pushing his glasses up on his nose and dusting off the cover of a book with the sleeve of his coat. He handed over a copy of *Middlemarch*. "Which is why I found this for you. I thought it might help you to pass the time tomorrow."

"Thank you," Hazel said, immediately opening the book to the first page. "I can't wait to read it."

"There's something else we need to talk about."

"What's that?" Hazel glanced up. "Nothing too serious, I hope."

"I wish that were the case. Come sit."

Hazel followed her father to the small seating area that was rarely used and sat on the small settee, across from her father's armchair.

"You've heard that Mr. Walters is unwell?"

"Yes, he hasn't been in the office in weeks. But we're expecting him soon. The surgeon said he only needed four to six weeks recovery time."

"Well, the procedure did not go quite as planned. Mr. Walters continues to deteriorate."

A sensation like an icy fist wound its way around Hazel's heart. Where would the paper be without Mr. Walters? Where would she be?

"Are you saying that Mr. Walters may not recover?"

"It's a possibility that I would like you to prepare for."

Hazel shook her head. "I don't think I can."

"You can and you will." Her father leaned forward, taking her hand in his. The book lay forgotten on the sofa next to her. "What's more, you must not tell anyone at the paper what I've told you. They'll find out when the official announcement is made. You understand?"

"Yes Papa."

"I know this is hard for you, but you must be strong. For Mr. Walters, and for his family."

"What will happen to the *Daily*? There's no one who can possibly fill his shoes."

"I'm sure Mr. Walters made a plan. Have faith."

CHAPTER FOUR

Duncan was having the devil of a time getting a carriage. He turned to his valet in frustration. "Where is everyone going?"

"Tomorrow is the anniversary of the aether rain, sir. It will be a national day of mourning."

"London still shuts down over that?"

"I believe so, sir," Myers said, looking up and down the street in frustration. They'd been left on the docks after the airship had landed and had managed to get a cart to pull their trunks to the street but they needed a hired carriage to get home

"The townhouse isn't terribly far from here," Duncan said. "I can go on foot and have the carriage sent for you and the trunks."

Myers' eyes were already watering from the aether fog. Duncan had forgotten how sensitive his valet was to the London air. "I should be the one to walk, sir."

"I need the exercise," Duncan said. "You stay with the trunks."

Duncan walked through the streets, out of the downtown district with its sidewalks crowded with vendors selling last minute wares, everything from indulgences like paper bags full of candied almonds to necessities like mercury filled aether detectors. Anything to help London get through the next twenty-four hours.

As he walked, the crowd parted, either because he was dressed like a gentleman or because of his broad physique, or perhaps both. Either way, he was grateful for it. Too long outside and he'd arrive home choking. The sea air had certainly spoiled him.

Emerging into the more residential area of London, Duncan slowed his pace. He noticed with some satisfaction that many of the grand houses of the Mayfair district, those whose doors had always been closed to him, were looking a little worse for wear. A few had faded trim. Some needed a shutter or two replaced.

Apparently, the aristocracy wasn't worth as much as it used to be.

He turned a corner and the familiar townhouse his parents had acquired when he was sixteen came into view. They might have climbed their way up the social ladder to a Mayfair address, but they hadn't been able to force their way into the *ton's* inner circle. Not that Duncan cared. He had no desire to participate in the Season.

As he walked up the front steps of the house that had never felt like his home, Duncan was relieved to see that things had been kept up. No missing railings or peeling shutters for his family.

For the briefest moment, Duncan stood on the top step and very nearly knocked on the door. Then, remembering this was technically his permanent residence, he walked inside.

Duncan paused in the foyer. His nostrils filled with the soapy scent of the lilies that his mother insisted on keeping in the main entrance.

"Master Duncan." Briggs greeted him with the same strait-laced posture that brought him back to his childhood. He had an overwhelming urge to hide from the butler.

"Mister, please," Duncan said. "I've not been master for many years."

"Of course, sir," Briggs said with a stiff nod. "Apologies."

"I need the carriage sent down to the docks," Duncan said. "My valet is there with our trunks."

"I'll see to it. Is there anything else, *Mister* Duncan?" Briggs emphasized the title.

"Is my mother at home?"

"She's in her drawing room," Briggs said, taking Duncan's hat and gloves. "Right this way."

Duncan fought the urge to point out that he didn't need to be shown the way to his mother's suite, but he bit his tongue. He needed to pick his battles and if the past was anything to go by, there'd be plenty of opportunity to have it out with Briggs.

"You have a visitor, Mrs. Walters," the butler said, opening the door. "Mister Duncan."

"Duncan?" His mother stood up and hurried toward him, enveloping him in a rose-scented embrace. "Oh thank goodness. I was so afraid you'd arrive tomorrow and there'd be no way to get you home."

"We made good time," Duncan said, closing his eyes for the briefest of moments as the tension he'd felt from seeing Briggs drained out of his body. He'd missed his mother. "The navy sent its best for me. But I think you knew that."

"You're so dark," Mrs. Walters said, holding him at arm's length.

"The sun will do that, Mother."

"And thin."

Duncan laughed. Only his mother would call his physique thin.

She turned to Briggs. "Have a tray sent up and tell Cook to make sure there's a plate of Duncan's favorite lemon tarts."

"Yes ma'am."

"Come, sit," his mother said, dragging Duncan to a satin covered sofa. The whole room was done in her favorite shades of pink: blush carpeting, striped coral wallpaper, cushions in patterns of deepest fuschia.

Nothing had changed.

"How's father?" Duncan asked as soon as he was seated.

"I'll bring you to see him as soon as you've eaten."

"Why am I getting the distinct impression that you're stalling?"

Mrs. Walters was saved from having to answer by the arrival of the tea tray followed by his sister, Flora, who was led into the room by Mrs. Clements, her companion.

"Say hello to your brother," Mrs. Walters said to her daughter. "He's just arrived."

"Duncan?" Flora asked, looking in her brother's direction, but not really focusing on him. "How nice."

While his mother poured tea and piled food onto a

plate for him, Duncan tried to engage with his sister. She sat on the settee directly across from him, Mrs. Clements at her side.

"How have you been, Flora?"

But his sister was staring off into space.

"Your sister has been doing quite well," Mrs. Clements, an older woman of his mother's generation, answered. "She's even taken up the pianoforte again, haven't you Miss Flora?"

"How nice," Duncan made sure to direct his comments to his sister. "Maybe I can hear you play later."

"I have a headache," Flora said, standing up. "I wish to lie down."

"Of course, dear," Mrs. Walters said. "But I'd like you to try to make it down for dinner."

"I'll see to it, Mrs. Walters," Mrs. Clements said, following her charge out of the parlor.

Duncan looked to his mother once they were alone. "She's still being medicated."

Mrs. Walters turned to the tea tray and poured herself a cup. "The visions returned."

"But she was doing so much better."

"She was," his mother agreed. "Then she started spouting some nonsense about the vicar's wife beating their youngest son at an afternoon tea and Mrs. Clements and I decided it was time to call Dr. Baker again."

"Mrs. Clements isn't her guardian."

"No, but she's been with Flora most of her life and I trust her opinion."

Duncan put his plate on a side table. "I'd like to talk to the doctor myself."

"Of course. He's due back tomorrow to check on your father."

The sound of a carriage pulling up in front of the house had Mrs. Walters hurrying to the window.

"That will be Myers," Duncan said. "We couldn't get a hired carriage."

"I'll go down to the foyer to direct the trunks," Mrs. Walters said, stopping next to the sofa to give him a hasty peck on the check. "It really is good to have you home."

CHAPTER FIVE

Hazel picked up her book for what felt like the hundredth time but, try as she might, she couldn't get into the story.

Between the Day of Mourning and worrying about Mr. Walters, she was feeling heavy, both in thought and in body.

The rain beating against the library window did little to help her mood.

She laid *Middlemarch* to one side and picked up the book she'd told herself she wouldn't read. It was a history of the major events surrounding the Great Sea War.

The volume opened to the page she read every year. The passage about the aether rains.

Though it was an uncharacteristically sunny day, the skies over London grew dark as a hundred American air balloons crowded the heavens and unleashed a toxic rain on the citizens below...

Hazel set the book down, rubbing her temple. Rain always made her head achy.

"There you are," Lilith said, pausing in the doorway. "What a dreary day."

"Hopefully the start of the Season will be better," Hazel said. There was nothing worse than getting in and out of carriages in the wet.

"Have you heard about Lady Felicity?" Lilith asked, coming into the room and settling in Lord Winchester's favourite wingback chair. "Her father had her committed."

A cold feeling settled in the pit of Hazel's stomach. Lady Felicity was one of their social circle. She and Hazel had made their come out in the same year. "What for?"

"Aether fever."

"But she hasn't had an attack in years."

"Apparently she had visions, mad ramblings in Lady Ashburn's drawing room of all places, and her father decided he'd had enough."

"Wretched man," Hazel muttered. She couldn't help remembering her own incident from the day before. But then, Hazel was fortunate to remain silent during her spells.

"On that we can agree." Lilith picked up a book from a side table and put it down again. "At least you've not had any relapses."

"Have you seen Mama?" Hazel asked, changing the subject.

"No, and I don't expect to. She rarely comes out on the Day of Mourning."

"I know, but I thought she might be getting better. It's been twenty-one years."

"I think the passage of time makes it harder. She lost

so much that day, we all did."

Hazel rubbed her temple. "May I ask you a question? You don't have to answer."

Lilith quirked a brow. "Now I'm curious."

"I know you were only three at the time, but can you remember that day?"

"Bits and pieces," Lilith said, leaning back in the chair. "I remember playing with my dolls in the nursery. Nanny Perkins was with us and I think she was fussing over my hair because I was crying and I always cried when she brushed out my curls. Perhaps she was readying me to make an appearance in the drawing room that evening. It was to be the opening ceremonies of the king's jubilee celebrations that afternoon, though I couldn't have known that at the time."

"And of course Mama was planning on attending? Despite her condition?"

Lilith laughed. "I don't think anything could have kept her away from such an event."

Lady Winchester was nothing if not consistent. Hazel doubted even the actual onset of labor pains could have kept her mother from attending the celebration of the year.

"Mama stopped by the nursery. I think I have such a clear impression of her arrival because she so rarely came to see me there. She was dressed in a cloak, ready to go out. Her stomach was puffed out. I must have called her fat because she got cross over something I said."

Hazel's lips curved, thinking of how her mother would have reacted.

"After she left, do you remember the rains coming?"

"No." Lilith shook her head. "I was probably napping because there's a gap. The next thing I remember is Papa barging through the front door, soaking wet and carrying Mama like she was one of my ragdolls. I was watching her through the railings. Everyone was running about, no one gave me a second thought. Nanny had abandoned me. I think they were calling for a doctor, but the doctor couldn't be reached. I imagine every woman in London who was with child was in similar distress. I must have gone to the window at some point because I remember seeing rows and rows of soldiers. And the rain running down the windows had a horrible reddish tinge."

"That's from the aether," Hazel said, she couldn't help glancing at the rivulets running down the library window.

"It left rusty puddles all over the streets. Even Mama's clothes were covered in it and the smell, I'll never forget it. It was like old eggs and vinegar. It filled the house for days."

"It sounds horrible," Hazel said. "You must have been quite upset."

"Fortunately Mama came around and it seemed as though no harm was done. That is until you were born a few weeks later. I woke from what I thought was a nightmare and went to find Nanny. That's how I arrived at Mama's door and realized the screaming hadn't been in my dreams after all. Everyone was in a panic because it wasn't her time. You were supposed to be born at least a month later."

"That's why I was so small," Hazel said.

"Yes. And everyone thought you wouldn't make it. There were so many stillbirths after the rains. Poor Papa was crying in the hallway. Of course, we were lucky. As we know now, if you'd been a boy you would have been dead."

"Yes," Hazel said. "How fortunate I am."

"How fortunate we all are," Lilith said, looking out the window but her eyes appeared to be focussing on something other than the rain. "I'd hate to be an only child."

His father was dying. Not today maybe. But soon.

Mentally, Duncan had known what to expect when he'd been called home. He'd known his father wouldn't be sitting at the desk in his study as Duncan last remembered him. Charles Walters hadn't even looked up from his morning paper as his only son stepped out of his life. But sitting next to his father's bed, watching the way he struggled to breathe in and out, it was more dire than he'd expected. Always a large man, he had lost nearly a third of his body weight and if the way his skin was hanging off him was anything to go by, it hadn't been a gradual transition.

Pushing past the tight feeling in his chest, Duncan turned to the doctor who stood at the foot of the bed, his examination complete.

"How much time does he have?" Duncan asked.

"Impossible to say," Dr. Baker answered. "The nature of an apoplexy of the brain is such that one can never know."

Duncan cleared his throat. "It happened during a procedure?"

"Yes, I was treating him for heart palpitations at the time."

Duncan noted the metal pole next to the bed with a glass bulb filled with a mostly clear fluid that ran into a needle in his father's right arm.

"Is he in pain?"

"No, we've prescribed a heavy dose of laudanum to keep him comfortable, as well as fluids. Your mother was most insistent that he be kept comfortable."

Duncan looked back at his father. "Why wasn't I called sooner?"

Dr. Baker cleared his throat. "Your father didn't think it was serious."

"He never does," Duncan muttered to himself.

"He may hang on for some time," Dr. Baker said, closing his bag. "I've known patients to hang on for weeks, even months."

"But will he regain consciousness?"

"It is unlikely."

This was not the homecoming he'd envisioned while he'd been at sea the last several months.

As Dr. Baker snapped his bag shut, Duncan looked up, remembering there was something else they needed to discuss.

"Before you go, Doctor, I'd like to talk to you about my sister."

"Miss Flora? She seems to be doing much better."

"That wasn't my experience," Duncan said. "She's extremely distant. Not herself at all."

Dr. Baker straightened his spine. "There are side effects to her treatment, but stopping the visions was the top priority."

"Whose priority?"

"Your mother's. And your father's before he took ill."

"What is it you're giving her?" Duncan asked.

"Persephamine."

"Anti-aether?"

"That's the street name for it, yes."

"And that's the only treatment you'd prescribe?"

Dr. Baker tapped his fingers against the side of his medical bag. "There is a place you could send her. Only about a half day from London and there's a doctor there doing some interesting work."

"An institution?"

"A facility for girls like your sister. It's worth thinking about."

Sending his sister away was completely out of the question. Duncan would have to look for an alternative.

"Thanks for your time," Duncan said and the doctor gave him a quick nod before leaving. Duncan continued sitting, watching his father's labored breathing. Something rustled behind him and he turned to see his mother enter the room.

"I saw Dr. Baker leave. Did he answer your questions?"

"As best he could."

His mother sat down next to Duncan, reaching for her husband's hand. "I'm glad you've come home. I always find today such a challenge."

Duncan had forgotten it was the Day of Mourning. Of course his mother would find it hard. Hell, he found it hard to think about and he'd only been five years old.

"I've had an invitation to Lady Germaine's ball," Mrs. Walters said, clearly looking for a lighter subject.

"How nice," Duncan said. "I imagine you and Flora will enjoy yourselves."

"Your name is on the invitation as well. I believe she'll be expecting you."

"I'm certain she will get over her disappointment."

"Duncan, be serious. You can't come back to town and ignore all the society events."

"Why not? When I left town I was a merchant's son and none of these old dragons would have allowed me near their drawing rooms. But now that I'm the imminent heir to a wealthy man I'm welcome to grace their exalted presence."

"This is what your father and I have been working for. This is your chance to have a place in London society."

"If you and Father had no place, then why do I need one?"

"You know as well as I do that the way forward is through the aristocracy. We're doing quite well for ourselves, but the War Tax is a constant threat to families like ours. You need to go out there and make a strong alliance."

Duncan glanced at his father. Though he wasn't able to contribute to the conversation, he knew his father would say the same thing.

"I'll go to the ball," Duncan said. "But don't get any ideas. I'm not marrying anyone."

His mother beamed. "This is a good first step. I'll go write our acceptance now."

"Am I to believe you haven't already gone ahead and written on my behalf?"

She released her husband's hand and turned to her son. She reached up and pushed a lock of hair off his forehead. "Well, I know my son and I knew you'd see reason."

CHAPTER SIX

"What do you think, miss?" Penny asked as she finished pinning Hazel's hair.

Hazel tipped her head from side to side, watching the curls bounce ever so slightly. She barely recognized herself when Penny did her up like this.

"You've done a lovely job, as usual," Hazel said. "But I have no desire to go out tonight."

"Why so melancholy?" Penny frowned. "I know balls aren't your favorite activity, but it hardly deserves such a long face."

Between her conversation with Lilith yesterday and her worries over Mr. Walters, the last thing she wanted was to dance at a ball.

"Do you think I could fake a headache?"

"I very much believe your dear mama would come up here and drag you downstairs by the curls. Lady Germaine's ball is the official start of the season. You won't get off that easily."

Hazel tried to take in a deep breath but the dress her mother had picked out required a tighter corset than she preferred.

"I wouldn't breathe too deeply in that," Penny said with a nod to her chest.

Hazel scrunched up her nose in the mirror as she took in the expanse of pale skin over the yellow gold satin that her mother had picked out. Aside from being cut fashionably low, the colour gave her auburn hair an orange tinge.

"I hate this dress."

She hadn't wanted anything new for her wardrobe, but her mother had insisted on at least one ball gown for her and Lilith. As though that were the missing piece that would catch both her daughters a husband.

"Come now." Penny crouched down to help Hazel into her dancing slippers. "Best to get the whole ordeal over with."

"You're right," Hazel said, slipping on her shoes and getting to her feet. "And perhaps I'll find something scandalous to write about in my next column."

"There's the spirit." Penny handed over her fan. "Try not to eat anything. I don't think that dress could take it."

Hazel took her reticule and headed out into the hall. She heard her mother's and sister's voices floating up from the foyer.

"We're late," Lilith said.

"All the fashionable people arrive late," her mother said. "We'll be noticed."

"We'll be left without any decent partners," Lilith said.

"Don't worry," Hazel called from the staircase. "If anyone asks me for a dance, I'll direct them straight to you."

"I'm sure I can get my own partners, thank you very much." Lilith opened her fan with a snap.

"Shall we go then?" Lady Winchester looked her daughters over. She gave Lilith an approving nod but her eye rested on Hazel's curls. "I do wish you'd let Penny wash your hair with coffee grounds. It would tone down the carrotiness."

"Leave her, Eleanor," Lord Winchester called from the staircase where he was doing up the buttons of his coat in the wrong order. "She looks lovely. They both do."

Lilith closed her fan and hurried to her father's side. "Do you think so, Papa?"

Hazel pulled her shawl over her shoulders, wishing she could keep it on all night, and followed her family to the waiting carriage.

Like many families, they rented a steam carriage during the season. The cost of keeping a private vehicle was prohibitive. Not only was there the cost of the carriage, but the driver and footman also had to be specially trained and they could barely manage their meagre staff as it was.

Hazel would have preferred walking, but her mother had been horrified at the very notion.

It wasn't how proper ladies arrived at a ball.

The outside of the carriage was a black metal casing. It looked much like the horse powered carriages that still existed in the countryside, but the windows were much smaller, just a porthole in the door. Instead of sitting up top, the driver sat in a seat on the front of the carriage, taking care of the steering while the footman hung off the back, operating the steam pump.

"Lord Fowler is still unmarried," Lilith said as Hazel was handed into the carriage and the driver closed the door behind them. The one good thing about the better carriages was the ventilation system that kept the air more or less pure. "And we hit it off so well last year."

"And there's Baron Dorset's second son," Lady Winchester said. "He's just returned from the Indies and hasn't had proper exposure to civilized society in years."

Lilith wrinkled her nose. "A younger son?"

"Don't rule him out," Lady Eleanor said. "Not at your age."

The hissing of the steam engines fully engaging cut off conversation for several moments until the carriage got under way.

"If I don't get a dance with Lord Dennison I will be most put out."

They continued their back and forth, requiring no input from Hazel or Lord Winchester, as their carriage eased into the waiting line in front of Lady Germaine's door.

"Of course Lord Fletcher is still single," Lilith said. "And so handsome."

"I don't think Fletcher ever intends to marry," Lady Winchester said. "We'll set our sights on someone more attainable."

Lilith frowned, but further conversation came to a halt as the carriage jerked forward into a rambling halt at the foot of Lady Germaine's stairs.

A scarlet liveried footman opened the door and helped the ladies down. The emissions from the line of carriages was almost overwhelming. Hazel covered her mouth and nose with the edge of her shawl as she kept to her sister's side, following her up the steps behind their mother and father as they all made their way inside to the receiving line.

It was at occasions such as these that Hazel appreciated her sister's ability to mix in polite company. With any luck Lilith would do all the talking for the two of them, leaving Hazel to her observations.

"Lady Germaine," Lilith said in a voice dripping with honey. "What a veritable squeeze."

"Lovely to see you Lady Lilith, Lady Hazel," she nodded at each of the girls. "If I were you, I would make haste to the ballroom while there are still dances to be had."

"Your ladyship," Lilith said, taking two dance cards from the butler and handing one to Hazel. As soon as they got to the end of the line Lilith grabbed Hazel by the elbow and dragged her in the direction of the ballroom.

"You're hurting me," Hazel whispered to her sister as Lilith pushed her way through the crowd.

"Hush," Lilith said as they emerged into the candlelit ballroom. Like the rest of Lady Germaine's house, the ballroom was decorated at the height of fashion from twenty years back with dark red papered walls and ornate heavy gold trim plasterwork on the ceiling.

If Lilith hadn't kept a grip on her elbow, Hazel would have been swept aside in the crush of people moving in and out the main doors to the room.

"Do you see anyone we know?" Hazel asked, trying to rise up on her tiptoes. Lilith had a good three inches on her and tipped her chin toward a cluster of young ladies in the far corner. "There's Rosamund and Kitty."

Hazel allowed Lilith to propel her forward and noticed that her particular friend, Miss Eloise Truman, was also present. As soon as they arrived at the group of ladies, Lilith allowed herself to be enfolded into the circle of her friends, leaving Hazel to Eloise.

"Your new dress is very becoming," Eloise said with her usual soft smile.

"Though, perhaps not my color," Hazel said, pulling out her fan. "It hardly matters when I am certain to disappoint my mother yet again."

"Don't say that." Eloise laid a gentle hand on her friend's shoulder. "This is your year. I can feel it."

Hazel forced a smile. Once upon a time she might have dreamed of being swept off her feet by a dashing gentleman. But then she'd had her first season and everything had changed. She hadn't been a wallflower exactly—she was too good at conversing for that—but she hadn't dazzled either. Her title was of little use to most of her peers as it came without a fortune and the few gentlemen who could overlook her lack of worldly assets had their pick of ladies.

No, Hazel had decided after that first year that no match was better than a desperate one. Besides, she had her employment to focus on and a husband would never allow his wife to write a society column for money.

"Dear Eloise, you are two years younger than I and therefore still have reason to be full of optimism and good intentions."

Eloise laughed, then her face turned serious. "Have you heard about Lady Felicity?"

"Lilith told me," Hazel said, a sick feeling settling

in her stomach again. "How could her father do such a thing?"

"And her birthday luncheon was set for next week too," Eloise sighed. "I'd already gotten her a present."

"Perhaps she'll be better by then," Hazel said, wishing not for the first time that she could breathe properly in her corset.

"That seems unlikely. They've sent her to Craven-wood."

"The asylum?"

"Her father wanted a permanent solution," Eloise said, directing her gaze across the room. "I do believe Mr. Ellis is headed our way."

Hazel looked up to see the rail thin form of Mr. Ellis bobbing through the crowd toward them. He stopped to her right, his pale features blending with the white of his shirt collar.

"Lady Hazel," he said with a bowed head. "I hope I am not too late for the first dance."

Hazel had hoped that they had indeed arrived too late to find partners for the first dance, or at the very least that she'd be able to escape to the gardens before the music started.

"Thank you," Hazel said with a tilt of her head. "I am much obliged."

"The honor is mine," Ellis said, offering his hand to her. Hazel allowed him to lead her out onto the dance floor for the first set.

"You are looking remarkably fetching this evening, my lady," Ellis said. She noted that his gaze was resting below her neck.

"Thank you," Hazel said, glancing around the room at the other attendees, and there were many of them.

Lady Germaine's ball was considered the official start to the season. She caught sight of the Duchess of Roscommon and a tall thin man with a hooked nose whose bearing indicated he must be the Duke. They were speaking to the Ashburns and the Earl and Countess of Randelwood.

"And what a lovely shade of yellow," Ellis continued. "Like a ray of sunshine."

Hazel bit the inside of her cheek to keep from rolling her eyes.

She was relieved of his inanity when the figures of the dance took them in opposite directions.

Her next partner was Lord Fletcher, the target of not only her sister's affections, but every lady between the ages of eighteen and eighty. Titled and independently wealthy, Lord Fletcher was the catch of the season.

He was also dashing, with dark brown eyes that settled on a lady, making her think she was the only person in the world. Yet, while he flirted shamelessly, everyone knew that despite his mother's intentions, he had no plans of marrying anytime soon.

Which made him one of Hazel's favorite dance partners.

"And how are you, Lady Hazel?"

"Quite well, my lord."

"May I say that you are looking especially charming this evening?"

"You have and you may," Hazel laughed.

"How are things at the *Daily*?"

This was the other reason Hazel liked Lord Fletcher

so much. No other gentleman in her acquaintance would ever think to ask about her employment.

"I've managed not to embarass myself too much, I think."

Fletcher took her left hand in his right as they formed an archway for another couple to go under.

"I think you managed quite a bit more than that," Fletcher said. "From all reports you've managed to do an excellent job of distinguishing yourself."

Hazel's smile faltered briefly. What kind of reports was he getting and from whom? She tried to think of a polite way to ask when she felt a prickling sensation in her left temple.

No, she thought to herself. *Not now.*

"Are you quite all right?" Ellis asked. Hazel hadn't even realized the figures had changed, throwing them together again

"I need some air," she said, backing up just in time to avoid a collision with the couple next to them. "If you wouldn't mind?"

"Of course." Ellis danced out of the figures and offered his arm, leading her off the dance floor. They had to maneuver through the crowd at the edge of the dance floor and Ellis paused to give Lady Ashburn his greetings. Hazel could feel the tingling sensation spreading. She attempted to move her hand, but Ellis put his hand over hers where it rested on his arm.

Lady Ashburn ended the conversation with Ellis and he once again moved through the crowd and outside onto the veranda. He led her to a bench right next to the open doors and sat next to her, patting her hand absently.

Hazel knew it was too much to hope that he'd lead her outside and then leave her on her own, but the way Ellis hovered around her made her want to run.

Which gave her an idea.

"Mr. Ellis, would you mind terribly going to fetch my father?"

"Your father?" He frowned. "Surely you'd prefer the company of your mother or sister if you are feeling indisposed."

"Thank you, but I don't want to alarm them, and my father can arrange for me to get home, if necessary. Would you mind?"

He looked as though he did mind, but being a gentleman, he made a bow and headed through the French doors back into the ballroom.

It was a clear night, and without the line of carriages that crowded the front of the house, the garden air was quite pleasant. Hazel let out a long breath, but the tingling did not subside.

She heard laughter and realized how close she still was to the ballroom. She needed to get herself out of sight. Hurrying down the steps and into the garden, Hazel headed straight into a hedge maze and rounded several corners before she felt safe to stop. The tingling was getting more intense and a wave of nausea was threatening to overtake her. There was a stone bench in an alcove next to a bird fountain. Hazel sat down and closed her eyes.

Red walls, swirling dresses. So many dull young ladies. Trying desperately to snag husbands. Not more than a handful of the girls were even worth a second glance and most couldn't hide the stench of genteel poverty that clung to even the best families.

She waved a lace fan in front of her face. London was better than this. They were all better than this.

"Miss?

Someone was calling her. She looked to her left and saw the Duke of Roscommon, sipping champagne, looking as bored as she felt.

"Are you ok?"

The room slipped away and the vision broke.

Hazel opened her eyes. She was sitting on the stone bench, a sheen of perspiration on her brow, and the most piercing blue eyes she'd ever seen were looking her over.

Duncan wasn't certain, but he did feel with a degree of confidence that this was the most tedious evening of his life.

He'd shown up at Lady Germaine's house with his mother on his arm and made his bow to the old battle ax and her line of well married daughters. Then he'd made his round of the ballroom, sidestepping the first set of country dances but unable to avoid making the acquaintance of several young ladies, none of whom had two coherent thoughts to rub together.

Or if they did, he wasn't to be blessed with hearing them.

"Your mother said you are newly arrived?" The question, asked for what felt like the hundredth time, came from a simpering young miss, a Lady Rosamund.

"Yes," Duncan said with what he hoped was a pleasant smile. "I returned not a week ago."

"You were traveling abroad?" she continued. "You

must have seen some interesting sights."

"Since my travels were mainly work related, I did not get much time for sightseeing," Duncan said and realized he'd broken a cardinal rule: He'd referred to work in Lady Germaine's ballroom.

An uncomfortable silence hung over his group for a moment until the young lady turned to his mother.

"You and Mr. Walters must be pleased to have your son home."

"Of course we are," she said, looking up at Duncan. "It has been an absolute blessing."

Behind him, on the dance floor, the set came to an end. Duncan saw the eager gleam in the eyes of the young ladies around him and knew swift action was necessary.

"Mama," he said, turning to his mother. "You'll excuse me for a moment? I see an old acquaintance I really ought to have a word with."

"Of course," his mother said. "And Mrs. Markle is across the room. Perhaps you could escort me on your way?"

Duncan held his elbow out to his mother and made his excuses. As they walked around the edge of the room, Mrs. Walters slowed her pace, forcing him to fall into step.

"You aren't enjoying yourself."

"What do you mean?" Duncan said with a laugh. "Did I not keep up my end of the conversation?"

"You're a perfect gentleman, but I can tell when you aren't happy, and you aren't happy here."

"I'm not used to confined spaces."

"Are boats not confined spaces?"

"The open air then," Duncan said. "I'm not used to so many people indoors. Perhaps if I took a short stroll in the gardens it would improve my disposition."

"As you wish. But don't be too long."

Duncan delivered his mother to round-faced Mrs. Markle and headed toward the veranda doors. Before he got there, a familiar figure walked toward him from the direction of the dance floor.

"Fletcher?" Duncan greeted his friend with a grin. Fletcher's main claim, aside from his fortune, was rakish looks. Taller than average, Fletcher sported chestnut brown hair that always looked slightly windswept, as though he were on the run from a matchmaking mama. Even in the middle of a set, more than one lady turned to watch him walk across the dancefloor. "I should have known you'd be here."

Fletcher wore the amused expression that he always sported at public events. "Did your mother drag you out as well?"

"She made it clear that my company was appreciated."

"While my mother made it clear my company was required."

Duncan laughed. "It's good to see you again."

"You as well." Though Fletcher's smile never faded, there was a serious gleam in his eye. "We should talk, sooner than later."

"Once I get business in order I will come to you. At the club?"

Fletcher nodded as the music started up again. "I'm off to find my next partner. You?"

"Stepping out for some air."

Duncan watched Fletcher stop at the side of Lady Rosamund, who puffed up like a peacock at the attention.

And if he didn't want to suffer a similar fate, he needed to move.

He moved out onto the veranda. It was an unseasonably warm night, but compared to the ballroom the air was cool on his face.

The sounds of a happy couple coming out the doors behind him, caused him to spring into action, and Duncan headed straight down the stairs into the garden and hedge maze that took up most of the yard.

He walked along, blissfully alone, until he turned a corner and saw a young woman sitting on a stone bench. She wore a fitted yellow-gold gown revealing a lovely figure, but it was her hair that caught his attention. In the light from a nearby gaslamp he could have sworn it was the color of fire.

At first glance, she appeared as unmoving as the stone bird bath she sat next to. But a faint intake of breath let him know she was fully alive.

The hairs on the back of Duncan's neck prickled. He'd seen this before. Years ago, when his sister had been young. She'd had quiet episodes like this before she'd developed the full blown attacks with uncontrolled ranting.

He walked over to the young lady, not wanting to scare her but knowing no one else could catch her like this. As he got closer, he noticed her unblinking eyes were a mossy shade of green and one of her curls had escaped from its pins and lay against the pale skin of her neck. If he were disposed to flights of fancy, he might have taken her for a wood nymph.

But, he reminded himself, he was not so inclined.

Remembering the other couple who'd followed him out onto the veranda and thinking they might come looking for a quiet alcove, Duncan knew he needed to act. He placed a hand on her shoulder, hoping to bring her around.

"Miss?" he said, hoping to catch her attention. Finally she blinked, the spell broken.

"Are you all right?"

She looked at him in wide-eyed shock. Finally she answered. "Yes, I'm fine."

"Perhaps you need a glass of wine?" Duncan continued. "I can get someone to fetch you one."

"It's just a migraine." The girl, woman really, stood up and ran her hands down her skirts. "I thank you for your concern."

She turned and hurried down the garden path, out of Duncan's line of sight. For a moment he thought to go after her, but he stayed put. Whoever she was, he'd have to wait and hope for a better time for an introduction.

CHAPTER SEVEN

"You look like you're a million miles away," Penny said, adjusting Hazel's hair into a simple braided bun.

"Sorry. I didn't sleep well."

"Do you want to talk about what brought you home from the ball early?"

Hazel fidgeted with a silver trinket box on her dressing table. She couldn't get last night out of her head. She'd been caught in the middle of a vision. It was a stroke of luck that it wasn't anyone in her circle.

"As a matter of fact, I do not."

"As you wish."

Hazel watched through the mirror as Penny finished her hair. She knew her maid would never push her for an explanation, but she also knew she needed her help.

"I would like you to reach out to Dr. Sahni for me," Hazel said. A true professional, Penny didn't bat an eye.

"Of course. Shall I ask the doctor for a Thursday appointment, when your mother and Lilith will be out visiting?"

"Yes, thank you."

Having made the request, Hazel felt a little lighter.

She stood up from the table and looked herself over in the mirror.

"All set for a day at the office," Penny said.

"Yes," Hazel agreed. "I believe I am."

The walk to the *Daily's* office took less than a quarter of an hour and though not quite sunny, the day was unusually bright, making for a particularly pleasing outing requiring no mask.

"Morning, Lady Hazel," Liza, the girl on the front desk greeted her with an eager smile. "How was Lady Germaine's ball?"

"About as you'd expect."

"I want all the details," Liza said. "Cup of tea and a chat?"

Hazel nodded. "That sounds lovely."

Hazel glanced through her notes while Liza went to the potbelly steam stove in the small room behind her desk. Hazel heard the hiss of the valves as Liza released the steam. The stove was a marvel that made boiling water a breeze. Hazel wished they could afford one for her kitchen at home. Liza returned a minute later with a cup and saucer in each hand.

"Thank you," Hazel said, taking one of the teacups and sitting on the wooden stool next to the desk. She told Liza about the food and the dresses and the many, many floral arrangements.

"What about the gentlemen?" Liza asked. "Did you run into anyone interesting?"

Hazel sipped her tea. She couldn't help thinking about the tall, dark haired man with the square jaw who'd come upon her in the garden.

Best not to go there.

"I danced with Mr. Ellis."

"The one what looks like he's got no eyebrows?"

"That would be him."

Liza leaned back in her chair, doing a poor job of hiding her disappointment.

"You can do better."

"I appreciate your confidence in me," Hazel said. "Especially given the serious deficit of eligible gentlemen in this day and age."

Liza rolled her eyes. "You grand ladies wouldn't have near as hard a time finding a husband if you weren't so opposed to marrying a man with a proper job."

"I have no doubt that if a man—gentleman or not—made enough money my mother and sister would find a way to see past where his good fortune came from."

"S'pose you can do that," Liza said. "Seeing as how you're a lady."

"I'd best get to work," Hazel said, picking up her teacup. "If you need me, I'll be at my desk."

"There's a staff meeting at eleven," Liza called and Hazel stopped in her tracks.

"Who called it?"

Liza held up a piece of paper. "I got a note this morning from young Mr. Walters' valet."

"He's taking over for his father then?"

"Certainly looks that way."

Hazel could feel her nostrils flare and she took a deep, calming breath. She'd never had the pleasure of meeting Mr. Walters' son. He'd been away for at least three years and prior to that he'd never had entry into society.

None of the Walters family had until their fortune had grown impossible to ignore.

"Just so long as the younger Mr. Walters doesn't get in my way."

"I think that would be best for everyone," Liza said with a laugh. Hazel went straight to her desk. It was still early enough that she was the only reporter in. Everyone else was either covering a story or sleeping off the last one.

She propped up her brown journal still open to her notes on Lady Germaine's ball. It would be a simple article; one she'd done dozens of times before. She'd include a description of the flower arrangements, references to prominent guests and a detailed menu.

One thing she would not be including was her encounter in the garden.

As she began typing, the newsroom came to life around her. Hazel looked up periodically to greet her fellow reporters or to check a detail in her notebook. She finished the article and reached for her tea. It was stone cold.

She stood up to get another when she noticed how quiet the newsroom had grown. The men were lined off in front of the windows.

Looking up at the clock on the wall, she saw it was less than five minutes to eleven.

"And they say ladies are busybodies," Hazel said under her breath.

"Have you seen him before, Lady Hazel?" Jignesh, a young typesetter, pulled himself away from the windows.

"No. Young Mr. Walters has been away for years."

"But he's been in town for a few days now," Jignesh said. "Been spotted at Burke's Club."

"Perhaps you should be the one writing the society columns," Hazel said.

Jignesh grinned. "My sister's a ladies' maid to one of Lady Germaine's daughters. Bina told me young Mr. Walters has been invited to several events during the Season."

"Really? I guess money can open any door now."

"Never took you for one of those League misses."

"You know I'm not," Hazel said, taking a quick look around the newsroom. Everyone was still occupied. "I wondered if you had any more leads for me?"

"You went down to the docks after?"

"I did. But it didn't exactly turn out as I'd hoped."

"You're looking for a bigger story?"

Hazel nodded. "You got one?"

Jignesh scratched his ear. "I don't know that I should be telling you this. Seeing as you're a proper lady."

"You know that's not true."

"All right." He glanced over his shoulder but none of the men in the newsroom paid them any mind. "King's Pawn Shop. Saturday night, there'll be a card game going on."

Hazel frowned. "Why would I care about a card game?"

"Because the owner of King's Pawn Shop has a share in every black market shipment coming in through the harbor."

"Fair enough," Hazel said, already making a plan in

her head for Saturday night.

At that moment everyone moved away from the windows and hurried to their desks, shuffling papers or tapping busily at typewriters.

"I guess the new master has arrived," Hazel said.

"I'd best get back to the presses," Jignesh said with a tip of his pageboy hat. "But be sure to get a good look at him for me. I promised my sister a full account."

"I'll do my best," Hazel said and returned to her own desk just as the door to the newsroom opened. She looked up, conjuring a polite smile to greet her new boss.

She felt her face freeze.

Standing before her with his hat in hand and a devilish grin on his face was the man from the night before. The one who'd attempted to comfort her in the garden. The one she'd run away from.

"Hello everyone," he said, addressing the crowd but settling his blue eyes squarely on Hazel. "My name's Duncan Walters and I'll be taking over."

Three hours earlier, Duncan had looked out the window as the dockyard came to life below. He'd arrived at the downtown shipping office at first light and had introduced himself to the staff there. He'd spent a pleasant hour with the manager and had discovered that his father didn't spend a lot of time at the shipping office. As a result, the manager, Mr. Idrissi, was fairly bursting with ideas.

A former captain, Idrissi had worked his way up from the Morrocan run and was boundlessly innovative and

Duncan found the enthusiasm contagious. He'd already approved a plan for later in the week to go over a full proposal for expanding the fleet route to Portugal and Mauritania.

"Mr. Walters?"

Duncan glanced away from the window. Myers was standing in the doorway. "There's a cab waiting downstairs."

With a sigh, Duncan had closed the files and stood up. "If we must."

Duncan had followed Myers down the staircase of the shipping office building and out onto the street.

"I'm sure we could walk," Duncan had said as the steam carriage sputtered forward. "It's as good a day as you can expect in London."

"But not in time," Myers said. "The note I left this morning said to expect you at eleven."

"What's the point of being in charge if I can't show up late?"

Myers hadn't bothered answering and they'd climbed into the cab, the metal door shutting them in as the coach lurched forward. Duncan had never liked riding inside the steam carriages. It felt like a mausoleum on wheels.

Between steam carriages and ballrooms, Duncan was more than ready for the wide open sea again. He hoped his mother wouldn't lean on him to accept any further invitations. The previous evening had been entirely dull.

With one marked exception. An exception with the most alluring—

The carriage jerked to a halt and both he and Myers grabbed onto the overhead handrails. Through the one small window in the door, Duncan could see the newspaper office.

As he got out of the cab, Duncan was fairly certain he saw a flickering in the windows.

"It appears your arrival hasn't gone unnoticed."

"Wonderful," Duncan had said. "I thought the day couldn't get better."

Taking a deep breath, and instantly regretting it as his lungs filled with London air, Duncan walked in through the front door.

"Morning, sir," a young woman stood up from behind the front desk. Duncan wasn't certain but he thought she might have curtsied.

"Good morning Miss—?"

"Liza Butler, sir. I run the front desk here."

"Nice to meet you, Miss Butler. I assume everyone knows I'm coming in this morning?"

"Oh yes. They're all waiting inside."

Taking off his hat, Duncan headed into the newsroom. It was a space he hadn't entered since he'd been a teenager. He wondered how anyone could get work done in such a wide-open, noisy environment.

Duncan was aware of more than a dozen sets of eyes on him, but there was one pair in particular that very much stood out.

Less the eyes than the hair. Such a flaming red.

Duncan's lips curled as he recognized the young woman from the gardens the previous evening.

And now, standing in front of the crowd, he realized his visit to the *Daily* had become very interesting after all.

Later, he couldn't remember what he'd said during his

speech; he'd been too eager to meet his staff and particularly a certain out-of-place female.

"William Hathaway, sir," a gray-haired man held out his hand. "Your chief copy editor."

"Nice to meet you," Duncan gave his hand a firm shake. "Perhaps you would be so kind as to introduce me to the other staff."

"Certainly."

Duncan followed William around the newsroom, feigning interest in modern photography techniques and front-page reports on the price of corn, all while waiting to finally meet the red-haired woman. At last it was her turn.

She looked up from her typewriter as he and William stopped next to her desk.

"And this is Lady Hazel Winchester. She writes for the society pages."

"How unusual. A lady reporter."

Lady Hazel didn't meet his gaze. Her cheeks turned a charming shade of pink and she pulled a paper out of the typewriter on her desk. "If you'll excuse me, I'm on a deadline."

Duncan bowed his head and moved on, but he couldn't stop himself from smiling.

CHAPTER EIGHT

Dr. Sahni adjusted her glasses, a sure sign she was thinking through some problem.

Hazel had come to the doctor's office as soon as her mother and sister had gone out to do their morning visits. The doctor's suite sat above a milliner's shop and was only accessible by stepping around the back. It was the perfect location for a private meeting.

Dr. Sahni's office was a small room, made smaller by the shelves of books and the large desk that dominated the space. The walls, what could be seen of them around the books, were papered in a forest landscape that a previous tenant had likely picked out. Behind Dr. Sahni, velvet green curtains were pulled over the window, giving them complete privacy.

Sitting across from the doctor, Hazel had just given a rundown of her recent incident at Lady Germaine's ball. She still felt jittery when she thought about it, and especially shaken about the fact that her new employer—he of the penetrating blue stare—had been the one to discover her.

"And you say this is your first episode since we started

the new regime?" Dr. Sahni asked.

"Yes," Hazel said, hesitating. "There may have been one or two minor incidents."

Dr. Sahni leaned her elbows on the desk, steepling her fingers. "Have you told anyone about your incidents?"

"No. My mother might try to force me back to that quack Dr. Baker."

"And I wouldn't wish his methods on anyone. But it would be helpful to have someone around observing you, someone who could verify how long the episodes are. It ensures I'm not over medicating."

"You think that's what happened?" Hazel straightened up in her seat. "I'm not taking the correct dose?"

With her black hair pulled back in a severe bun and her spectacles sitting on the end of her nose, Dr. Sahni could pass for a governess or librarian. Few would guess she was one of the leading medical minds of their time. "When do you turn twenty-one?"

Hazel frowned. "In three weeks. Why?"

"I've noticed in several of my patients that as they near their twenty-first birthdays, they've begun to suffer a relapse, if you will."

Hazel bit her bottom lip. "I don't like the sound of that."

"I don't believe there's any need to worry. Once the medications are tweaked, things seem to normalize."

"It's not just that the episodes have returned. The visions have become more...realistic."

Dr. Sahni reached for a fountain pen and pulled a paper closer. "How so?"

"I don't know how to explain it, not without sounding

mad."

"You know that's not how I think."

"I know." Hazel took a deep breath. "But when I was in the vision, it was like I was inside someone else's head, seeing what they were seeing, feeling what they were feeling."

Dr. Sahni made several notes. "And you were in the present moment?"

Hazel nodded.

Dr. Sahni adjusted her spectacles again. "Interesting."

"How serious is this?"

The doctor looked down at her notes. "Your story is remarkably consistent with two other patients I have. The timing isn't always the same. One patient feels like they've been sucked into the past, the other into future events."

"I was very much in the present," Hazel said, then she frowned. "I understand being in the past, but how would a person feel they were in the future?"

"It was described to me as an impending sensation, like something is going to happen."

"That must be uncomfortable."

"I imagine so." Dr. Sahni put down her pen and read through her notes. "Based on what I've learned from you today, and what I observed in my other two patients, I'd like you to continue checking in with me on a more regular basis."

"Is something wrong with me?"

Dr. Sahni pursed her lips in a thin line. "I'd like to keep an eye on you. I've noted that more and more young women of your age are being checked into institutions."

Havel couldn't suppress the shudder that ran down

her spine. "I don't like the sound of that, one of the ladies in our circle was admitted to Cravenwood."

"Yes, that seems to be the common choice. There's a Dr. Cadavy there who believes he's got a better treatment."

"Does he?"

Dr. Sahni pushed her notes to one side. "Not from what I've seen."

"Well, I appreciate your efforts." Hazel loosened her hands, letting them rest in her lap. "What do you suggest I do?"

"For now, the best thing you can do is take an extra blocker every other day."

"You think that will fix it?"

"I think it will help," Dr. Sahni said. "My other patients have reported a reduction in symptoms."

"A reduction? But not gone completely."

"No."

"There's no way to make the episodes go away altogether?"

"Not without using Persephamine."

Hazel shuddered. "I don't want that."

"And I would never prescribe it. You're better off waiting out the visions when they do come. In the years I've been treating patients, the one thing I can tell you is that I have never seen any negative physical side effects from having a vision."

"Unless you get caught by your mother," Hazel muttered.

"As far as I can see, that's society's problem. Not yours."

Hazel felt her lips form a smile for the first time that morning. "I'm very fortunate to have found you when I did. I'd hate to think of my life otherwise."

Dr. Sahni sat back in her chair, returning her grin. "Now that business is over, I want to know about the *Daily*. I hear there's a new editor-in-chief?"

Hazel frowned. "You've heard correctly."

"What's he like?"

Too handsome for his own good, Hazel thought to herself, remembering the way his dark hair fell over his forehead when he'd stopped at her desk.

Not at all like the properly groomed gentlemen of her class.

"I hardly know," Hazel said when she realized the doctor was waiting for her answer. She'd been doing her very best to avoid him since their brief meeting in the newsroom.

"Well if he's anything like his father, the paper will be in good hands."

"I very much hope so," Hazel said, but she didn't share the doctor's confidence.

Duncan sat at his father's desk, looking out at the busy newsroom.

He'd forced himself to spend the day at the paper, observing the staff, watching the presses. He wondered if it would ever feel like his.

The shipping office, on the other hand, felt more like a home than the house he'd grown up in. He loved his family, but the merchants who came into the shipping office were his friends. They didn't care about the season, they didn't care whether there was mud on his boots or that he preferred to walk everywhere.

Newspapers on the other hand, they were a different business altogether. Peddling information was so different from filling a ship's hold with cargo. For one thing, the upper levels of society were far more interested in the front page than they were in what arrived at the docks.

"Mr. Walters?"

Duncan looked up to see William standing in the doorway. "Come in."

William came in and took the seat across from Duncan. "I wanted to see what you thought of the front page?"

Duncan picked up the paper that was lying on his desk. "Yes, it looks fine."

"I don't believe you read it."

"No need. It always looks fine."

"Glad it's all to your taste then, sir. If there's nothing else, I'll be going home for the evening."

"Actually, I wanted to ask you about Lady Hazel."

William's face lit up. "A fine young lady."

"Indeed, she must be a rather unique lady to fit in so well at a newspaper."

"She is," William agreed. "Not many ladies of her birth would be able to manage in this industry. Most women forced into labor are working for milliners or dressmakers."

"What do you mean forced? Couldn't her family pay the idle tax?"

William shook his head. "There's not one posh family in five that can afford not to have some family member working. Lady Hazel's just doing her part."

It should have occurred to Duncan that Lady Hazel was part of the national movement aimed at getting more Londoners into the workforce. It was the only way to compensate for the increase in navy recruitment.

For some reason it disappointed him to think that the only reason she was there was because her family couldn't afford the tax that would have exempted her household from working.

Duncan pushed the thought aside.

"You believe this Lady Hazel is a sensible woman?"

"I absolutely do."

There was a tapping on the door and Duncan looked up to see Myers there.

"You have the Ashburn ball this evening, sir. If you leave now there will be just enough time to get ready."

"Thank you, Myers," Duncan said. "I'd be lost without you."

William stood up, a smile on his face. "Enjoy your evening, sir."

"If only I could."

CHAPTER NINE

"You should see him," Hazel said. "Mr. Walters the younger. Walking in off the street like he could just fill his father's shoes."

"Well legally he can," Penny said, pulling a brush through Hazel's hair.

"But not morally." Hazel crossed her arms over her chest. "What does he know about newspapers? He's been away for years. I give him three months. Six at most."

"I'm sorry I asked about work," Penny said, putting the brush on the table and dividing Hazel's hair into sections. "I'd like to try something new. A braid across the crown of your head."

"You know I don't care," Hazel said, shifting in her seat.

"Well stay still unless you want me to get the curling iron."

Hazel stopped fidgeting.

"He said he'd be taking over, like he owned the place."

"Which, I imagine he will one day."

"But not yet. Ouch!" Hazel frowned into the mirror.

"Do you have to pull so hard?"

"Can you sit still?"

"Apparently not."

"Then yes, I have to pull."

With a sigh, Hazel reached for the silver backed brush and flipped it over, running her fingers over the bristles while Penny fixed her hair.

"Do you think he'll be at the ball tonight?" Penny asked, tucking the end of a braid behind Hazel's right ear.

"I'm sure I don't care if he is," Hazel said, looking away from the mirror. She hadn't told her maid about their encounter in Lady Germaine's garden and she didn't want to be reminded of it now.

"As you say, my lady." Penny pushed a pin into Hazel's hair and stood back. "I think that'll do it."

Hazel looked up and saw her hair formed a braided crown around her head.

"It's lovely, Penny."

Penny smiled into the mirror. "It is, isn't it?"

"I fear your talents are wasted on me."

"I prefer being where I'm needed most." Penny moved away from the vanity table so Hazel could stand up.

"Here you go." Penny handed over a fan and a pair of gloves. "Try to have a good time tonight."

"I will do my best," Hazel said.

She walked down the stairs and was surprised to see that, for once, she was the first one down.

"Oh," her mother came down the stairs behind her. "It's you."

"You look lovely as well, Mama," Hazel said. Her

mother gave her a once over and frowned.

"You got that dress last year."

Hazel glanced down at the green silk with the modest neckline. "Yes, I know."

"But I don't like that dress."

"You aren't required to wear it."

Lady Winchester snapped her fan open. "What's the point of working like a commoner if you aren't going to use the money to better present yourself in society?"

Hazel was saved from making a retort by the arrival of both her sister and father. Lilith immediately met with her mother's approval in an ice blue gown in the latest fashion.

"I knew that color would suit," her mother said. "Your skin is like porcelain."

Lilith beamed. "Do you think Lord Dennison will like it? He danced with me twice at Lady Germaine's."

"If he doesn't, one of his brothers is certain to," Hazel said. "There are so very many of them."

"Are we ready to go?" Her father glanced at his pocket watch. "Or can I return to my study?"

"Don't be so silly, Papa," Lilith said, eying her sister. "Unless you'd like to change into a newer dress?"

"No thank you. I'm quite comfortable."

"Yes, I hear comfort is what all the French modistes are obsessed with this year."

Hazel followed her parents out to the carriage, easily stepping in while Lilith had to struggle with her train. They arrived at the Ashburns within moments but had to idle in a line of carriages.

"It'll be quite a squeeze tonight," Lilith said, craning

her neck to see out the small window in the door. "If I don't dance every other set I'll be extremely put out."

As the carriage inched along, Hazel felt a sense of dread overtake her. What if Duncan Walters did show up tonight. It seemed likely given he was at Lady Germaine's. She couldn't avoid talking to him forever.

And perhaps she was making more of their first meeting than she needed to. There was no reason to think Mr. Walters hadn't believed her when she said she had a migraine. Now that she thought of it, how many gentlemen would really know what an aether episode looked like anyway?

She caught sight of her sister out of the corner of her eye, preening in her reflection from the carriage window.

The carriage rolled forward and came to a rocking stop.

"You must have a word with the driver," Lady Winchester said, bracing herself against the window ledge.

The door swung open and the stairs were lowered. Hazel waited until her mother and sister were handed out before departing the carriage. It wasn't a clear night and aether fog filled the air, but the entrance to the Ashburn's house was close enough that Hazel didn't bother to take out a handkerchief.

In the foyer, Hazel stood with Lilith and watched her sister adjust her gloves and pinch her cheeks while they waited in a receiving line.

"Don't you love the Season?" Lilith asked, her eyes glowing with excitement. "Dances, dresses, sparkling wine."

"Waiting in carriage lines, waiting in receiving lines,

waiting in ballrooms for unworthy gentlemen to request a dance."

Someone snorted behind Hazel, and she felt her face heat. She could tell by the way her sister stared at her that she'd made a cardinal error.

Never speak your mind at a ball.

She kept her eyes forward and her mouth shut as her parents approached the receiving line ahead of them.

"Lady Lilith, Lady Hazel," Lady Ashburn said with a regal nod. Not to be outdone by her remarkable hats, Lady Ashburn's hair was arranged in a high, cascading style that increased her height by nearly half a foot.

"Good evening, Lady Ashburn," Lilith said. "Thank you for the invitation."

Hazel nodded to her hostess and continued into the ballroom with her sister. Unlike Lady Germaine's ballroom, which had been preserved over three generations, Lady Ashburn's changed with each season. This year the theme was white. White walls, white curtains, white roses, white candles.

There was something truly enchanting about a room of white.

"A bold choice," Lilith said. "This decor will give you something to write about."

"It's like dancing inside a cloud," Hazel said, already composing in her head. "The column writes itself."

Lilith waved at someone across the room. "See you on the dance floor," Lilith said with a laugh before heading off toward her friends.

At the same time, Hazel caught sight of Eloise talking to their friend Lady Beth Eustace.

"Lady Hazel," Beth said with a smile. "Thank heavens you're here. You're always so amusing."

"Well I've already made a spectacle of myself." Hazel waved her fan in front of her face and recounted what she'd said in Lady Ashburn's receiving line.

"Are you sure it was a snort?" Eloise asked. "Perhaps he had a cough and didn't hear you after all."

"I'm certain it was a snort," Hazel said.

"More importantly, who was it?" Beth asked. "That's what I'd like to know."

"Whoever it was, if I meet up with him again I'll be sure to give him a lesson in manners," Hazel said. "Eavesdropping is never appropriate."

"Indeed," Beth said with a smirk. "I think I'd give up my favorite bonnet to see that exchange."

Hazel rolled her eyes. "Change the subject. Please."

"The music is about to start," Eloise said. "And Mama says if I don't dance at least three sets she's sending me to Scotland for the summer."

"That's a severe punishment," Beth said. "Even for your mama."

"I have cousins there." Eloise fidgeted with her dance card. "She thinks I could make a match."

"You probably could," Hazel agreed. "The population of young men in Scotland is higher than here in London."

"I don't want to live in the highlands." Eloise crossed her arms over her chest.

"Well stop whining and put on a smile," Beth said. "And maybe some charming young men will come by and ask us to dance."

"I don't see anyone to tempt me," Hazel said.

"Oh, I don't know," Beth said, scanning the room. Her eyes came to a stop and she gave a quick nod. "What about him?"

Hazel turned around, ready with a scathing dismissal, when she caught the eye of Duncan Walters and her mouth went dry.

"He's a handsome fellow," Eloise agreed. "I haven't seen him before. I wonder who he is?"

"The Duke of Northam has many relatives on the continent," Beth said. "Perhaps he's one of them."

"French or Dutch?" Eloise asked. "My mama would never let me marry a Frenchman."

"With a figure like that, I believe your mama would let you marry the very devil himself."

"Lady Beth!" Eloise's eyes widened and she glanced over her shoulder. Fortunately her mother was busily talking to the Duke of Roscommon. "Really, you can't say such things."

But Lady Beth was unrepentant. "I do believe I might swoon if he comes this way. Do you think he'd pick me up? He certainly looks strong enough."

Hazel finally found her voice again. "That's Mr. Walters. The younger."

"Really?" Beth's eyes lit up. "So you've met him."

"Just at the paper," Hazel said. "Nothing formal."

"Well formal or not, he's coming this way."

Hazel glanced over her shoulder and her stomach dropped as she realized Beth was right.

"I want an introduction," Eloise whispered. "That will definitely get me into Mama's good graces."

"Good evening, Lady Hazel," Duncan said in a voice as smooth as warm honey. "I hope you are enjoying yourself?"

"Indeed, Mr. Walters," Hazel said, though she hoped he would simply move along, but when he continued looking at her, she became intensely aware of the expectant gazes from her companions. "May I introduce you to my friends? Lady Beth Eustace and Miss Eloise Truman."

"A pleasure to make your acquaintance," Duncan said with a bow.

"Lady Hazel says you've just arrived back in London," Beth said. "Are you happy to be home?"

"How could I not be?" Duncan asked with an easy smile that Hazel didn't trust. Not when he clearly knew she'd just been talking about him. "When there is such company to be had?"

Both Beth and Eloise giggled behind their fans. Hazel pursed her lips.

"However, I must confess, I had an ulterior motive for coming over here."

"Oh?" Beth asked with raised eyebrows. "Do tell."

"I wondered if Lady Hazel would accompany me in the next set? I've been away so long, I can hardly remember the last time I had an opportunity to dance in such exalted company."

"She'd be delighted!" Eloise clapped her hands together. "Wouldn't you, Hazel?"

Hazel was about to suggest perhaps Lady Beth might take her place when Duncan quirked a brow at her.

"Assuming, that is, that she thinks I am a worthy partner?"

Hazel's cheeks grew hot and she could tell by the gleam in Duncan's eye that he could sense her discomfort.

Dratted man. He'd been the one behind her in the waiting line.

"Of course, Mr. Walters. It would be my pleasure."

She allowed Duncan to lead her out to the dance floor. As the music began, Hazel realized it was to be a waltz.

Leave it to Lady Ashburn to open a ball with a waltz.

As Duncan held a hand out for hers, she stiffened.

"Is something wrong?" Duncan asked.

"I don't waltz."

Duncan frowned. "You mean you don't know how?"

Hazel cleared her throat. "That's not what I said."

Duncan took her hand, placing it on the crook of his arm and led her off the dance floor. He leaned in and whispered in her ear.

"Fan yourself."

"Pardon?"

"If anyone asks why you left the dance floor it will be easy enough to say you were overcome and needed refreshment."

"Anyone who'd believe that doesn't know me very well," Hazel said, but she took out her fan anyway.

Duncan led her into the refreshment room, and she picked up a glass of lemonade.

"If you return now you can likely get a partner for the next set," Hazel said. "Since you were so keen to dance."

"What on earth gave you that idea?"

"You said you hadn't been in a ballroom in ages."

"I haven't," Duncan agreed. "Yet I haven't missed it."

"That's not the impression you left Lady Beth and Eloise with."

"Yes well, I needed to be polite," Duncan said, guiding Hazel to a quiet corner. It was still early enough that most of the guests were in the ballroom or the card room.

"You don't feel the need to be polite with me?" Hazel asked, sitting on a gold backed chair.

"We'll be working together," Duncan said, sitting next to her. Hazel shifted so their knees didn't touch. He really was rather broad. And tall. As ever, Beth's observations were on point.

"I'm still a lady."

"You didn't sound especially lady-like earlier in the receiving line."

Hazel fixed a strand of hair behind her ear. "A gentleman wouldn't have been listening."

"And I'm not a gentleman. Good we got that out of the way."

Hazel sipped her lemonade. Duncan was smiling again and it was throwing her off. She'd never thought of a smile as dangerous before, but she was fairly certain if she wasn't careful she could get lost in this one. She needed to get the conversation back on safer ground.

"How is your father?"

Duncan shook his head. "Not well, I'm afraid. He's not been conscious for several days now."

"Ah," Hazel said, swallowing hard and staring into her glass. "I am sorry."

"I get the impression you and my father get along rather well?"

Hazel nodded. "He gave me an opportunity that few

men of his generation would have considered."

"Few men of any generation would welcome a lady of breeding in their place of work."

Hazel raised an eyebrow. "Am I about to be out of a job?"

"Not at all. Your column is far too popular with the ladies of the *ton*."

"I am gratified to hear that I will continue to have employment."

"You were in doubt?"

Hazel shrugged. "I don't know you. And you did seek me out at a ball for a tete-a-tete."

"Perhaps I enjoy the company of charming young ladies?"

"Then I will be sure to point some out to you."

He laughed, and Hazel found she liked that even more than his smile. "Actually, there was something else I wanted to talk to you about."

"Oh?" Hazel wondered if she was about to get lectured for her earlier faux pas in the receiving line.

"The other night, when I encountered you in Lady Germaine's garden it appeared you were...indisposed."

Hazel knew her cheeks were turning pink. She opened her fan with her free hand. "I believe I told you I had a migraine."

"I think we both know it was more than that."

She knew she was flicking her wrist far too quickly and she forced herself to slow the fan. "As I said, it was a migraine."

"I'm just looking for advice," Duncan said, leaning closer and dropping his voice. "About your course of treatment."

"My treatment?" Hazel's voice was strangled. She was shocked she could get any words out at all.

"Yes. It seems you manage quite well despite your condition."

Hazel had enough. She stood up, her glass spilling her lemonade in her haste.

"I believe you were correct in your earlier assessment, Mr. Walters. You really are not a gentleman."

And with that, Hazel left her glass with the nearest footman and stormed toward the ballroom.

"I gather the ball went well, sir," Myers said as he entered the bedroom to find Duncan slouched in an armchair, next to an empty fire grate with a brandy snifter in his hand.

"I was a smashing success," Duncan said, draining the contents of his glass and laying it on the nearest side table with a thunk.

"I can tell by the state of your cravat," Myers said. "Give me your foot, I want those boots before you do any further damage to the shine."

Duncan lifted his foot. "I don't want to talk about it."

"Then I promise not to ask." Myers gave the Hessian a hard yank and braced himself to keep from falling backward.

"I hate society functions."

"Other foot."

Duncan raised his other boot. "All simpering and chatter."

"And dancing," Myers added. "Now your cravat, please."

Duncan hooked a finger into the fabric at his neck and unwound it in one fluid motion.

"I danced four sets," Duncan said. "I don't even know how it happened. I hadn't intended to dance more than one."

And the one he'd planned was to be with a green-eyed lady who'd been the one to elude him.

"By all appearances, your mama was very pleased with your foray into the Season."

Duncan snorted.

"I gather you disagree?"

Duncan pointed at his empty glass. "Would you?"

With a sigh, Myers reached for the brandy decanter and refilled the glass. "I assume there's a reason you require such remedy"

"I fear I was a touch indelicate," Duncan said. "With a lady."

Myers' face turned beet red. "You do not have to continue, sir, I believe I understand."

"No." Duncan laughed. "I'd have had a far better night if that were the case."

His mind wandered back to his conversation with Lady Hazel. How much better it would have been if instead of quarrelling over lemonade they'd been in a darkened corner getting to know each other in a different way. Perhaps he could take her hair out of its braid and see it in all its fiery glory—

Duncan frowned. Those were dangerous thoughts. Especially about a lady. Not just a lady, a lady he'd see on a professional basis.

"What was the problem then?" Myers asked, bringing him back to his current predicament.

"I was hoping she'd give me a piece of information," Duncan said, remembering how upset she'd looked hurrying out of the room. More than upset; she was scared. And he was the cause. "But instead I managed to cause offense."

"Might I ask what the nature of this information was?" Myers folded the cravat and placed it in a drawer.

"Something personal to her."

"And did it occur to you to explain why you needed that information?"

Duncan scowled. "I'm not used to having to explain myself."

"You aren't used to being in the company of ladies. I'd recommend you readjust."

"I don't think she's going to want to talk to me long enough to give me another try."

Myers thought for a moment. "Then, perhaps you are the wrong messenger."

Duncan's expression brightened. He sat up straight in his chair.

"Of course. Myers, you're brilliant."

"I'm glad you think so, sir."

CHAPTER TEN

Hazel sat in Lady Germaine's drawing room with a cup of tepid tea in her hand and an even more tepid conversation swirling around her despite the fact that she was with her friends Eloise and Beth.

She'd gone into the paper first thing in the morning and had handed in her column outlining the ball from the night before, giving an extensive account of the decor and the guest list.

By happy coincidence, her early arrival and departure meant she hadn't seen Mr. Walters at all.

"You are looking tired, Lady Hazel," Lady Germaine interrupted her thoughts. "I hope you aren't working yourself too hard."

"No, my lady," Hazel said, forcing a smile. "I had trouble sleeping last night after all the fun at the Ashburn ball."

"Indeed," Lady Germaine gave her a nod. "But do take care. A girl of your years needs her rest. Especially when being presented next to the young ladies in their come-out season."

"As always, I am beholden to your excellent advice."

Having made her point, Lady Germain turned her attention to the next group of young ladies.

"She's such a dragon," Beth whispered. "My mama says the only reason anyone listens to her is because her daughters married within their first three seasons."

"And my mama says that's reason enough to listen to anyone," Eloise said.

"Have you been to Hyde park this morning?" Beth asked. "The construction of the temporary pavilion for the Princess's birthday celebrations is well underway."

"Mama says it's a terrible waste," Eloise said. "Not to mention tempting providence, especially after the last royal celebration."

While Beth and Eloise argued over the sensibility of the celebrations, Hazel's mind went back to the issue that had kept her up all night.

What was she going to do if she lost her employment? Stalking off as she had, Mr. Walters could hardly be blamed for firing her. And if he did, she'd have to find another job. Her father simply couldn't afford the taxes for her to stay home.

She'd end up trimming hats. How horrid.

While Eloise and Beth continued their back and forth, their group was joined by Miss Clara Evans, a sweet girl, still in her second season, with a reasonable dowry and pretty brown eyes.

"Did you enjoy the ball last night?" Eloise asked.

"I did," Clara said. "But I wish there had been more gentlemen to choose from. I'd have liked more dancing partners."

"For a lady of breeding, there will always be options,"

Lady Rosamund said with a sniff. She'd been walking past with Lilith and had overheard the conversation. Clara's cheeks colored and Hazel recalled hearing that her father had made his fortune in trade.

"I believe you danced with Mr. Walters last evening, Rosamund?" Hazel asked. It hadn't escaped her notice that after their encounter, Duncan had gone on to dance no less than four sets with young unattached ladies. Not that Hazel cared.

"Why yes, I did," Rosamund answered. "And he was quite charming, considering his background."

"I think he was far more than charming," Beth said. "Did you see those arms? I near fainted just to have him catch me."

Lilith set down her teacup with a clink. "I don't believe there is any need for such talk."

"Why?" Beth continued. "He's a handsome man. Why shouldn't I acknowledge it?"

"It isn't ladylike," Lilith said.

"Being perfect ladies hasn't landed us husbands yet, has it?"

Hazel bit the inside of her cheek to keep from grinning. Lilith looked ready to explode.

"Some of us have been waiting for the right moment," Rosamund said, narrowing her eyes at Beth. "We're not all unmarried because we can't find husbands."

Beth shrugged off the attempt at a set down. "As my papa says, there's no time like the present. Mr. Walters is attractive, rich and charming."

"I heard he had a terrible falling out with his father," Clara said, her voice dropping to a whisper. "And that's why he hadn't returned to England in years."

"What was it over?" Hazel asked, the question coming out of her mouth before she could stop it.

"A girl," Clara said. "At least, that's what my maid told me."

"Ancient history," Beth said with a dismissive wave. "Besides, it's clear his mother dotes on him. I saw him escorting her around the ballroom several times."

"Did anyone see Mr. Ellis last evening?" Eloise asked. "I believe he drew on eyebrows."

As the conversation shifted, Hazel sipped her tea. It had never occurred to her to wonder why Mr. Walters the younger had left London. It was quite common for sons of wealthy men to spend time abroad, especially if there was work to be done.

But he was Mr. Walters' only heir. Shouldn't he have stayed home to help his father?

Lady Hazel was avoiding him.

She'd been coming in early for a week.

Of course, it was the Season. That meant afternoon and evening engagements, so of course she'd need to alter her hours.

But coming in at six in the morning was a bit much.

Duncan paced his small office. Myers had not been pleased with the early call. He hadn't gotten time to properly adjust his cravat and his boots were not up to standard.

And Duncan couldn't have cared less.

Grateful to have spent a quiet night at home, he'd left

home at the crack of dawn. So early that he encountered more than one group of revelers coming home from the night before.

But he needed to talk to Lady Hazel.

"Morning sir," Jignesh, one of the print boys, paused at the door. "I got a paper here, hot off the presses."

"Thank you," Duncan said, taking the still warm paper in his hands as the boy went off to organize the stacks for the paperboys.

As he unfolded the newsprint, the warm scent of fresh ink filled his nostrils. He imagined that if he were inclined to be a newsman, this would be a welcoming sensation.

He looked at the front page. It was a story on a debate in the House of Commons about increasing the merchant taxes. Again.

Fortunately, it had been voted down. But just barely.

He looked through for anything that might be of interest to himself or the other agents, not that he expected to see anything spelled out, but sometimes there were clues in the strangest of places.

There was a stirring out in the main area, and he looked out to see a shadowy figure head toward one of the central desks. She turned up the gas lamp, illuminating her drab gray day wear and bonnet.

But he'd seen her in much more flattering attire. He knew where her waist curved in and where certain other assets curved out...

Duncan gave himself a mental shake. That was no way to think of an employee.

She sat down, taking off her bonnet and gloves before typing.

He waited, watching as her gaze never left the paper in front of her. When she seemed to be finishing up, or at least slowing down, Duncan took his cue and left his office.

"Good morning, Lady Hazel," he called. "You're in early today."

She visibly jumped.

"You scared me," she said. "I didn't think anyone else would be in the newsroom."

"Well, apparently that's the only way to track you down."

"Was there something you needed to discuss?" Hazel said. "You could have left a message with Liza."

"I don't think I could give this particular message to Liza."

Duncan watched her turn back to the paper in the typewriter. Whatever was going through her head, she wasn't going to share it.

"What did you want to discuss?"

The light from the gaslamp flickered, illuminating the shades of red in her hair and Duncan was momentarily distracted.

"I shouldn't have asked you about your condition the other night," he said, forcing himself to focus. "That's your personal business."

"Yes, well, I have everything under control. It won't affect my work."

"I wasn't worried about that."

She raised an eyebrow. "You weren't?"

"No."

She looked around, taking in the empty newsroom.

"And you came in here at this hour just to reassure me of that?"

"Actually, I came with an invitation from my mother. She would like to invite you and Lady Winchester to tea tomorrow afternoon."

"You're inviting me to tea?"

"My mother is. She isn't entertaining much this season. But I think some company will lift her spirits."

"I would love to visit with Mrs. Walters," she said, standing up with her journal and press pass. "I'm on assignment this morning but I will ask my mother about it this afternoon."

"Where are you heading off to so early?"

"An airship tour."

"Really?"

Hazel nodded. "The *HMA Triumph* is about to be decommissioned and the newspapers are getting one last look."

"I'm not usually envious of your assignments," Duncan said. "But this one sounds rather fun."

Lady Hazel pulled the paper out of the typewriter and left her column about the previous evening's soiree on her desk. "Luckily you can read all about it in tomorrow's edition."

CHAPTER ELEVEN

Hazel adjusted her bonnet as she headed through the downtown streets toward the London dock. A weak sunlight streamed through the ashy clouds overhead, not quite touching the lines of people heading to work for the day.

But it was enough to hold the fog at bay, which meant she could forgo the mask.

She'd never come down to the docks during the day. It was not a place for a lady and even though she was on assignment, she wouldn't be telling her mother about today's excursion.

At least, not before her story appeared in the paper.

Reaching the docklands, the smell of fish and salt assailed her nostrils as she came upon a fishing boat unloading baskets of dried cod. She passed two sailors speaking German and a small crew gutting fish and speaking a mix of English and Hindi. As she moved down the dock, the ships progressed in size from smaller fishing boats to bigger merchant ships. She paused when she saw the logo for Walters' shipping on a massive vessel painted a shiny black and trimmed out in red and gold.

Much like a pirate ship.

"Wotcher miss!" a young male voice called and Hazel lifted her skirts just in time to skip over a broken mast lying in her path.

She mixed in with a stream of passengers disembarking from a ship from France, then dodged a group of young men unloading barrels from a trading ship.

The tall ships grew sparser and so did the people as she reached the end of the docklands. An eight-foot tall wrought iron gate complete with spikes, marked the entrance to the military section of the dockyard.

A squat figure stood guard outside the gate like a fat, metal soldier and Hazel smiled with delight. She rarely got to see a mech up close. This one had a large round head and was painted in navy and gold and his squat body made him look like a heavy-booted giant had stepped on a tin soldier.

Hazel pulled a pass card out of her reticule and stuck it in the mech's hinged mouth. There were a series of clicks followed by a punching sound as the card was spit out and the gates swung open.

She walked through, careful to keep the skirts of her day dress from catching on a pointed iron spike.

"Can I help you with something, Miss?"

Hazel looked to her right to see a young naval officer hurrying toward her.

She pointed at the huge white balloon hovering overhead.

"I'm here for the tour."

"The tour?" The officer repeated.

With a sigh, Hazel pulled her press pass out of her

reticule and handed it to the officer.

"You're Lady Hazel?"

"I am."

"My mother loves your column."

"Glad to hear it," Hazel said.

"The rest of the reporters are straight ahead and to the right."

"Thank you," Hazel said, fighting the urge to point out that she probably could have found her way without his directions.

She put her pass back in her reticule and headed off. As she rounded a corner, *HMA Triumph* came into view. Hazel paused for a moment to get the full impact of the ship. The gondola, or vessel, rested in the water in full navy and gold perfection. Its figurehead stared ahead proudly, a winged woman, ready to guide them through the clouds.

The Triumph could almost be mistaken for any other naval ship if not for the massive white balloon hovering over it, attached to the masts instead of sails. Once the aether engines started that balloon would pull the ship into the air, ready for flight.

Hazel heard a clicking noise and turned to her left to find Matilda Martin standing next to her, capturing the airship in all its glory.

"What do you think?" Matilda asked, taking the brass and mahogany camera down from her face and looking at Hazel.

"It's quite impressive."

"It's smaller than I'd imagined," Matilda said pushing a stray curl under her bonnet. "Not the balloon part, but the ship."

"On an airship that part's called the gondola. And it's the biggest HMA to date."

Matilda wrinkled her nose. "I think I was expecting a full-size navy ship attached to a balloon."

"Then you'd have been disappointed with the early models. They were barely bigger than dories."

"I assume this isn't your first time on an airship then?"

"No," Hazel shook her head. "But those were just pleasure cruisers. Nothing like this."

"I forget sometimes that you're a lady," Matilda laughed. "Of course you were probably a Duke's guest on a holiday."

Hazel half smiled. "It was an earl, actually."

The two women walked forward, joining the line of reporters on the dock waiting for the tour to start.

"You in the right line, ladies?" A man with a crooked nose raised an eyebrow. "I don't think they're serving tea on board today."

The man next to him laughed and though Matilda visibly bristled, Hazel didn't bother answering. She eyed Matilda's camera instead.

"Do make sure you get a photo from the upper deck when you get a chance," Hazel said. "The view of the city should be impressive from up there."

"Already planning on it," Matilda said, messing with the lens on her camera and holding it up to her eye. She had a satchel slung over her shoulder with more parts. Hazel had no idea how the contraption worked—Matilda had constructed her own device—but there was no mistaking a print by M. Martin.

"I'm glad William sent you with me," Hazel said. "Last time I had Benny and he wasted his plates on a group of tavern maids and had nothing left for when we made it to the event."

"Never fear," Matilda patted her satchel. "I never run out of materials."

As the line of reporters began moving toward a gangplank, Hazel frowned.

"That's the cargo bay. We're not entering through the main deck."

"There's probably a good reason," Matilda looked around Hazel to get a better view of where they were going. "Have you heard who's doing the tour this morning?"

"No," Hazel shook her head.

"Captain Merritt Lancaster."

"Really?" Hazel turned to look at her friend. "Whose wrong side did he get on to have to do a job like this?"

"I think the Navy wants to make sure we all walk away with a good impression. They're trying to justify the expense of a replacement airship."

Hazel looked up, taking in the balloons again. From this angle she could see that the balloons themselves were easily three times the size of the ship.

"I heard her Majesty was in favor of a new ship."

"Yes, but Parliament is divided."

"Stupid Parliament," Hazel said. "When are they going to let women in the press gallery?"

"Probably when we force them, just like everything else."

The line continued moving forward until Hazel and Matilda found themselves at the end of a gangway with a young officer ready to greet them. They handed over their press passes.

"Straight ahead ladies," the officer said after looking at their credentials. "Have a pleasant day."

The gangway led to the cargo bay of the airship where barrels and crates stood with French labels.

"I would have expected to see weapons," Matilda said in a low voice. "Are those brandy barrels?"

"The ship must have just returned from France," Hazel said. "Our French neighbors often use goods to pay us for our security."

The women went to stand with the dozen young men who were there for the tour. Based on their accents, Hazel figured a number of them had come from out of town to report on the rare glimpse into a former gem of the British fleet.

An officer walked toward them from the other end of the bay. Hazel recognized him from the dozens of pictures she'd seen in the papers. Captain Merritt Lancaster, defender of the Empire.

"His photograph doesn't do him justice," Matilda whispered, holding up her camera.

A flurry of flashes went off, capturing a smiling Captain Lancaster in his uniformed glory. Matilda had been correct, his photograph had not done him justice. For one thing, no black and white image could capture the gold hair that could be seen crowning his head under the brim of his hat.

Once the photographers finished, he began speaking.

"Thank you all for joining us today," the captain started, his cheery voice echoing off the solid walls. "It's my pleasure to show off the *HMA Triumph* before she leaves our service for use by private citizens."

Two more officers joined the captain, and they began their tour in earnest.

"I had you come in through the cargo bay so that you could all experience the ship from the bottom up," the captain said, leading them toward a rounded doorway. "Let me assure you it only gets better from here."

They went up a staircase, into the galley, its long wooden tables already set for dinner.

Hazel figured you could easily feed two dozen officers at once.

While the captain called the cook out to give examples of the daily menu and Matilda set up to take a photograph of a sample meal, Hazel studied the oil paintings on the wall. They were all of various battles fought during the Great Sea War.

The first two showed the English triumphing over the crew from the Americas, but the third depicted the battle of Greenland and the sinking of *HMS Glory*. It had been such a staggering defeat and such a waste so close to the declaration of the truce.

What was particularly interesting to Hazel was that all the paintings were of sea vessels, but then most of the great battles happened before the British air fleet had gotten fully off the ground.

"Perhaps you want to be taking notes?" The crooked nosed reporter came up behind Hazel. "Won't your lady readers be most interested in what the officers like to eat?"

There was a general burst of laughter from the reporters around her and Hazel saw Matilda straighten, ready for a fight.

"Actually," Hazel said. "I think the *London Daily* readers will be most interested in the torodial engine. But by all means, if you need more time in the galley, I won't stop you. Which of the country papers did you say you came from?"

There was a snicker behind her and Hazel turned around to see Captain Lancaster cover his mouth and cough. She wasn't certain, but she could have sworn he winked at her.

"I was under the impression the engine room was off limits," crooked nose said.

A young officer hurried into the galley and went up to the captain. They had a quick exchange before the captain addressed the group.

"If you'll excuse me for a moment," Captain Lancaster said. "Officer Shaw will show you the next section and I'll meet you on the deck."

"The next stop will be the visitor's deck," Shaw said. "If you'll follow me."

The reporters lined up and followed Shaw out of the room. Hazel and Matilda joined the end of the line.

"How do you feel about taking a detour?" Hazel whispered.

"Really good," Matilda said.

Watching the line move up the stairs, Hazel and Matilda went around the corner toward the center of the ship.

"What are we looking for?" Matilda asked.

"The engine room."

They crept through the hallway and arrived at a large round door edged in brass.

"Do you hear that?" Hazel asked. "The door is humming."

"It's not the door," a familiar voice called. Hazel felt her cheeks start to burn as she turned around to see Captain Lancaster standing behind her.

"We seem to have gotten lost," Hazel said, clearing her throat.

"Somehow I doubt that." He grinned, opening the door and walking into the vibrating room. "All I ask is that you keep this room off the record."

Hazel braced herself to see the ship's engines but instead found herself in a round room with floor to ceiling brass tubes. There was a low hum in the air and she reached out, running a gloved hand over the nearest tube. It vibrated.

"This is the communications room," Captain Lancaster said. "We not only receive and send messages via telegraph, but also have an intra-ship communication system, which is what the tubing is for."

"How does it work?" Hazel asked.

"Each main room is set up with a morse inker. The message travels through the tubes to the designated room via vibrations. It isn't necessary for everyday use, but when in the midst of battle it could be of the utmost importance to get a message from the cannon deck to the wheelhouse."

"It's quite the innovation," Hazel said. "Are you going

to send us back to the visitor's deck now?"

"Not quite yet."

Next to the communications room was a door with a large wheel instead of a doorknob. Captain Lancaster turned it twice counterclockwise, then once back. The door swung open.

At first, all Hazel could see was gold.

"As you know, only pure metals can conduct aether," the captain said. "And this is the largest engine of its kind so there's a lot of precious metal in this room."

The engines were the centerpiece of a circular room, all shining silver wheels and valves. Towering a good twenty feet above them and culminating in a solid gold sphere. A narrow walkway with a railing surrounded the room, letting engineers and visitors maneuver around the engine.

Even though the engines weren't currently running, the walls and railings still glowed with a reddish tinge from the aether residue.

"I wish I could take a picture," Matilda sighed.

"You'd never do it justice," Hazel whispered.

"We've removed a few elements, the kind that allow for long range travel," the Captain Lancaster said. "So while it's no longer classified, your friend is correct. It isn't possible to do it justice."

"How does it work?" Hazel asked, stepping closer to the engine.

"It's a state secret," Captain Lancaster said, then he smiled. "Also, I'm not an engineer."

Hazel looked down. The enginestack went right to the lower deck.

"You must know something," Matilda said.

The captain pointed at the gold sphere above them. "I know when that starts turning there's enough force created to bring this whole vessel into the air."

"How splendid," Hazel said, her eyes on the sphere.

"I'm a pilot," he continued. "This is all the work of engineers. When we're flying, my job is to keep us in the air and set a course. Their job is to make sure the aether smoke is properly ventilated, away from the helium in the air balloon."

"It sounds dangerous," Hazel said.

"We're soldiers," he shrugged. "But the main work is in the upkeep. When we're in the air there's not much to do in here, particularly for a short range trek."

There was a tapping behind them and two naval officers entered the engine room. "We're ready for the demonstration," one of them said.

"Excellent." Captain Lancaster clapped his hands together and broke into a smile that reminded Hazel he wasn't actually that much older than her and Matilda. "Ladies, I must insist that you come with me to the upper deck."

With one last look over her shoulder, Hazel followed the captain and Matilda up the stairs, through the main part of the ship to a deck surrounded by windows on three sides, allowing for the loveliest view. The other reporters were already there chatting in small groups while the photographers took pictures. Matilda started setting up her camera next to the railing.

"You're going to want to wait about five minutes," the captain said. "Trust me on this."

As he spoke, the decking beneath their feet began to

vibrate and Hazel hurried to join Matilda, holding onto the railing as the balloon began to pull the gondola up out of the water.

"Where are we going?" Hazel asked as Captain Lancaster joined them at the railing.

"Does it matter?" Matilda called from behind the camera lens. "This is bloody brilliant!"

"It's just a short demonstration. We'll putter around London and then back down for tea."

As the city grew smaller and smaller below them, Hazel couldn't help but remember the purpose of the airship.

"It's truly remarkable," Hazel said, catching the captain's attention. "But I wish it wasn't a battleship."

"You don't think the British navy deserves the best?" Captain Lancaster asked.

"We're at peace," Hazel said. "The Americans haven't attacked in over a decade. Isn't the war over?"

He looked out over the city of London, the tower looming in the distance. "Perhaps for now, but we were caught off guard once before."

A shiver ran down Hazel's spine. She'd grown up with the stories of London being set on fire, of men and women screaming in the streets from toxic rains pouring down from the American air balloons.

"In the event the Americans get any ideas of coming after us," Captain Lancaster continued. "We're going to be ready. They won't take us by surprise. Not again."

CHAPTER TWELVE

Duncan walked into Burke's club and saw Lord Fletcher, leaning against a mantle and holding court with several young gentlemen of the *ton*, all of whom were vying for his attention. He approached the group but wasn't particularly interested in the conversation.

"There's nothing like the mama of a well-bred lady to strike terror into the heart of a confirmed bachelor," Fletcher said to a chorus of laughter. "It very nearly makes one want to head for the continent."

He was dressed in shades of brown that on any other gentleman would look drab, but on Fletcher it suited his coloring perfectly. Duncan had never mastered how to wear color other than gray and black and as a result suspected he always looked overly severe.

"But there are a number of pretty ladies about this Season," said Mr. Ellis.

"Any young lady in particular?" asked Lord Harkness, a fresh-faced youth who looked like he was playing dress-up in his father's coat.

Mr. Ellis stuttered, but before he could speak another young man cut him off.

"He's been trying to catch the attention of Lady Hazel Winchester."

Duncan looked over to Ellis, a frown on his face.

"Oh that will never do," Lord Fletcher said with a click of his tongue. "She's far too independent for a lad like you. She needs someone more like...Duncan? Is that you skulking in the corner?"

"Not skulking," Duncan called back. "Just waiting for you and your entourage to stop taking all the air from the room."

Fletcher laughed. "Is there something you want to talk to me about?"

"The outrageous tax on lumber from your lands?"

"You know I don't set the tax law."

"But you do enforce it," Duncan said.

The other young men, sensing an uncomfortable discussion, began to shift their feet and look at each other.

"I say Ellis," Lord Harkness said. "You fancy a drink?

Ellis and the other young men agreed and headed to the dining room, leaving Duncan and Fletcher alone.

"Well, you certainly know how to clear a room," Fletcher said.

Duncan grinned. "You're welcome."

"Am I to assume you got my message, then?"

"And here I was thinking you wanted a social visit."

"It's always a social visit with me," Fletcher laughed. "But you're right. Come along and step into my office."

Duncan followed Fletcher into one of the private dining rooms. Like much of the rest of the club, it was decorated in dark paneled walls, rich green carpeting, and high-backed leather upholstered chairs.

"Two brandies," Fletcher said to the footman. "And leave the bottle."

Once the footman had filled their glasses and left, Fletcher turned to Duncan. "I spoke to Meri recently. He had a few hours to spare after dropping you off. He said there was nothing to report in Iceland?"

"If the Amer-Irish Guard is there, they are buried underground."

"Then I would say it's very lucky you are in London. The Agency could certainly use your expertise here."

Duncan frowned. "What could possibly be of concern on English soil?"

Fletcher sipped his brandy, a serious expression on his face. "There is a threat, though we don't yet know the extent."

"What kind of threat?"

Fletcher tapped the side of his glass with the family crest ring he wore on his right hand. It made a clinking sound.

"Have you heard of Cravenwood?"

Duncan thought for a moment about why the name was familiar, then remembered his conversation with Dr. Baker. "The institution for delicate young women?"

"That's the one."

"What about it?"

"Several young ladies have disappeared from it."

Duncan had been in the process of lifting his glass to his lips and stopped. "How's that possible? I was under the impression only the best families were sending women there."

For a moment, all Duncan could hear was the ticking

of the clock over the mantle. Finally Fletcher answered.

"It appears that the families of the ladies involved have not been forthcoming in filing reports."

"Why not?"

"That's the mystery. One thing we do know is that all the ladies who are missing were diagnosed with aether fever."

Duncan set his glass down, half full. All he could think of was his sister and how his mother had considered sending her there.

What if he hadn't come home?

"What's the plan?"

"First we need more information. We don't know why the ladies are missing."

"But you feel their disappearance warrants Agency involvement?"

Fletcher reached for the bottle of brandy, refilling his glass. "The physician overseeing their cases, a Dr. Cadavy, came from Western Ireland. He arrived five years ago as an asylum seeker."

"And you don't trust him?"

Fletcher swirled the brandy in his glass before taking a healthy sip. "I trust no one."

Duncan straightened in his chair. "What would you like me to do? Fish out information?"

"This isn't like your usual cases. It's one thing to go undercover on the streets of Iceland but these are ladies of breeding we're talking about. You'll have to navigate the drawing rooms of the *ton*."

Duncan reached for his glass. Though it was still half full, he topped it up. "Not my forte."

"Don't sell yourself short," Fletcher said. "You are, after all, very rich."

"Lovely."

"Still, I'm not sure you can do this alone." Fletcher tapped his finger against the arm of his chair. "Not with so many ladies involved."

Duncan narrowed his eyes. "What are you suggesting?"

"Ideally, we need to have a lady on this job."

"Adelia is the only active female agent in the alliance," Duncan said. "And she's tied up in a production."

It was true. Adelia Dumont, the belle of Covent Garden, moonlighted as one of Her Majesty's agents.

"She's also an actress," Fletcher said. "And not likely to be taken into the confidence of a member of the aristocracy, and that's what we need. We need to know what's happened to their daughters."

"Then what do we do?"

"We'll need to recruit."

Duncan leaned back in his chair, sipping his brandy. "A lady?"

Fletcher nodded. "And I know just the one."

"Of course you do."

"Lady Hazel."

Duncan coughed, his drink burning a path down his throat.

"I don't think it's as bad as that." Fletcher frowned. "She's quite intelligent, especially for a lady."

"She's definitely smart enough," Duncan agreed, clearing his throat. "But can we trust her?"

"I don't see why not. She's got a good head on her shoulders and if she were as delicate as her counterparts she'd never write for you in the first place. She has the potential to infiltrate the Ladies' League. Which, as we both know, is beyond our scope of entry."

Duncan grimaced. "Surely it's not necessary to get involved with the League?"

Fletcher reached into the inside pocket of his jacket and pulled out a square of cardstock and handed it to Duncan. It was an invitation to Lady Ashburn's country party. Duncan and his mother had also received one. Duncan flipped it over, but there was nothing written on the back. He looked back to his friend.

"I don't understand."

"Cravenwood lies adjacent to the Ashburn estate and is under Lady Ashburn's patronage. If we had a lady with us, this would be the single best opportunity to get in there to have a look around."

"You don't think we could do it ourselves?" Even as Duncan asked the question, he knew the impropriety of his words. Two men could not ask for a tour of an asylum for ladies.

"I think this situation highlights the need for a lady to join our ranks."

"And you're set on Lady Hazel?"

"I am."

Duncan reached for his glass. "I don't care for it."

"Fortunately, you're not in charge of recruitment. We need to get Lady Hazel an invitation to the house party."

"I assume you have a plan?"

"I do. You're going to court her."

Hazel got out of the carriage behind her mother.

"I didn't expect they'd be in such a fashionable part

of town," Lady Winchester said, looking up at the town-house.

"They're merchants," Hazel said. "Not stray dogs."

"You always misconstrue everything I say," Lady Winchester said, climbing the steps to the front door. "I am quite pleased that your employer is so well-placed."

"Thank you," Hazel said. "And I'm sorry. I shouldn't have spoken to you like that."

Her mother gave her a pat on the arm. "It's natural to be nervous. Mr. Walters is a very eligible man."

Hazel blinked. Twice. "That's not what this is about."

But her mother had already stepped forward and picked up the door knocker. They were greeted by a tall, dour faced-butler.

"Good afternoon Lady Winchester, Lady Hazel," he nodded at each of them in turn. "Do come in."

Hazel accompanied her mother inside, following the butler up to the drawing room where they were announced.

"How lovely to see you, Lady Hazel," Mrs. Walters stood to greet them. Hazel had met her before, she'd come to the offices once or twice to visit her husband. To her left was a young lady whose resemblance to Duncan had to make her his sister.

"Mrs. Walters," Hazel walked into the room. "Thank you for your invitation. May I introduce my mother, Lady Winchester?"

"A pleasure." She nodded her head in greeting. "And may I introduce you both to my daughter, Flora?"

Flora looked in her mother's direction, but her eyes didn't fully focus. With a twist of her stomach, Hazel realized what was wrong.

"Flora dear," an older lady, presumably her companion, held out a cup and saucer. "Have your tea."

Flora took the cup without looking at the woman. Her mother continued talking as though nothing were out of the ordinary.

Hazel and her mother settled on a settee together and took tea from an attending maid.

"We haven't had an opportunity to have many visitors," Mrs. Walters said. "Between my husband's illness and poor Flora's relapse, it has been a difficult time."

"What caused the relapse?" Hazel asked. She felt a dig in her ribs and knew her mother was unimpressed with her question. But Mrs. Walters didn't appear bothered.

"It happened around the time her father took sick," Mrs. Walters said. "Poor Flora has never been able to handle stress."

"But she's gotten better in the past?" Hazel could almost feel her mother's gaze boring into the side of her head.

"For short periods," the companion said. "But now we, that is to say Dr. Baker, believes that medication is a permanent solution."

"But surely you can't mean—" Hazel started, but her mother took over this time, cutting her off.

"It must be nice for you to have your son at home."

"Oh yes." Mrs. Walters set down her cup with a smile. "It has been a relief to have him deal with the business."

"And he's quite handsome," Lady Winchester continued. "Don't you think so, Hazel?"

Hazel sipped her tea and gave what she hoped was a sound of agreement. His looks weren't the issue. It was his behaviour.

"It's nice to see him take part in the Season for once. He left home before...well, before he could really have a place in society."

"Best let the past stay in the past, is what I always say, don't I, Hazel?"

"Indeed," Hazel muttered.

"But really, Mrs. Walters," her mother continued. "You must tell me who does your draperies."

Not caring at all about Mrs. Walters drapes or the sad state of carpet imports, Hazel watched Flora. The poor girl stared absently into the empty fireplace while her companion occasionally fussed in her general direction.

Half an hour later Hazel found herself back outside being handed into the carriage with her mother.

"What a charming woman," her mother said. "And she seems to accept you, despite your appalling manners."

"I simply wanted to know about her daughter. Is that so terrible?"

"No one wants to talk about the fever." Her mother shivered. "I'm so grateful that you grew out of it."

Hazel recalled the night of Lady Germaine's ball. "Yes, I'm very lucky."

"And I think it's safe to say, if you play your cards right, you could get a proposal from this Mr. Walters."

"Pardon?"

"Don't look so shocked. Why else would a man invite you to meet his mother?"

Except, Hazel thought, it wasn't Mrs. Walters she'd been sent to meet.

CHAPTER THIRTEEN

Duncan sipped his brandy and looked around at the various tables where young men of good breeding stood shoulder to shoulder with colorfully dressed ladies of the night and threw away their fortunes on games of chance.

"Fancy meeting you here."

Duncan looked up with a smile as Meri sat at the bar next to him and ordered straight gin.

"How long are you in town?"

"Forty-eight hours," Meri said.

"Long enough to take in some entertainment?" Duncan asked.

Meri looked around, there was a squeal of delight from a woman at a nearby table as she blew on the dice of a particularly inebriated gentleman. "Is that what this is?"

"So I've been told."

Meri leaned in and lowered his voice. "Why did we have to come here again?"

Duncan set down his glass. "Fletcher wants us to keep an eye on Banks."

"I thought he was run-of-the-mill black market? Hardly our business."

"Still, you know Fletcher. He likes us to have our ears to the ground."

They nodded as Lord Dennison walked by with two women, one decked out in red, one in blue. They each clung to an arm as though they were drowning and the gentleman between them was a raft.

"Denny appears in good company," Meri said.

"When isn't he?" Duncan sighed. "We're getting too old to come to these places."

"And too poor," Meri said. "I haven't got a fortune to lose."

"I can't believe it, a naval hero like you?"

"Awards and ranks don't pay like they used to and every penny has to go towards marrying off three sisters."

"Of course, if you just married well yourself, you'd have the funds for proper dowries."

"Have you been talking to my mother?" Meri asked, waving to the bartender. "We'll have another round."

"She's putting on the pressure?"

"I'd rather not discuss it," Meri said. "Tell me more about your meeting with Fletcher. He's got you on the Cravenwood file?"

Duncan picked up his glass, watching the brandy swirl before bringing it to his lips. "He does."

"And?"

"And what?"

Meri punched him in the arm. "And it's clear something's bothering you about it."

Duncan pulled on his cravat. Myers had definitely tied it too tight. "He wants me to recruit Lady Hazel."

"The columnist?"

"Yes."

Meri grinned. "That's a great idea."

"Fletcher had this harebrained idea about bringing her in to help investigate Cravenwood."

"And you disagree?"

Duncan sipped his drink instead of answering. Meri shook his head. "Surely you could do much worse for a partner."

"I can't invite Hazel into our group."

Meri quirked a brow. "Hazel, is it?"

Duncan scowled. "Lady Hazel."

"Why not? Having another woman on our side can only help."

"I'm not sure she's a good fit for our organization. She's been gently raised."

"I know you don't think particularly highly of the gentry, but I think Lady Hazel has shown real gumption working in a newspaper. Not many ladies could do that. I rather like her spirit."

Duncan didn't disagree with Meri's assessment, but he didn't like the glowing way his friend spoke about Hazel. Not when Duncan had just taunted him about finding a wife.

Which was ridiculous. Why should he care what either of them did?

"Hazel is a member of the *ton*. You can't expect her to be comfortable in the type of work we do. She isn't a spy."

Not to mention there was the very real issue of the fever which she appeared to suffer from. A fact Duncan would be keeping to himself.

Meri turned to take in the room, grinning as his eyes settled on a young man moving between the tables. "She seems to be doing a rather decent job of it tonight."

"What?" Duncan turned around, seeing the same young man. "She wouldn't."

"Apparently she has."

Reminding herself to fix her gait, Hazel eased her way between tables of gentlemen throwing away their inheritances on a roll of the dice. It was both freeing and strange to walk around without skirts.

She paused to watch a young man escorting a brightly clad woman on each arm. There was something familiar about him.

As the women laughed over something the man said, Hazel listened in fascination. She knew the women were ladybirds. She'd come across their kind before in her night travels and had even been propositioned once, to her delight.

"Oh Denny," the woman to his right, slapped his arm. "You're too much."

She wore a scarlet red gown that caught the light of the gas lamps. Her friend, the lady in blue velvet that made Lilith's necklines look downright modest, was not to be outdone. She took out a feathered fan and tickled it against the man's cheek.

Which is when it struck Hazel. The women had called him Denny, the nickname for Lord Dennison. She'd need to see his face to be sure, but she was already confident that this was the man Lilith had been gushing over on her way into Lady Germaine's ballroom.

And here he was now, with not one but two hired women.

Hazel reminded herself that she needed to stay on track. She'd been chatting with one of the footmen and learned that the owner of the pawn shop, Mr. Banks, had an office just down from the gaming room.

She walked down the hall, looking straight ahead. In her few short excursions dressing as a male, she'd come to the conclusion that a confident man could walk about without interference.

Hazel tried two doors. The first was a closet. The second was also a closet.

How many closets did a man need? Hazel frowned to herself.

Her third attempt was a success.

She walked into the office and closed the door behind her. A gas lamp burned low on the wall. Hazel didn't dare turn it up.

There was a ledger on the desk. Hazel took her red journal out of her coat pocket and began looking through the book. The first pages appeared to be related to the pawn shop but near the back were a set of columns that most certainly related to shipping.

Hazel smiled to herself. This was the key to unlocking the black market ring. She ran her finger down a column itemizing brandy, sugar and tea, but stopped when she came across a list of flowers.

Rose, Iris, Daisy, Marigold...

Odd. Why bother shipping flowers? Especially

through London?

Just as she was about to take notes, Hazel felt a familiar pins and needles sensation in her temple.

"No, no, no," she rubbed her head, trying to remember if she'd taken the extra blocker but was fairly sure she'd forgotten.

As the tingling intensified, Hazel looked around the office. She needed to find somewhere private to wait out the episode.

There was very little furniture in the room, but the windowsill was wide enough to sit on. Hazel sat on the ledge, pulling her knees up to her chest, and swinging the curtain closed.

The vision overtook her and she could feel her mind move back down the hall to the main gaming room...

Fear, like a fist in her stomach. She watched the poker tables, the games of chance, but wasn't interested in any of the activities. She'd come because she'd been summoned.

There was a tug on her arm, and she looked to her right to see a woman in red bat her lashes. She gave her a slow easy smile, but it was forced…

The vision passed and Hazel was once again aware of her immediate surroundings. Taking a deep breath, she felt her heartbeat slow to a normal pace.

She reflected back on what was familiar about the vision, or more particularly the person whose mind she'd imagined herself inside of.

The arm dressed in garish red satin. One of Lord Dennison's ladies.

How odd that she'd imagined herself in a man's head.

She really needed to do a better job of remembering to take her medication.

Checking her reflection in the window and seeing that her hat was still in place and none of her hair was showing, Hazel was about to jump down from the ledge when she heard footsteps, followed by the office door swinging open.

"I say," a man's voice boomed. "Do you want to tell me what this is about?"

"Oh I think that's more than clear, Denny," a second male said. "I think my books will show that I've been remarkably patient with you."

Hazel's foot was falling asleep but she didn't dare move. She was pretty sure that the man threatening Lord Dennison was Mr. Banks.

And, likely, not someone who would be impressed to find a street urchin eavesdropping while he threatened a gentleman.

"I never travel with cash," Denny said. "You know I'll be good for it."

"You've been saying that for weeks now," Banks said. "This is bigger than me, Denny. The men you owe need to be paid and I'm afraid they're going to need something more than your word. Perhaps a lovely lily?"

Why would a flower get him out of trouble? Hazel wondered.

Before Denny could answer, there was a knock on the door and a familiar voice called out.

"Banks? You in here?"

What was Duncan Walters doing there? Hazel caught sight of her reflection in the window and saw her own surprised face look back at her.

"Mr. Walters," Banks said, his voice taking on a much more even tone. "Enjoying yourself, I hope?"

"As always," Duncan agreed. "But I wondered about a ring I saw downstairs in your window. A rather fine-looking emerald."

"Sounds like you've got business here," Denny said. "I'll leave you to it."

"One moment," Banks called and there was a scurrying noise as he left the room. Whatever exchange they had, Hazel assumed it was in the hallway because she could no longer hear what they were saying, only vague murmuring. In the meantime, Hazel was intensely aware that Duncan was still in the office on the other side of the curtain. She could hear him pacing, near the desk.

His footsteps moved around the room and Hazel saw his broad shouldered shadow against the curtain.

She held her breath. Perhaps she was visible to him too.

"Apologies," Banks said, reentering the room. "You wanted to see a ring?"

"If it isn't an imposition," Duncan said.

"I don't usually conduct shop business during these events," Banks said. Hazel could hear the opening and closing of a drawer and the sound of keys. "But seeing who you are, I'll make an exception."

"I appreciate it," Duncan said.

Hazel waited until the door closed and their footsteps disappeared down the hall before pulling back the curtain and peeking out into the room.

She hopped off the ledge, her satchel hitting her thigh. It felt oddly light. Hazel reached inside with a sinking feeling. Her journal was gone.

Which is when she remembered she'd had it out on Mr. Banks' desk, taking notes.

In the low light from the lamp, Hazel searched the desk. The sinking feeling grew. There was no sign of the journal. She checked the floor under the desk and inside the drawers.

Her journal was gone.

CHAPTER FOURTEEN

"Good morning sir," Liza said, her usual cheery smile falling off her face as she looked at Duncan. Which was his first indication that he was wearing his feelings.

He took a deep breath and tried to school his features.

"Is Lady Hazel in yet?"

"No sir," Liza said. "I'm not expecting her for another hour."

"Please let her know that I would like to see her. As soon as possible."

"Yes, sir."

Duncan walked into the empty newsroom. He intended to go straight to his office when he saw Hazel's desk.

Reaching into his pocket, he took out the red journal and propped it up on her typewriter where she couldn't possibly miss it.

In his office, Duncan took off his hat and sat at his desk. There were already copies of the morning papers both the *Daily* and its competitors, but he found he couldn't settle into reading.

He would rather be at the shipping offices. Everything

that had to do with importing and the fleet was intensely interesting to him.

The newspaper on the other hand, that was a different beast.

Duncan had never got the hang of it. It was his father's greatest disappointment. Charles Walters had made it clear that he'd acquired the *London Daily* so that his son wouldn't have to dirty his hands at the dockyards with the shipping business. But Duncan had never taken to it, not like the shipping business.

Once upon a time he'd thought he could follow his father's wishes. Then the Honorable Miss Cora Blackwood had walked into his life and for a few short months he thought he'd met someone who'd make sitting in an office day after day worthwhile.

The daughter of a baron, Duncan had thought himself in love after meeting Cora at the theater. Her father had even entertained his proposal, and for three months he'd paid court, until a better offer had come along.

Sir Blackwood had actually told Duncan it was a relief not to have to give his daughter to a common merchant.

After the fiasco with Cora, Duncan had told his father he would not take over the paper, instead he'd thrown himself completely into the shipping business. It was that, as much as anything, that had put the final nail in the coffin that was his relationship with his father. All Charles Walters had ever wanted was for his son to advance in polite society.

Which brought him back to Lady Hazel. No wonder his father had hired her. She was everything he admired: intelligent, hard working and aristocratic.

But what the hell had she been doing parading around dressed up as a man? And based on what he'd seen of the journal she'd left on Banks' desk, it hadn't been her first such excursion.

She certainly had the capacity to work as an agent. She was intelligent, determined, and willing to go undercover. But Duncan didn't relish the idea of having a partner. He didn't need the distraction of looking after someone else.

He was a lone wolf. It was better that way.

Looking out through the window in his office door, he watched as the newsroom came to life. He picked up the paper on his desk. The headline was about another complaint concerning the birthday celebration.

The palace was over budget. Again.

Duncan read the headline. It was written by one of their top news reporters.

The other papers on his desk, the ones from his competitors, carried the same story.

Maybe it was time to change tactics.

"Good morning sir," William poked his head in the door. "You're in early."

Duncan dropped the papers back on his desk. "I wonder if you can arrange an interview with the palace?"

William stepped further into the office. "With the palace, sir?"

"None of these articles about the birthday celebrations actually quote anyone from the Queen's office."

"No, but they aren't very complimentary."

"Just the same, I'd like to see if the palace will comment."

"I'll make a request. Is there anyone in particular you'd

like me to put on the story?"

Duncan looked past William, out into the newsroom. "As a matter of fact, there is."

Hazel had never felt nervous walking into the newsroom, not even the day she'd gone in for an interview with the elder Mr. Walters. She remembered walking into his office and feeling a tremor of anticipation run up her spine at the thought of working on a real newspaper. It hadn't even bothered her that she'd spent her time primarily writing societal columns for fashionable ladies.

But today, as she approached the main door her stomach flipped over.

"Don't be such a goose," she muttered to herself. Just because Duncan had been at King's Pawn Shop and just because her journal was now missing did not mean that the two incidents were in any way connected.

"Good morning," Hazel said to Liza as she entered the foyer.

"Good morning, my lady," Liza replied. Her usual bright smile was replaced by a worried frown and Hazel's stomach flipped over again.

"Is everything all right?" Hazel asked, looking past Liza to see into the newsroom.

"I have orders to send you into Mr. Walters' office. Immediately."

"Immediately?" Hazel repeated.

"That's what he said."

Taking as deep a breath as her corset would allow, Hazel marched into the newsroom. If she was about to get fired, at least she'd do it with her head held high.

She stopped at her desk, preparing to leave her bonnet and gloves when she saw something that made her heart stop.

The red journal.

Glancing around the newsroom, and seeing no one watching, she slipped the diary into a drawer before heading past the desks of her colleagues to the editor's office. Through the window in the door, she could see that Duncan's eyes were down, looking at the newspaper on his desk. She raised her hand and tapped on the door once.

He looked up and motioned for her to come in.

She stepped into the office and halted in the doorway. She'd never get used to seeing someone other than the elder Mr. Walters sitting behind the desk.

"You can close the door," Duncan said, barely looking in Hazel's direction. Beating down her annoyance, she did as instructed and came to stand in front of the desk.

"You wanted to see me?"

"No," Duncan said, looking at her with piercing blue eyes. "I want to see the boy that snuck into a card game last night."

Hazel could feel sweat beading on her forehead. She cleared her throat. "I beg your pardon?"

"Stop pretending, Hazel."

"It's Lady Hazel," she said, automatically.

"Not in this office you're not. And for heaven's sake sit down."

Hazel sat in the wooden chair across from Duncan's desk, gripping her hands in her lap.

"Shall we speak frankly?" Duncan asked.

"About what?"

Duncan leaned back, looking up at the ceiling. "I read the journal."

Hazel's jaw tightened. "You had no right."

"Even if I hadn't, I have eyes. Your disguise might work for someone who has never seen you before, but it's hardly going to work on me."

Hazel looked away. Through the office windows she could see the bustle of the newsroom.

"Am I fired?"

"Fired?" Duncan frowned. "No, you're not fired."

The tension Hazel hadn't realized was coursing through her body eased just a little.

"But your alter ego is."

"What I do in my own time is none of your concern."

"Why is it so important for you to wander the streets as a boy? Are drawing rooms and balls not exciting enough for you?"

Hazel drew her lips into a thin line. "You're being offensive."

"I'm asking a question."

"I can't make a difference," Hazel said. "Ladies rarely can. But as a man, I can expose real criminal activity."

"Real criminal activity? Like taking down the black market?"

She clenched her jaw. "I see you were thorough in your reading of my journal."

"Why do you care about cheap goods flooding the streets of London? Some would argue it's too damn expensive to live in this city."

"Yes, but the way to fight that is to go after the tax

hikes. The poorer merchants, the family run shops, those are the ones who are suffering. They're getting it from both sides. Less people in their stores and increasing taxes."

Duncan leaned back in his chair. "And you want to help them?"

"I want to make a difference," Hazel reiterated.

"What if I told you that I need you to walk away from this line of inquiry?"

"Why? Because I'm a woman?"

"No. Because there's something bigger at stake."

"Bigger than the London black market?"

Duncan shrugged. "Possibly."

Hazel narrowed her eyes at him. "Are you going to tell me what it is?"

Duncan scratched his chin. "I'm not sure you're up to it."

Hazel crossed her arms over her chest. "Try me."

"I will tell you something, but it must remain between these four walls. Can you agree to that?"

"Of course," Hazel said, leaning forward in her chair.

"My time abroad wasn't devoted entirely to my father's business interests. I've also been acting on behalf of the British Crown."

"What were you doing for the Crown?" Hazel asked, then her mouth formed an O as her brain worked to make the necessary connections. "Are you saying you're a spy?"

"Is that so hard to believe?"

"Yes."

"You don't have to take my word for it," Duncan said. "I'll prove it to you."

Hazel leaned back again, looking at her employer through fresh eyes. Could he be telling her the truth?

"How do you expect to do that?"

"Are you free to go to the theater tonight?"

"The theater? What does that have to do with anything?"

"All will be made apparent. Are you free or not?"

"Yes, I believe so."

"Then I will make sure there's a box waiting for you and your family. And while you are there, there's an important interview I would like you to conduct."

CHAPTER FIFTEEN

The production of Macbeth was sold-out, but Duncan had expected no different. Not when Adelia Dumont was playing the lead role.

"Thanks for getting the seats on short notice," Duncan said to Meri.

"I would never shirk my patriotic duty," Meri said. "Besides, it's never a chore for me to watch Adelia perform."

"You two are still just friends?" Duncan asked.

Meri's usually pleasant features turned to a frown. "Must you ask?"

"The rumors are that she's your mistress."

"Rumors which are beneath you," Meri said. "Adelia and I are good friends. That's all."

"Well I'm counting on your good friend to sell the Agency to Lady Hazel."

"Adelia knows what to say. You're worrying unnecessarily. Lady Hazel will be an asset."

"Perhaps. But Lady Hazel wasn't raised like the fair Adelia. She's been brought up with the sensibilities of the *ton*."

"Speaking of which," Meri nodded. Duncan turned to see Hazel, along with her sister and parents, make their way toward the box.

"Mr. Walters," Lady Winchester stopped in front of him. "Thank you so much for the seats."

"May I introduce my friend, Captain Merritt Lancaster. This is Lord and Lady Winchester."

Lady Winchester's eyes widened. Evidently she recognized the captain from the papers.

"It's an honor to meet you, Captain," she said. "These are my daughters, Lady Lilith and Lady Hazel."

"Lovely to meet you," Lilith held out a hand, her eyelids a flutter.

Meri took Lilith's hand briefly, then turned his attention to Hazel.

"Lovely to see you again, Lady Hazel."

"You've met?" Lady Winchester looked at her daughter.

"I had an opportunity to interview Captain Lancaster," Hazel said. "When I was on a tour of the *Triumph* for the *Daily*."

Lady Winchester pursed her lips and turned back to Duncan. "I believe the play is about to start."

Duncan waited while Lord and Lady Winchester entered the booth and watched while Meri offered his arm to Lilith, leaving him to lead Hazel to her seat.

"Is it just me, or does your mother dislike any reference to your work?"

"How observant of you," Hazel said. "Perhaps you should be a reporter."

"I think I'll leave that to professionals," Duncan said,

leading her to the seat in the front of the box, next to her sister.

"Are you going to tell me about this interview I'm supposed to do?"

"Adelia Dumont."

"She's starring in the show, I know," Hazel said.

Duncan grinned. "She's also your interview."

"These seats are delightful," Lilith whispered. "Rosamund will be green with envy. Everyone in the whole audience can see us."

"The view of the stage isn't bad either," Hazel said, though she wasn't feeling nearly as excited as Lilith. Usually a trek to the theater was a highlight of the Season, but she was far too anxious to really enjoy herself.

"It was very nice of Mr. Walters to get us a box," Lady Winchester leaned in from Hazel's other side. "He must be very impressed with you."

Hazel drew her mouth into a thin line. Between the tea with Mrs. Walters and the tickets to the theater, her mother was getting the wrong idea.

Fortunately, there was no time for further conversation as the theater lights dimmed and the gas lamps around the stage turned up.

Macbeth wasn't one of her favorite plays, but Hazel found herself completely taken in by Miss Dumont. Her rendition of Lady Macbeth was truly tragic and even went so far as to have Hazel feeling a little sorry for the ambitious king by the time the curtain dropped on the final act.

When the lights came back up, Hazel made her way to the back of the box where Duncan was chatting with Meri.

"What did you think of the performance?" Meri asked.

"Overall it was quite good," Hazel said. "But Miss Dumont really does steal the show."

"How fortunate you're about to meet her," Duncan said.

Hazel's smile faltered. She very much wanted to interview Adelia Dumont. The problem, of course, was getting past her mother. Lady Winchester did not believe that meeting actresses was an appropriate pastime for one of her daughters and she had no problem telling Hazel as much when she told her mother what she planned on doing.

"It's an interview, Mama," Hazel explained. "I do them all the time."

"Not with actresses, you don't," Lady Winchester said.

"I'll act as her escort backstage," Duncan said. "And deliver her back to you within a quarter of an hour."

Lady Winchester's demeanor completely shifted as she turned to Duncan. Hazel could almost see the scales working in her head, weighing her daughter's reputation against an opportunity to further her interests with a suitor. Marriage potential won out.

"That's very good of you, Mr. Walters. Perhaps a short interview wouldn't be altogether inappropriate."

Hazel took Duncan's arm and allowed him to lead her away before her mother changed her mind. They walked down the hallway, away from the box seats and into the main lobby of the theater. She nodded at several friends and acquaintances along the way and knew she and Duncan would be the subject of gossip in several drawing rooms the next day.

It wasn't a pleasant prospect.

As they headed into the backstage area, Hazel's spirits lifted significantly.

"Do you think those are real?" she asked Duncan as they passed a props table. She desperately wanted to pick up one of the bloody swords to see if they were as heavy as they looked but Duncan propelled her along.

"I wonder," Hazel said as they passed a rack of men's costumes, "are you anything like the Duncan in the play?"

"In *Macbeth*, you mean?" Duncan asked and Hazel immediately shushed him as they were glared at by a group of actors.

"You can't say that name back here," Hazel whispered. "It's cursed."

"That makes no sense," Duncan frowned. "How on earth can they put off an entire production if no one can say the name?"

"Very carefully," Meri's laughing voice called from behind them. As they turned around, Meri's attention was on Hazel. "And to answer your question, I believe he is very much like the Duncan in the play. Set upon earth to do God's will in the face of evil."

"You're ridiculous," Duncan said. "Make yourself useful and lead us to Miss Dumont's room."

Meri did as directed and they went further backstage

stopping at the first in a row of dressing room doors.

"Come in," a voice called and Meri opened the door. Hazel paused for a moment before entering. The space was exactly as she would have imagined a dressing room for a great actress. Costumes hanging from pegs and a decorative screen in Chinese silk dominated one corner while a plush rose-colored settee took up the middle of the room.

Adelia was sitting in front of a mirrored dressing table. She'd changed out of her costume and was wearing a deep pink evening gown. Her face, now removed of makeup, looked young and fresh.

Up close, Hazel realized that they must be of similar ages.

"Lady Hazel," Adelia stood up and walked to the door, hand outstretched. "It's lovely to meet you."

"And you," Hazel said, taking Adelia's hand.

"I don't mean to rush us along," Duncan said. "But Lady Winchester was less than thrilled with the idea of her daughter being backstage."

"Right," Adelia nodded and indicated the settee. "Do sit down then."

Hazel sat while Adelia pulled the plush stool from her dressing table over. Duncan and Meri remained standing near the door.

"Am I correct in assuming I'm not conducting an ordinary interview then?" Hazel asked.

"You didn't tell her why she's here?" Adelia frowned at Duncan.

He cleared his throat. "I didn't get into the full background of the Agency, no."

Adelia looked Hazel over, a small line forming between her brows.

"What makes you think she's ready to join us then?"

"She's very good at her job," Meri said. "And at getting into places she doesn't belong."

"A little too good," Duncan added.

Hazel drew her lips together. "I don't like being talked about as though I'm not present."

"Sorry," Adelia pushed a blond curl off her temple. "We have to be sure though, before letting in anyone new."

"She's uncovered several leads into the black market," Duncan said. "All on her own steam."

While they continued discussing her strengths, Hazel looked around the room. A soldier, an actress and a businessman.

"Are you all part of some kind of club then?" Hazel asked.

"Club?" Meri laughed. "I guess you could say that. We're part of the HMSA."

"HMSA?" Hazel furrowed her brow. "I've never heard of it."

"Her Majesty's Secret Agency," Adelia said. "Our job is to protect Crown and country."

"You work directly for the queen?" Hazel asked. "Seriously?"

"We do," Meri said.

Hazel crossed her arms over her chest. "The queen has her own set of secret agents? Since when?"

"Since it became apparent that attacks on the Crown have not ended despite the truce," Meri said. "The queen wanted to have her own set of agents who report directly to her. The group is small and includes members of the aristocracy, the armed services and the political realm."

"What about you?" She asked Adelia. "How were you recruited?"

Adelia smiled. "Meri came to watch me in Romeo and Juliet. When he requested a meeting after the show, I assumed his proposal would be for something less...wholesome. I was ready to turn him down. Then he told me about the Agency."

"Adelia has been a major asset," Meri said. "She can move in circles that the rest of us cannot."

"Yet I cannot move in other circles." Adelia turned to Hazel. "Which is where you come in."

"What can I do?" Hazel asked. "You want me to keep sneaking around the docks?"

"No," Duncan's voice was emphatic. "No more dressing up as a man."

"You've been sneaking around in men's clothes?" Adelia grinned. "How charming."

"But it's not necessary," Meri added. "What we actually need is for you to continue doing your job and, most importantly, acting the lady, with some minor tweaks."

"What kind of tweaks?" Hazel asked Meri, but it was Duncan who spoke next.

"You and I are going to start courting."

CHAPTER SIXTEEN

"So she said yes?" Fletcher sipped from a champagne glass in Lady Tremayne's drawing room. For once, Duncan had managed to find his friend on his own at a social event. At this moment the object of their conversation was standing with a group of young ladies that included her sister and Lady Rosamund.

Lady Hazel was wearing a burnt orange ball gown that, while not completely suited to her coloring, nevertheless gave her a cheerful appearance. Like a ray of sunshine, Duncan thought.

Which was a foolish notion.

"She's strongly considering it," Duncan said.

"Excellent," Fletcher said, looking in the same direction as Duncan. "We need a lady of breeding to round out our numbers."

Duncan watched as Hazel turned her head to smile as her friend Lady Beth approached the group. He'd already conceded that Lady Hazel was generally pretty, but when she smiled, Duncan had to admit she was stunning.

He gave himself a mental shake. They were entering a fake courtship, not a real one.

"There isn't much time to waste. The house party is in just over a fortnight. I'd suggest you stop wasting time and invite her to dance."

"Of course you would," Duncan said.

"Also, if you'd like further opportunities to meet with her, you can always ask her to go for a ride in the park."

"Thank you," Duncan said. "Whatever would I do without your advice?"

"I shall await you here while you go beg for a set."

Duncan walked over to Hazel's group, fully aware that Fletcher watched him as he moved across the room and was immediately greeted by Lady Rosamund.

"Good evening, Mr. Walters," she said. "How lovely to see you this evening."

"And all of you," Duncan said.

Rosamund tilted her head to one side, her curls bobbing. "May I ask what brings you over to our side of the room?"

"I was very much hoping that I wasn't too late to secure the first dance with Lady Hazel."

"How kind of you." Rosamund's smile faltered. "I'm sure she isn't engaged, are you Hazel?"

"No," Hazel said. "My first dance is free."

"I imagine it's not the only one," Rosamund said and Lilith hid her snickering behind a fan.

Duncan forced himself to ignore their jibes.

He was already singling Hazel out, he didn't need to add to gossip by doling out a setdown to Lady Rosamund.

"I'll leave you ladies to your conversation until the first set," Duncan said, directing his nod to Hazel.

As he returned to Lord Fletcher's group, he was unsurprised to find that his friend was now surrounded by his usual entourage of lords and barons. One of the young men in particular seemed to have been watching Duncan's previous exchange.

"I see you've engaged Lady Hazel already," Mr. Ellis said, eying Duncan in a way that made it clear he found him lacking.

"I have. She's a most charming young lady."

"Yes well, some of us have noticed that for some time now," Ellis said. "Those of us who've not been called away in trade."

The quartet struck up the first notes of the dance and Duncan was saved from further conversation.

"If you'll excuse me, I must go find my dance partner." He walked back across the room and found Hazel awaiting him.

"I find I am keen to dance this evening," Hazel said as she took his hand.

"Does that have anything to do with the company you are keeping?" Duncan asked.

"How observant you are," Hazel said. They took their places for the country dances and all discussion turned to polite observations about the music, the room and the number of couples on the floor.

There were simply too many others around them to talk about anything else.

When they were done, Duncan seized his opportunity for further conversation.

"Might I accompany you to the balcony for some air? I assure you it will not be a repeat of our last conversation."

Hazel's lips quirked into a smile. "That would be love-ly."

Since it was a clear evening, there were several other couples out on the balcony, but they were spread out, allowing Duncan and Hazel to speak without fear of being heard.

"Have you had time to think about last evening?" Duncan asked.

"I find I've thought of little else," Hazel said. She flipped her fan open and waved it in front of her face. "It's a most extraordinary proposition."

"It is," Duncan agreed. "And not one to be taken lightly. I remember when I was recruited. I assumed Fletcher was making fun of me."

"It's the sort of thing I've always dreamed of doing," Hazel said, waving her fan back and forth. Duncan was close enough to feel the gentle breeze. "Serving the queen. I'm sure if I'd been born a boy I'd have been a naval officer."

"Indeed?" Duncan couldn't help laughing at the thought of Hazel in uniform. "What a strange young lady you are."

Hazel's own smile faltered. "Indeed. I'm sure I must appear that way."

Duncan cleared his throat. "I didn't mean to offend."

"I assure you, none was taken."

He'd taken a misstep, he knew he had. He racked his brain for a way to fix it. What's something Hazel would care about?

He remembered a conversation he'd had with William

that morning. His assignment editor had been thrilled over a call from the palace.

"I received word this morning that the *Daily* has been given an opportunity to interview Her Royal Highness, Princess Evelyn."

Hazel's eyes widened. "The Queen's sister?"

"The very one. What's more, I'd like you to conduct the interview."

The fan in Hazel's hand picked up speed. "Me? But that will be a front page story."

"I imagine it will."

"I won't let you down, sir," Hazel said, glancing over her shoulder. "Do you think we've been out here long enough to draw attention?"

"Perhaps a few more minutes," Duncan said, finding he was in no hurry to return to the ballroom. "Do you think you could call me Duncan? At least while we're working together?"

Hazel bit the inside of her lip, apparently thinking. "I suppose I could."

"Excellent. Do you have any questions about our assignment?"

"Why is it necessary that we appear to be courting?"

"It was Fletcher's idea," Duncan said. "He thought it more likely that you'd get an invitation to Lady Ashburn's this way."

"Indeed." Hazel looked out over the garden, waving her fan in an absentminded manner.

"Is courtship with me really so terrible?"

She looked at him, a startled expression in her eyes. "No, I'm only thinking of how we'll end it without a scandal."

"I don't plan on staying in town forever," Duncan said with a shrug. "Isn't it possible that once I go back to sea you'll be justified in pursuing other gentlemen?"

A frown line appeared between her eyebrows. "What about the paper?"

"I'll make sure there's a good editor in place, for when I'm away."

Duncan had the distinct feeling he'd made a misstep, but before he could question her about it, Hazel snapped her fan shut and a look of resolve in her eyes.

"What happens if we can't convince Lady Ashburn to extend an invitation? How else will we get into Cravenwood?"

"We'll worry about that if it happens. You aren't nervous about going there?"

"Why should I be?"

"There may not be anything out of the ordinary going on there, but several young ladies seem to have gone missing. I'm sure it won't be dangerous, but I'll be there just in case."

Hazel's eyes widened and Duncan thought she'd gone pale, but he couldn't be sure without better light.

"Are you feeling all right?" He asked. It struck him that perhaps she was about to have another spell. Flora sometimes got pale right before an episode.

"I'm quite well," Hazel said, though her voice was low and husky.

"If this is too much for you, I'm sure we can find another way to investigate."

But Hazel shook her head even before he finished

speaking. "I'll do it. I'll go to Cravenwood."

Hoping to get rid of her worried expression, Duncan searched his brain for a way to change the subject. "Your interview is scheduled for Tuesday next, in the afternoon."

Her face lit up, all worry momentarily forgotten.

"I'll get started on a list of questions," Hazel said, her voice stronger. "You won't regret assigning me this story."

"There's one other thing you may want to consider," Duncan said, looking down at her brightly colored dress.

"What's that?"

"Perhaps you could get something new to wear?"

Hazel raised an eyebrow. "Indeed?"

"Adelia knows the very best dressmakers in the city—"

"I'm certain she does." Hazel turned back toward the doors to the ballroom.

Duncan stepped forward, as though to accompany her, but she held up a gloved hand. "Thank you for the dance, Mr. Walters. I'm sure I can find my own way back inside."

CHAPTER SEVENTEEN

Hazel walked into Café Marrakech and was hit by the smell of sweet spices. She spotted Adelia at a corner table with a green embroidered cloth. Though she was dressed in a simple pale pink skirt and jacket, with her honey blond hair and clear blue eyes she still stood out amongst the other patrons.

"Hello," Adelia said, standing up as Hazel approached the table. "I went ahead and ordered for us. I hope that's all right?"

"Yes, of course," Hazel took the seat across from her.

"And you found the café without any trouble?"

"Duncan gave me directions."

Adelia nodded. "I thought it best to avoid the more fashionable areas. It wouldn't do for you to be seen about London in my company. Not when you're about to conduct an interview at the palace."

A short, gray haired waiter brought a tray with a silver carafe and a plate of pastries to their table before bustling off again.

"I should have asked if you drink coffee? I can order tea as well."

"Coffee is fine," Hazel said, though she didn't drink it often. "And thank you for agreeing to meet me."

"It's a pleasure." Adelia poured two cups of coffee and handed one to Hazel. "It's quite rich. I'd recommend adding milk and sugar."

"Thank you." Hazel could smell the strong brew. She added milk and a pinch of sugar before taking a sip. Adelia was right, it was strong, but not as bitter as she'd expected.

"These are almond pastries," Adelia said, pointing to the platter. "It's their specialty and quite good."

Hazel put one on a side plate, but didn't take a bite. She looked back at Adelia in her day dress. She looked perfectly turned out.

"Apparently I am in need of some proper guidance on how to dress."

Adelia laughed. "Duncan stepped in it, didn't he?"

"He made it clear that I couldn't go to the palace in my current state. I'm afraid I have only plain, gray work dresses, or garish evening gowns chosen by my mother."

"Try not to think too badly of him. He's not used to the company of ladies. He'll come around in time."

Hazel picked up her pastry. It looked good with its dusting of powdered sugar. "I don't need him to come around."

"Indeed?" Adelia raised an eyebrow. "I'd thought perhaps there was something between the two of you."

Hazel set her pastry back on its plate, untouched. "He's my employer."

"He was," Adelia agreed. "But now he's your partner, and you could do much worse. If there's one thing I can tell you about Duncan it's that he will absolutely have your back."

"Do you speak from experience?" Hazel's voice cracked. She sipped her coffee in an attempt to clear her throat.

Adelia grinned. "Not personally, no. I've seen the reports though."

"Right. That's a comfort."

"It should be." Adelia took a delicate bite from her pastry, not spilling any crumbs or getting sugar stuck to her lips. "And by the way, there's nothing wrong with how you dress. You're a pretty girl with an even prettier brain. Other girls need the feathers. They'd be lost in the crowd without their plumage."

"That may be the nicest thing anyone has ever said to me."

"Which is all well and good, but on this occasion Duncan is right. We won't think of it as plumage though. You're going to the palace. It'll be your armor."

"Where does one obtain such armor on short notice this late in the season?"

"Why from the very best, of course. Now eat your pastry."

Madame de Meliodor had a storefront in the theater district. On a block of bland boarding houses and cheap cafes, it shone like a brightly colored peacock in a sea of pigeons. The shop was a light gray with bold blue trim. A picture window dominated the front with the most elaborate display Hazel had ever seen. There were two full size mannequins—one male, one female—decked out in matching red and gold silk with feathered masks covering their featureless faces.

But that wasn't all, behind the mannequins was a painted scene, a full ballroom with more couples twirling about. Scattered on the floor at their feet were another dozen masks, each one more stunning than the last.

Hazel could have spent a good five minutes looking at the display, but the air outside wasn't good. She followed Adelia through the shop door and if the display window hadn't told her, the inside would have made it absolutely apparent that this wasn't a typical London dressmaker.

For one thing, the show room was crowded with racks of fur-trimmed coats, brightly colored skirts and mannequin heads wearing the strangest selection of hats and headwear Hazel had ever seen. There was a man's tricorn next to a white bonnet in early puritan style, which was next to an intricate circlet of bronze from the medieval era.

Hazel took off her aether mask, dropping it into her reticule and stretching her jaw.

"Is Madame a costume designer?"

"Indeed," Adelia said as a large, barrel shaped woman bustled out of the back room. She was dressed head to toe in shades of purple.

"Who's there?" the woman called in a cockney accent.

"So not French then?" Hazel whispered to Adelia.

"Not French," she agreed. "Former actress."

"Adelia darling, is that you?" Madame de Meliodor squinted in Adelia's general direction.

"It's me, Madame M," Adelia said in a loud voice,

though the woman was looking right at her. "You need your spectacles."

Madame M reached into her corset and pulled out a monocle. She looked Hazel up and down. "Who've we got here?"

"This is my friend, Lady Hazel Winchester."

"What's a lady doing in this part of town?" Madame M frowned. "I ain't got time to do fancy dress for a *ton* ball."

"No fancy dress," Adelia said. "An interview at the palace for next Tuesday."

Madame M laughed, a loud booming sound. "You ain't serious."

"Very serious," Adelia said. "We'd be ever so grateful."

"Is she one of your lot then?" Madame M dropped her voice.

"You know I have no idea what you're talking about," Adelia said, a bland expression on her face.

"Right then." Madam M toyed with her monocle and gave Hazel a second going over. She snapped her fingers and two women—one blond and one brunette—came shuffling out of the back. Both were dressed in identical black dresses. Madame M pointed at Hazel and told the women to take her measurements. Within moments, Hazel found herself dragged to a corner of the showroom where curtains were pulled aside to reveal the largest gilded mirror she'd ever seen.

One assistant pulled off her jacket and had her arms out to her sides while the other began unbuttoning her blouse.

"Look at that corset," the blond said. "You could get two more inches at least."

The brunette reached behind, undoing her strings and pulling tighter. "There now, that's better."

"I can't breathe," Hazel said.

"Don't worry about that," Madame M walked past with silk and velvet fabrics in a rainbow of colors tossed over her shoulder. "You'll look amazing."

"We're going to need a hat too," Adelia called. "Something fabulous."

Madame M came up behind her and Hazel watched her reflection in the mirror. She picked up a lock of Hazel's hair.

"Is this your natural color?"

"I certainly wouldn't have chosen it on purpose," Hazel said.

Madame M took a step back and picked up her monocle again.

"Greens, I think," she said, and her two assistants nodded their agreement.

"It will be most flattering," the blond said as Madame M dropped the fabrics on the counter and began discarding the reds, blues and yellows. The brunette assistant stood to the side, arms out, catching the castoffs.

Hazel allowed herself to be poked and prodded until the blond assistant was done recording her measurements and she was allowed to get dressed again.

"We'll have it sent over Tuesday morning," Madame M said, tapping her temple with the monocle. "I've already got the preliminary sketches up here, just leave us your address."

"Yes ma'am," Hazel said, fishing a card out of her reticule. Madam M took it and slipped it into the side of her cleavage.

"As always, your discretion is much appreciated," Adelia said as they headed for the door.

"Mum's the word, Miss."

Hazel followed Adelia outside, back into the street. It was late afternoon, most of the factories had closed for the day and the air was much clearer.

"Ices I think," Adelia said, turning to her left.

"Sorry?" Hazel had been gazing into shop windows and not really paying attention.

"There's a dandy little Italian place just around here that does fabulous lemon ices."

"Lead the way."

The cafe did not disappoint. It was small, charming, and the ices were indeed delightful.

"I need to get out of my neighborhood more," Hazel said, dipping her spoon into the glass dish.

"I'd say you get around a fair bit," Adelia said. "For a lady."

Hazel paused with her spoon halfway to her mouth. "Can I ask you a question?"

"Sure."

"What do you do for the Agency?"

Adelia appeared to think for a moment. "I mostly spy at parties, you know, listen in on conversations, look for anyone or anything that doesn't quite fit in. An actress can get an invite into a lot of places."

"I imagine you could."

"But my next assignment is in Ireland," Adelia continued. "With Meri. I'm going to do a short run in Dublin and he's going along as my escort but really the whole thing is a fact-finding mission."

Hazel scooped up the last melted remains of her lemon ice. "How do you do it? An actress and a spy?"

"At the root of it, an actress is a spy. I watch people all the time to get the mannerisms for my different characters."

"I have to say, you are absolutely fascinating to watch."

Adelia's face lit up. "Thank you. I don't often get compliments from ladies."

"We're a stuffy lot."

"Oh, I don't know." Adelia looked Hazel up and down. "I think there's a great deal of promise in you."

"Are there any other females in the Agency?" Hazel asked.

Adelia shook her head. "Not yet. It took a great deal of convincing on my part to be allowed in."

Hazel pushed her empty dish aside. The cafe was emptying out and she knew she couldn't stay out too much longer.

"Is it dangerous?" Hazel asked. "I won't back out, but I am curious."

Adelia thought for a moment. "I've never felt at risk, at least not yet. But there are bad people out there, and I don't mean just the American threat. There's also unrest much closer to home, in Ireland and possibly other parts of Europe."

This wasn't news to Hazel, she read the papers.

"Just make sure you keep your head about you," Adelia continued. "And have a care with who you trust."

CHAPTER EIGHTEEN

"Why are you looking so somber?" Fletcher asked as he climbed into Duncan's carriage. Even in the middle of the afternoon, the lamps were on in the carriage interior. The one small window didn't permit enough light to seep in. "We're going to a lady's drawing room, not a funeral."

"I'm not somber," Duncan said. "Just serious. As you should be too. These are serious times."

Too serious to be hanging out in drawing rooms having tea, but with all the preparations for the palace interview, Hazel hadn't time to come into the office and the best way to meet up was during her mother's at home day.

Aside from which, he was supposed to play the part of the interested suitor.

"Who says one cannot enjoy themselves during such trials?" Fletcher leaned back in the carriage.

"You forget, I'm not one of your usual entourage. I know you well enough to see through the facade."

"You may continue to think I have hidden depths," Fletcher said. "But I know myself. There's nothing there."

"Yet you have chosen to be part of the Agency."

"I know my duty. At least where protecting the Crown is concerned."

Duncan glanced out the window. He could tell they were getting closer to Winchester house.

"I'm afraid I may have offended Lady Hazel," Duncan said.

Fletcher rolled his eyes. "What have you done now?"

"I suggested she get a new dress for her interview with Princess Evelyn."

Fletcher let out a bark of laughter. "You didn't?"

"I didn't intend her to take offense."

"And yet she has? What an unreasonable woman."

Duncan pulled at his neckcloth. Myers had tied the knot too high. "I'm glad I've amused you."

"And I'm glad we've found a sensible woman of breeding to include in our numbers," Fletcher said, his expression turning serious.

"I'm afraid we are putting too much pressure on her." Duncan frowned. "She's not been raised like us."

"What?" Fletcher snorted. "Like a man? I should think that for a woman such as Lady Hazel a country party and a visit to an asylum is hardly asking too much."

The carriage came to a stop in front of Winchester house and Duncan followed Fletcher up the front steps.

The butler took them straight through to the drawing room. It was an elegant space, though Duncan couldn't help noticing that, like most other grand houses, the floors showed wear and the furnishings were in need of recovering.

But then, if they'd been one of the few well-off aristocratic families, there'd be no need for Hazel to be working at his newspaper.

Lady Winchester was the first to come greet them.

"Lord Fletcher, Mr. Walters, how good of you to join us this afternoon."

"The pleasure is ours," Fletcher said. "Particularly when we are certain to be in excellent company."

Duncan fought the urge to roll his eyes but apparently Fletcher's words did the trick. Lady Winchester was completely charmed.

"Do come sit with my daughter Lilith, Lord Fletcher," Lady Winchester said. Then she turned her attention to Duncan. "And I'm sure Hazel will want to thank you for the flowers you sent, Mr. Walters."

Duncan wasn't certain Hazel would want to do any such thing, but he gave Lady Winchester a brief nod and went in search of Hazel. His eyes settled on her immediately. She was wearing an afternoon dress of gray blue. It was simple, particularly compared to what the other ladies were wearing, but Duncan believed it was the most attractive thing he'd ever seen her wear. It's simple cut showed off her narrow waist and her graceful figure. Her hair was also uncovered and in a simple braid around her head, like a crown.

As though sensing she was being watched, she turned her head to look in his direction as he approached. She was in conversation with a pair of young ladies he'd met at Lady Germaine's ball but could not remember their names.

"Good afternoon," Duncan said as he joined their

group. He thought Hazel's posture stiffened as he spoke, but when she turned to him, she wore a pleasant smile.

"Good afternoon, Mr. Walters," Hazel said. "You remember my friends, Lady Beth, Miss Eloise."

"Of course," Duncan said. He made a mental note of their names.

"Eloise," Beth turned to her friend. "Please come with me to speak to Lady Germaine. My mother wanted me to send along her wishes."

Eloise frowned. "Must we do that now?"

"Yes," Beth took her by the elbow and smiled at Duncan and Hazel. "If you'll excuse us?"

Duncan watched Hazel's face as her friends walked across the room. She let out a sigh.

"I must apologize for Lady Beth," Hazel said, turning back to him. "Subtlety has never been a strength of hers."

"Well, I'm glad to get a moment to speak to you," Duncan said. "Tomorrow is the big day."

"I've hardly forgotten," Hazel said, raising her teacup to her lips. "My new dress will arrive in the morning. With any luck I won't be an embarrassment to either myself or the *Daily* when I go to meet the princess."

"I am sincerely sorry for offending you," Duncan said.

"And yet, it doesn't make it untrue."

"I could have been more tactful."

"Is that why you sent flowers?" Hazel nodded at the mantelpiece where an arrangement of orchids took center stage. "My mother was overjoyed when they arrived."

"And what about you?"

Hazel cleared her throat. She didn't look at Duncan

when she spoke. "If the goal is to imply we're courting, I think the message has been received."

Duncan glanced in the direction of Lady Winchester. She smiled back at him.

"All it took was flowers?"

"And the theater tickets. And the invitation to take tea with your mother."

Duncan paused a moment, awaiting the feeling of dread that flowed through his veins at the mention of courtship, but it didn't immediately hit him.

Likely, he was tired. He'd been at the office early that morning.

"Would you like me to be more discrete?" Duncan asked. "Especially where your mother is concerned?"

"I should think that would defeat our purpose," Hazel smiled, but the expression didn't quite reach her eyes. "Besides, I've disappointed my mother before where matches are concerned and I'm certain to do it again after this."

"Is it the worst thing in the world? Having our peers assume I have an interest in you?"

Duncan watched while Hazel picked her tea cup up once more. She was biting the inside of her lip.

"No, perhaps not the worst thing." As she spoke Duncan realized she was trying not to laugh at him. "Besides, it does make meeting up easier."

Duncan didn't want to examine the feeling of excitement he felt at her words, so he changed the subject instead.

"I meant to tell you the other night, my mother was most pleased to meet you."

Hazel smiled. "I'm glad you brought our meeting up. I

hope you don't mind, but I sent a note to Dr. Sahni, about your sister."

"Dr. Sahni?"

"My physician," Hazel said. "That is why you invited me to tea with your mother? So I could meet your sister."

"I wanted you to see why I was so curious about your condition," Duncan said. "I wasn't intending to be rude."

"I assumed as much. At any rate, she sent a reply this morning to say she'll be happy to see your sister."

"I appreciate it," Duncan said. "You have no idea how much."

"Oh, I think I do," Hazel said, raising her cup to her lips. "On that you can be certain."

True to her word, Madam M sent a dress box first thing Tuesday morning. It was accompanied by a large round hat box.

Hazel was sitting at the breakfast table with her mother and Lilith when the packages were brought in.

"Oh my!" Lady Winchester clapped her hands over her eggs and toast. "You've bought a new dress?"

"Yes." Hazel put down her napkin and addressed the young maid holding the boxes. "Please bring them upstairs and let Penny know they've arrived."

"What did you order?" Lilith asked, straightening up in her chair.

"A new day dress," Hazel said. "And a hat."

"How on earth did you get Mrs. Portsmith to work so quickly?" Lady Winchester asked. "She takes weeks."

Hazel cleared her throat. "I went to someone new. A

Madame de Meliodor."

"Never heard of her," Lilith said. "I do hope you saw her work before placing an order."

"Of course," Hazel said, picking up her toast, though she didn't have much of an appetite. In truth, she wasn't completely confident that the dress would be up to scratch.

What if it had feathers? Or fur.

Or both?

"If you'll excuse me," Hazel stood up from the table. "I need to prepare for my interview."

"Of course," Lilith said. "We can't forget your excursion to the palace."

Hazel hurried up to her room and discovered Penny already there, with the dress box open in front of her.

"I don't know who you ordered from," Penny said, picking the dress up by the shoulders as though it was a rare artifact. "But this is sheer perfection."

The day dress was a deep cream color with forest green trim and a simple ruffle skirt and a short green jacket. The matching bonnet was wide brimmed with long ribbons in a matching shade of green.

"Let's try it on then," Hazel said. "If it doesn't fit we'll have to pull something else together."

"I'll make sure it fits," Penny said, a gleam in her eye.

Penny helped her into the corset and pulled tight.

"Oww," Hazel huffed. "That's enough."

"Half an inch more," Penny said, pulling. "Got it."

"I don't think I can breathe."

"If you can talk, you can breathe."

Hazel slipped into the top of the day dress while Penny adjusted the skirt before doing up the jacket buttons.

Penny took a step back. For a moment, Hazel thought her maid's eyes were filling with tears but she sniffed and pulled herself together. "It's the nicest dress you've ever owned."

"What does that say about the rest of my wardrobe?" Hazel asked.

Penny didn't answer, instead she handed over the hat. "You'd best be going. I can hear the carriage coming around to the front of the house."

"You can't possibly hear that," Hazel said, walking over to the bedroom window only to discover that the carriage had in fact just pulled up in front of the door.

"Told you," Penny said.

Hazel pursed her lips and grabbed her reticule off the dressing table.

When she got to the foyer she was surprised to see her father awaiting her.

"Papa! What are you doing here?"

"I wanted to wish you luck on your interview."

Hazel tipped her face up for her father's kiss and allowed him to walk her out. It was a foggy day, but he hurried toward the carriage, helping her in without the aid of the driver.

"You'll be splendid," he assured her through the handkerchief he held up in front of his face. He closed the carriage door and Hazel crouched in front of the small window to wave him off before sitting back as the carriage began to move. She settled in for a twenty-minute ride through the afternoon traffic, taking out her notebook to review her questions for the hundredth time.

She'd been to the palace once, like all young ladies of the *ton*, during her come out to meet the queen. But while she'd dressed in her white gown and waited in the line of teenage debutantes for her opportunity to make her curtsy, Hazel had come forward, been presented, and left with the certainty she'd made no impression at all.

It had been a rather sobering experience. Her mother had been less than thrilled. Some of the young ladies had been invited to engage in conversation with her Majesty, Lady Felicity had even been asked about the particulars of the lace trimming her dress and had held up the line for a full three minutes, but Hazel had simply made her curtsy and been escorted out.

She very much hoped to make a better impression today.

Hazel was jarred back to the present as the carriage slowed. Through the window she could see the palace gates go by and she forced herself to take a deep breath. Almost there now.

The carriage continued along toward the main door. Hazel put her journal in her reticule and prepared to step down as her door was opened by a liveried footman, dressed in scarlet and gold. She stepped onto a red carpet, taking in the glass walled tunnel that led from the main gates. It gave the illusion of still being outdoors while protecting from the worst of the aether filled air outside.

Realizing the footman was holding the door open for her, she hurried up the stairs where she was greeted by a lady in her mid-twenties with white blonde hair dressed in pale blue.

"You must be Lady Hazel," she said. "I'm Mrs. Fortnam, Her Royal Highness' private secretary."

"It's a pleasure to meet you," Hazel said. "We at the *Daily* are very grateful for an opportunity to speak to her highness."

A footman took her bonnet and gloves and Mrs. Fortnam led her down a large hallway with walls covered in gold trimmed moldings and glass globes filled with soft aether lighting.

It was a marvel, the lamps that conducted aether rather than gas. Each one made of pure metal. Hazel could have spent half an hour just looking at them. The installation of aether light was far too expensive for most households because of all the precious metal required to conduct the energy. Even the Ashburn's couldn't afford such luxury.

"Right through here," Mrs. Fortnam stopped outside a set of double doors. They waited a moment as two footmen opened the doors and Mrs. Fortnam entered with Hazel following.

They walked into the most magnificent sitting room that Hazel had ever seen. She knew it as the room where heads of state greeted the queen. It had been photographed often, but no black and white picture could do it justice. The walls were decorated in ivory paper with a quatrefoil pattern while the furnishings were deep blue. The artwork on the walls had been gifted to the palace from allies around the world and included a four foot long desert sunset from his Majesty, the King of Mauritania.

The most dominant works, however, were the three portraits over the marble fireplace. In the centre was the former king, depicted in his military uniform with a goatee. He was flanked on each side by his two wives, both of whom he'd married in attempts to strengthen alliances with other nations, and both of whom had died tragically young. To his left was his first wife, Queen Delphine of France, mother to the current monarch. She'd been a vision with gold blond hair and a complexion like porcelain. To his right was Queen Jiao of the Chinese Empire, mother to Princess Evelyn. She'd been a striking woman, with high cheekbones and dark eyes.

Mrs. Fortnam took a step forward and cleared her throat. "Lady Hazel Winchester, your highness."

Hazel knew from the newspapers that Princess Evelyn was a slightly unusual young woman. The younger sister of Queen Catherine, she'd had an interesting upbringing, even going so far as to enroll in the navy for a spell.

Based on photographs Hazel was expecting to see a striking young woman with black curls kept somewhat shorter than fashion usually dictated.

What she wasn't prepared for was her height. Princess Evelyn stood at just over five feet. Her small frame was accentuated by a day dress of pale gray with narrow skirts.

In her plain dress, the princess could have easily switched places with her private secretary.

"Your highness," Hazel dropped into a curtsy.

"Do sit," the princess indicated one of the sofas and Hazel took a seat across from her. Princess Evelyn looked up at Mrs. Fortnam. "I'll call you when we are done here."

Mrs. Fortnam looked uncertain. "It is customary for a member of staff to remain during interviews."

"Indeed," Princess Evelyn said. "Yet, I believe I will manage."

Mrs. Fortnam looked as though she wanted to argue but instead gave a quick curtsy and left the room.

"That's better," Princess Evelyn turned to Hazel. "How would you like to begin?"

Hazel glanced down at her list of questions. "I was thinking I could ask you about the plans for your twenty-first birthday celebrations."

"To be frank, the whole idea was largely my brother-in-law's doing. The prince consort was keen to do something to encourage the economy and the Queen agreed that it was time for my first public celebration."

"You don't think there's a bit of a pall hanging over the event? Given what happened at the last royal celebration?"

The princess frowned. "Obviously we don't think so or we would not have encouraged the event."

"Of course—" Hazel began but was cut off.

"If you've come to do a negative piece on the birthday celebrations you are far too late. I believe every doomsday prediction has already been made."

Hazel felt her stomach drop. She needed to get back on track, quickly. "That is not my intention, your highness. But I am not blind to the issues that have been raised. I thought you might like an opportunity to address the concerns publicly."

"Of course," Princess Evelyn cleared her throat. "There has been so much negativity, you'll have to forgive me for making assumptions."

"I believe you are within your rights to question the motives of any reporter," Hazel said. "But I want to write a fair article."

"The celebration is more than a birthday party, it's a symbol of hope for the future. A wish to move forward and leave the bleakness of the past behind."

Hazel made a note in her journal. "What is it you are most looking forward to?"

Princess Evelyn continued answering questions for the next thirty minutes until Mrs. Fortnam interrupted to let the princess know she had another engagement.

"Thank you for your time," Hazel stood and gave a curtsy.

"It was nice to meet you," Princess Evelyn said. She looked almost as surprised to say the words as Hazel was to hear them.

CHAPTER NINETEEN

Ordinarily, accompanying his mother to a musical performance at the home of Lord and Lady Wexley would have seemed like a chore. But Duncan found he was most eager to get out of the house.

"It's nice to see you so enthusiastic about going to *ton* events," Mrs. Walters said as she came down the stairs to find Duncan pacing in the foyer. "I hope I haven't kept you too long?"

"Not at all," Duncan said, bending down to give his mother a kiss on the cheek. "You look lovely this evening."

"As do you."

Duncan glanced at the staircase. "Will Flora be joining us?"

His mother seemed fixated on adjusting her gloves. "We thought it best to keep her in this evening."

"Whose 'we,' exactly?"

"Dr. Baker, Mrs. Clements, and I."

Duncan clenched his jaw. "I don't think a musical performance will be too taxing for her."

"It's not about that," Mrs. Walters said. "But it's hardly appropriate to parade her in front of the *ton*. Not in her condition."

"Well I think it's high time we fixed her condition," Duncan said. "I've arranged for Flora to see a new doctor."

"A new doctor?" Mrs. Walters frowned. "But Dr. Baker has been treating her since she was a little girl."

"Exactly."

"We can discuss it later," Mrs. Walters said. "I don't want to be late."

His mother spent the carriage ride talking about the soprano they were going to see. Duncan knew she was trying to avoid talking about Flora.

"I'm sure it will be lovely," Duncan said.

"And I imagine Lady Hazel will be in attendance."

"Yes, I should think so," Duncan said, remembering why he'd been eager to set out in the first place. He wondered how her palace interview had gone.

He caught sight of his mother smiling in the light from a gas lamp.

"She's a charming young lady."

Duncan wasn't sure that would be his preferred adjective.

He'd probably choose nosy.

No, that wasn't totally fair. She was resourceful and intelligent. And her hair was such an interesting shade of red...

"And she's got a title," his mother continued. "That would go a long way to solidifying your place in society."

"I'm not interested in a society that requires me to solidify," Duncan said as the carriage came to a stop. He had yet to tell his mother that he didn't intend to stay in London, at least not permanently. He'd see how his father progressed, then he had every intention of putting a proper editor in place.

Seeing his mother's wistful expression, it occurred to him as he opened the door, not waiting for the footman to hand his mother down, that Lady Winchester wouldn't be the only mother disappointed by the inevitable end to his courtship with Lady Hazel.

Then why end it?

The thought snuck into his brain and Duncan waited for the feeling of revulsion that inevitably appeared to creep in when he thought of marriage, yet it didn't appear.

The event at Wexley house was smaller than the balls he'd attended recently and Duncan was grateful for it. As he and his mother made their greetings to Lord and Lady Wexley and were led to a drawing room that, based on the heavy green damask, hadn't been updated in some years.

"Excuse me, dear," Mrs. Walters said. "I'm going to go speak with Lady Winchester.

"Of course." Duncan watched his mother walk over to a group of ladies that included Hazel's mother. Which meant the daughter shouldn't be far.

He located her across the room near a set of French doors, sipping champagne while in conversation with Mr. Ellis.

"Good evening, Mr. Walters." Duncan turned to find Hazel's friend, Lady Beth, at his side.

"Good evening, my lady," Duncan gave her a nod. Her lips quirked into a smile.

"Shall we go save Hazel from her tedious conversation?"

"Do you think she needs rescuing?"

Lady Beth's eyes fairly sparkled with mirth. "Oh, most definitely."

Duncan allowed Lady Beth to lead him across the room and as they came to a stop next to Hazel and Ellis, Duncan was glad to see a look of relief cross Hazel's features.

"I hope we're not interrupting?" Duncan asked. Ellis looked as though he was about to speak but Hazel beat him to it.

"Not at all," she said. "Mr. Ellis was just telling me about his last shooting excursion."

"Indeed?" Lady Beth spoke up with more enthusiasm than Duncan would have thought possible. "You must come tell Eloise all about it. She adores shooting."

Duncan thought that was highly unlikely, but Ellis seemed reluctant to argue with a lady and allowed himself to be led away.

"You sure we weren't interrupting?"

Hazel finished her champagne and placed her glass on the tray of a passing waiter. "If I had to hear another story about birds falling from the sky, I think I'd expire from boredom."

"May I ask instead how your afternoon went?"

"You may ask, though I'm not at all sure of the answer."

"Ah," Duncan said. "I hear the princess is somewhat

enigmatic."

"I think the interview went well," Hazel said, raising her fan. "I was in there for over half an hour."

"Well done," Duncan said and he noticed Hazel's cheeks flush at the compliment. Behind them, Lady Wexley called for the guests to enter the ballroom, which had been set up for the recital.

"May I escort you?" Duncan asked.

Hazel glanced over her shoulder and bit her bottom lip. "I'd best go in on my own. My mother has been watching us with eagle eyes. I know we're courting, but perhaps we should slow things a little. I wouldn't want you trapped into an offer."

"No, of course not," Duncan said, watching as she turned her head away from him. A strand of hair had fallen from it's braid and lay curled against the nape of her neck. His fingers itched to touch it.

"All the same," he continued. "I don't think there's any harm in my escorting you into the room. You can still sit with your mother and sister."

She bit the inside of her lip, but gave a nod. Duncan held out his arm and though she wore gloves, he could have sworn he could feel the heat from her skin through the heavy material of his evening jacket.

As they entered the music room, Duncan noted that several heads turned their way. He delivered Hazel to her mother and sister before going to join his own mother.

"You should have asked her to join you," Mrs. Walters said as he took the seat next to her.

He needed to get his mother's expectations in check. She didn't know he worked for the Agency and he could hardly tell her he'd recruited a lady as a spy. "Hazel works with me, Mama. That is all."

"I believe you mean Lady Hazel."

Duncan's eyes wandered to the other side of the room where Hazel was listening to something her mother was telling her.

"She's the talk of the room you, know," Mrs. Walters leaned in close and whispered. "Not many young ladies get to interview a princess."

"Yes, we are very fortunate to have her at the paper," Duncan said. They were also lucky to have her at the Agency, though he kept that to himself.

CHAPTER TWENTY

Hazel glanced from her notes to the typewriter and back again, tapping the keys. She had almost finished typing up her interview with Princess Evelyn.

"You look like a common worker."

Hazel looked up to find her sister, standing beside her desk, looking as out of place as a hothouse flower.

"Lilith? What on earth are you doing here?"

"I thought I should deliver this," Lilith held out an envelope in her gloved hands. It was addressed directly to Lady Hazel Winchester.

"Thank you," Hazel said. "But I'm sure it could have waited."

"That seal is from the Ladies' League."

"Is it?" Hazel flipped the envelope over for a better look. There was a stylized double L on the scarlet seal.

Lilith rested a hand on her hip. She was wearing her best daywear, a matching skirt and jacket in deep mauve. "Would you just open it?"

"Fine." Hazel reached for the letter opener on her desk. Inside was an invitation.

"You should be wearing gloves," Lilith said, taking in her sister's ink stained hands.

"I'm invited to tea," Hazel said, ignoring Lilith's remark. "Wednesday afternoon. At Lady Ashburn's."

"That's not just a tea." Lilith picked the envelope up off Hazel's desk. "You've been invited to a private league gathering."

"Oh." Hazel read the invitation again. "I wonder what that's about?"

"I assume it has something to do with your new suitor," Lilith said, bitterness slipping into her voice as she looked around the newsroom. "I suppose it's serious then?"

Hazel hesitated before answering. "I don't really know yet."

Lilith sniffed. "Well I'd best be on my way. I'm going bonnet shopping with Rosamund."

Hazel watched Lilith leave the newsroom, holding her skirts so they didn't hit off anything on her way out. Her sister was upset, worse than that, Lilith was jealous. She'd been desperate for an invitation to a League event for years.

Picking up the invitation, Hazel went straight to Duncan's office.

"Come in," he called, not bothering to look up from his papers at her knock.

"Look at this," Hazel said, holding out the invitation.

"What is it?" Duncan asked, reaching for the card. His fingers brushed against Hazel's and though they were a bit calloused, his touch set a tingle of awareness through her.

Hazel cleared her throat. "It's an invitation to tea. At Lady Ashburn's."

"A league tea?"

Hazel nodded. "I guess word of our courtship is getting around."

"You think that's why you've been invited?"

Hazel sat down in the seat opposite Duncan. "I doubt they want to chat about my work here, even if I did just interview the sister to the Queen of England. No, it's much more likely that they've seen us together and are assuming you can be persuaded to pay the exorbitant fees for your future wife's membership in their society."

"Future wife?" Duncan let a smile play over his lips as Hazel flapped her arm in dismissal.

"That will be their take on it."

"Well, it's a step in the right direction," Duncan said. "And hopefully you can get more invitations out of them."

"Right." Hazel stood up. "Best foot forward and all that."

"Exactly."

Hazel frowned. "Oh no."

"What is it?"

"I'm going to have to visit Madame M again."

Duncan laughed. "Are new dresses really the end of the world?"

"I suppose not." Hazel was heading for the door when Duncan called her back.

"Good work on getting the invitation."

"Thank you," she said and hurried back to her desk, trying to ignore the happy feeling bubbling up inside of her at Duncan's compliment.

Duncan waited outside the drawing room while Dr.

Sahni finished her examination. Both his mother and Mrs. Clements had wanted to be present but Duncan had insisted that the doctor see Flora alone.

Duncan had immediately liked Dr. Sahni. She had intelligent eyes and she spoke kindly to Flora and not around her, which was more than could be said for Dr. Baker.

"I don't like this," Mrs. Walters said, pacing back and forth. "I don't like it at all. One of us should be in there with Flora. We don't know anything about this doctor."

"Flora is in good hands," Duncan said for what felt like the hundredth time. "Dr. Sahni comes highly recommended and what's more, I've met a number of her patients and they all seem very satisfied."

"Perhaps they don't suffer as badly as your dear sister," Mrs. Clements said. She stood near the door, her hands clenched over her plain brown dress. "Miss Flora is so very delicate."

Duncan felt the heat of his temper rise but he fought it back. There'd be time enough to deal with Mrs. Clements after they got the doctor's report.

The door to the drawing room opened and Dr. Sahni stepped out.

"I've finished my examination."

Duncan, Mrs. Walters, and Mrs. Clements followed Dr. Sahni into the drawing room where Flora was sitting on a settee, staring off into space. His mother and her maid sat down on either side of her while Duncan took a seat across from the doctor.

"What's your conclusion?" Duncan asked.

The doctor cleared her throat. "I believe your sister would do well from a trial of magnesium blockers."

"How will that work with the Persephamine?" Mrs. Walters asked.

"Well, the goal would be to reduce that dosage," Dr. Sahni said.

"Reduce it? By how much?"

"Ideally to nothing."

Mrs. Walters and Mrs. Clements exchanged a look.

"What's the benefit of the blockers?" Duncan asked.

"It doesn't matter," Mrs. Walters stood up. "There's no possible way we can consider taking Flora off the Persephamine."

"We're going to hear the doctor out," Duncan said, then he turned back to Dr. Sahni. "Please continue."

"Clarity is the main one," Dr. Sahni said. "Persephamine causes a mental fog that makes it difficult to focus. I don't think you are unaware that Miss Flora is suffering from extreme mental displacement."

"Yes, but her episodes have stopped," Mrs. Walters said. "And that's the most important thing."

"I understand your feelings on that matter," Dr. Sahni said. "But there's a cost. Long-term use—"

"I don't mean to interrupt," Mrs. Clements said, cutting the doctor off, "but it's time for Flora's afternoon rest. Dr. Baker said it's best to keep her to a strict routine."

"Flora isn't going anywhere," Duncan said. "Not until we've heard the doctor out."

"You can stay and listen if you like," Mrs. Walters took her daughter by the hand and pulled her to standing. "But I'm taking Flora back to her room."

Duncan wanted to tell his mother to sit back down, but it was obvious she wasn't ready to listen. He watched the trio leave the room, Flora walking between them.

"Sometimes it takes time," Dr. Sahni said, fixing her jacket as she stood up. "Your mother may come around yet."

"What if she doesn't?" Duncan asked. "I don't want to have to pull rank as the head of the family."

Dr. Sahni adjusted her spectacles. "You'll have to make that decision, but my recommendation is the sooner you can get her off the Persephamine, the better."

"Thank you for your time."

Duncan walked Dr. Sahni out to the hallway where Briggs fetched her cloak and bonnet. As he waved the doctor off, he intended to instruct Briggs to get his own overcoat, but took a step back inside instead.

He found himself walking up the stairs and down the hall to his father's room. As usual, a nurse was sitting next to his bed. It was his mother's wish that her husband never be unattended.

"Mr. Duncan." The nurse stood up and bobbed a curtsy.

Charles lay in the bed, eyes closed. "How's my father today?"

"Much the same, sir," the nurse said. "We're keeping him comfortable with fluids and medicine."

"But he hasn't woken?"

She shook her head. "No sir."

Duncan paused at the end of the bed, watching as his father struggled with shallow breaths.

"Would you like a moment alone, sir?"

"No." Duncan took a step back toward the door. "Perhaps later."

CHAPTER TWENTY-ONE

She could have walked to Lady Ashburn's in less than ten minutes, but she strongly suspected her mother would have an apoplexy if she didn't take a carriage. Instead, Hazel settled in for the ride through the afternoon traffic.

Though she'd revisited Madame M and ordered two more day dresses and an evening gown at Adelia's recommendation, they'd yet to arrive so she'd elected to wear the same dress she'd worn to interview the princess.

At least she had a copy of the *Daily* to keep her company. She looked at the front page again and couldn't help the shiver of delight that ran through her at the sight of her byline under the banner headline.

Princess Evelyn gratified at interest in birthday celebrations

She'd gone into the office first thing that morning to pick up a copy. Part of her had expected Duncan to be there, but William had told her he had an appointment at the docks that morning. She would have liked to see his reaction to her front page story. He was her employer after all.

The carriage slowed in front of Lady Ashburn's home before coming to a hissing halt. Hazel waited for the driver to open the door and help her out, invitation in hand.

"Good afternoon," the butler said, taking her invitation as she entered the white marble foyer, waited while a maid took her bonnet and gloves before bringing her through to the drawing room. "Right this way."

Hazel was shown to a formal drawing room decorated in cream and gold. There were already several ladies grouped around settees and tea trays.

She realized with a sinking feeling that only a handful of ladies near her age were present, none of whom she was close to. Lady Carmella pulled herself away from her friend, Lady Cora Cartwright, and came over to greet her.

"Lady Hazel," Carmella looked her up and down. "Aren't you looking well this afternoon?"

"As are you," Hazel said.

"That shade of green does wonders for your hair. Makes the red so much more tolerable."

"That's truly a relief," Hazel said, scanning the room for a friendly face.

"Come," Carmella said. "I believe Lady Ashburn wanted to speak to you as soon as you arrived."

Hazel accompanied Carmella across the room and was well aware that several sets of eyes followed her.

"Lady Hazel," Lady Ashburn greeted her with a nod. The afternoon light hit off the large stone in the ruby ring she always wore over her gloves. "So good of you to make it."

"I could hardly refuse such an esteemed invitation."

"I am gratified to hear it," Lady Ashburn said. "Particularly as your presence will be requested at my future events."

"Indeed?" Hazel asked in surprise.

"I would like you to come to my annual house party. It's a highlight of the season."

"It is," Hazel agreed. She could hardly believe her good fortune. "I would be delighted to attend."

"Normally I only invite League Ladies, but Mr. Walters made it more than clear that your presence would go a long way in persuading him to accept his invitation."

Of course she'd never want to have Hazel attend any other way. She pasted a smile on her face. "I'm sure Mr. Walters will realize his good fortune at receiving an invitation."

"I'm sure you'll help him see the benefits. Lord Ashburn is most interested in bettering their acquaintance."

"Thank you for your consideration, my lady."

Lady Ashburn gave a regal nod before moving on. Lady Carmella came back to her side, grabbing her arm. "Did you get an invite to the house party?"

"I did."

"You'll have such a good time. I can't wait for you to marry Mr. Walters and join the League. We'll have such fun!"

Hazel hoped the smile she gave Carmella looked genuine.

"Are you sure you wouldn't rather drive?" Duncan

asked as another couple rambled by. It was a particularly clear day with a few patches of blue sky and not even a hint of aether in the air. Duncan had received a note from Hazel the day before to let him know her tea with the Ladies' League had gone exceedingly well. He'd taken the opportunity to come by that morning to invite her out for a drive but she'd elected to walk instead.

"I spend more time cooped up in carriages than I'd like," Hazel said. "A walk is a nice break."

They headed down the lawn in Hyde Park, Hazel with a parasol even though the sun was barely breaking through the clouds, her right hand on Duncan's arm.

"How was your tea yesterday?" Duncan asked as a group of ladies passed them, exchanging nods and pleasantries.

"I received an invitation to the house party," Hazel said. She looked up at him with sparkling eyes. She'd forgone her usual office gray and was wearing a day dress of lawn green with a matching velvet jacket. "Though that shouldn't be a surprise, since I hear you made it clear to Lady Ashburn that my presence was appreciated."

"She told you about that?" Duncan said.

"She did. She also made it clear that Lord Ashburn is keen to have you there."

"That man is always talking business," Duncan said.

Hazel burst out laughing. "That's something, coming from you."

The corners of his mouth tugged up in a reluctant smile. "I suppose it is. The difference being none of Lord Ashburn's investment ideas are very good."

Duncan followed Hazel to a bench under a nearby tree and sat down next to her. He tipped his hat as Lady Germaine passed in an open-air steam carriage. One of her many sons-in-law was attempting to steer the vehicle. It was a battle he was losing as a cloud of red dust sputtered behind them.

Despite the commotion, Lady Germaine still managed to return Duncan's greeting, running her gaze over both him and Hazel.

"Well if that isn't going to make us the talk of the *ton*, I don't know what will," Hazel said.

"Does it bother you?"

She shrugged a shoulder, her perfect posture making the casual gesture appear elegant. "Courting certainly makes it easier to speak together."

"I'm not too much of a chore then?"

Hazel raised her brows. "Am I?"

He shook his head. "Not at all."

Which was a surprise. Based on his previous experiences, Duncan hadn't thought it possible to enjoy the company of a lady of the *ton*.

But Hazel wasn't like other ladies. He'd actually miss her company when he went back out to sea.

In the not so far distance, they could see the frame of the pavilion for the princess' birthday celebrations.

"It seems the papers were wrong. The structure will be up in no time."

"That's not a surprise to me," Hazel said. "I knew the work was on track."

"And how did you discover that?"

Hazel twirled her parasol. "I spoke to the construction workers myself one day on my way to work."

"Why am I not surprised?"

She grinned and Duncan felt his stomach flip. She

smiled frequently, but rarely at him.

"I forgot to thank you," he said as two couples strolled past. He recognized at least one of them from Fletcher's entourage.

"Thank me for what?"

"For recommending Dr. Sahni."

"Ah." Hazel's expression sobered. "How was her visit?"

"Most enlightening."

"Are you going to let her treat Flora?"

Duncan shifted on the bench. "I would like to. Unfortunately, my mother has a different plan."

"That must be challenging. I am grateful my mother no longer interferes in my treatments."

"Can I ask you a question about your condition? I mean without you walking off and leaving me on my own to be ridiculed by all our peers?"

Hazel scratched her temple with her gloved hand. "What do you want to know?"

"What's it like? The visions?"

"I can only say for myself."

"That's all I can ask."

She took a deep breath before speaking. "It's like being inside someone else's head. Like feeling someone else's feelings, seeing what someone else sees. But I know it isn't real."

"What makes you so certain it isn't real?"

Hazel pursed her lips. "If you're going to be ridiculous I am going to get up and walk away."

"I'm being serious."

"Perhaps you're the one who needs a doctor."

Duncan watched in the distance where he could barely make out the movements of the men working on the pavilion.

"When I was twelve, my father employed a tutor to help me prepare for going off to boarding school. The tutor was not...the kindest man."

"What did he do?" Hazel's voice was quiet.

"Let's just say he had a tendency to be heavy handed with his corrective methods."

"Did you tell your father?"

"I told no one. Which is why I was so surprised to discover Flora knew exactly what was going on."

"Perhaps she saw something?"

"Oh, she most definitely did, only not with her own eyes. She saw through mine."

Duncan looked at Hazel. Everything about her had gone still, even her parasol. Yet he couldn't stop talking.

"I left the schoolroom after a particularly difficult session and there was Flora, running at me in a panic. She knew what had happened. She said she'd seen it as though she'd been in my head. Flora knew how scared I was and had come to find me."

"How can you be certain she wasn't outside the schoolroom?"

"Because her nurse came running after her. She'd just had an episode and the doctor was coming to sedate her."

Hazel turned away, looking off in the distance. When she finally spoke her voice was hollow.

"The visions feel so real."

"Is it possible that they are?"

Finally she turned to look at him, her eyes wide, almost frightened. "I very much hope not."

CHAPTER TWENTY-TWO

One of the benefits of courtship was that Hazel's mother hadn't blinked twice at the idea of her taking a morning to go shopping with Duncan.

"Enjoy yourself." Mrs. Winchester barely looked up from her breakfast.

"Are you at least taking Penny with you?" Lilith asked.

At least one of them was concerned about her reputation.

"As we are going by carriage, Penny will be joining us."

Lilith put down her teacup and looked to her sister. "Where are you going? Perhaps I could come along. I need some new ribbons."

Hazel could have bitten her own tongue. Of course she should have seen it coming that her sister would want to join in on a shopping excursion. Her brain worked furiously to come up with a place Lilith wouldn't want to go.

For once, she was saved by her mother.

"Leave it, Lilith. Let Hazel have her morning with Mr. Walters."

"Thank you, Mother," Hazel said. "I won't be more than an hour or two."

"Take your time," Lady Winchester called as Hazel went out to the foyer to meet up with Penny.

"Must we go in a carriage?" Her maid asked. "I do hate being in such a small space."

"We must," Hazel said. "The fog is terrible this morning and it's much too far to walk. Besides, Mr. Walters has his own carriage, not a rented one. I'm sure it's quite lovely inside."

Penny made a snorting sound but before she could give further opinions there was a knock at the door. It was Duncan's driver, face mask firmly in place, ready to help them into the waiting carriage. As a red fog was swirling around outside, Hazel hastened inside, Penny following closely behind.

The driver closed the door firmly behind them and it took Hazel's eyes a moment to adjust to the lighting inside the carriage. She could see that she'd been right in informing Penny that it would be nicer than the hired carriages they usually rode in. The seats were covered in deep blue velvet, and the carriage walls were painted in a matching shade with gold accents.

It was almost cozy.

Duncan himself was dressed in his usual gray day wear. Hazel didn't mind. It suited him.

"This is my maid, Penny," Hazel said, realizing the inappropriateness of presenting her maid to a gentleman. "If you'll pardon the introduction, but Penny is often with me and I thought you'd feel more comfortable knowing her name."

"Of course," Duncan smiled. "It's a pleasure to meet you, Penny."

Suddenly incapable of speech, Penny dipped her head and muttered something about being pleased in return.

The carriage huffed to life and they were soon moving through the streets of London. Penny mostly looked out the small window while Hazel searched for topics of conversation to pass the time.

She asked Duncan about his mother, his sister, and his father. To which she learned that his mother was well, his sister was still a concern, and his father was unchanged.

In return Duncan asked about Hazel's family. Then there was a silence that stretched between them and Hazel came very close to discussing the weather when the carriage came to a stop.

Penny looked out through the porthole shaped window and frowned. "Is that a milliner's shop?"

"It is," Hazel agreed. "And you're going to wait there while Mr. Walters and I go to a short meeting upstairs."

Penny let out a sigh. "I should have known it wasn't a normal excursion. Nothing with you ever is."

Duncan descended from the carriage first and handed out Hazel. He offered a hand to Penny as well which Hazel was amused to see caused her maid to turn an alarming shade of pink.

"We won't be long," Hazel said, trying not to breath in the foggy air. She took Duncan's outstretched arm and went around to the back of the shop and up the rickety staircase to the second floor. Once they were inside Dr. Sahni's waiting area, Hazel took a deep breath.

"You should have worn a mask," Duncan said, looking at her with a furrowed brow.

"It's fine, I just don't like the taste."

"No one does," a young woman with blond curls stood up behind the desk in the middle of the waiting area. She picked up a crystal dish of striped candies and offered Hazel one.

"Thank you, Irene." Hazel popped the candy in her mouth. She noted that Duncan declined the offer. "Can you let Dr. Sahni know we're here?"

"Of course," Irene bobbed a curtsy before tapping on the door behind her and going into the office.

"The decor isn't what I would have expected," Duncan said, taking in the masculine green walls and wood trim.

"I imagine it's probably exactly as the doctor found it the day she moved in," Hazel said.

"What do you suppose was here before?"

Hazel's lips quirked. "It was a high stakes gambling hell, I believe."

"Above a hat shop?"

She laughed. "Why not?"

The door to the office opened and Irene popped her head out. "Dr. Sahni will see you now."

Hazel led the way in, taking one of the two chairs in front of the doctor's desk as Irene closed the door on her way out.

"Thank you for agreeing to see us," Hazel said. "Especially on such short notice."

"It's lovely to see you both." Dr. Sahni peered at them through her spectacles. "If a little unexpected."

"We actually came to talk to you about your research,"

Hazel said, noting that while Duncan was watching her exchange with Dr. Sahni, he was letting her take the lead. "More specifically the visions some of your patients are having. Patients like me."

"I can talk in a general way, of course," Dr. Sahni stood up and went to a cabinet shoved in between bookshelves. She took out a stack of papers. "I can't give details on any of my patients though."

"I would never ask it," Hazel assured her.

"Why the sudden interest in my work?"

Hazel looked to Duncan, unsure how much she could give away.

Duncan cleared his throat. "There's concern over some of the patients suffering from aether fever, over their safety and care. Not your patients, but we thought your insight might help."

Dr. Sahni paused beside her chair, her eyebrow raised as she took in the pair before her. "And somehow this has become your concern?"

"In a very preliminary way," Duncan said, his voice smooth. "I have a friend in Scotland Yard. We'll be turning any relevant information over to the appropriate authorities."

"Seems like a strange hobby," Dr. Sahni said, taking her seat once again. She began leafing through her papers. "Do you have specific questions?"

Hazel caught Duncan's eye and he gave her a nod. The ball was back in her court.

"The last time I was here, I told you about my visions, about how real they felt and you said I wasn't the only lady to have a similar experience."

"That's right." Dr. Sahni adjusted her glasses. "For years the prevailing theories have been that the visions are a sign of mental instability and their appearance is purely random. However, I've been cataloguing some of these visions. What I've noticed is several instances where the experiences of the lady predict actions of those around them."

"Could it be a coincidence?" Hazel asked.

"Anything is possible, but I don't think so. The visions are too specific and there's often evidence that were correct—sometimes the vision shows information that the lady would have no way of knowing."

Duncan shifted forward in his seat and Hazel wondered if he was thinking of his sister.

"You've never published your findings?" Duncan asked.

"No," Dr. Sahni said with a sad smile. "Not only do I not have enough research, this is the sort of information that could put my patients at risk."

Hazel cleared her throat. She wasn't sure she wanted to ask her next question, but she had to know. "At risk how?"

"Assuming anyone believed my findings—which in and of itself is quite debatable—what would prevent people from attempting to use these abilities for their own means?"

Hazel's head was spinning and for the first time she understood what other ladies experienced when they felt faint. She took a deep breath. "Are you saying you think women like me have the ability to experience the thoughts of others through our visions?"

Dr. Sahni adjusted her glasses. "I think it's a distinct possibility."

Hazel knew she should have more questions, but what she wanted more than anything was to get out of the doctor's office. She stood up with a mumbled good day and was unaware that Duncan was following her until they were outside.

She hurried down the stairs, taking shallow breaths. All Hazel wanted was to walk and breathe in clean air, neither of which was possible at that moment.

"Here." Duncan took her arm and led her to a tea shop just across the street. Hazel didn't protest as he set her up at a round table with a lace cloth and ordered a tea tray from a freckled waitress with a wide smile.

"You're pale," Duncan said, reaching for her hands, pulling off her gloves.

"You shouldn't do that," Hazel said as he cradled her hands between his own.

"You're freezing."

She couldn't argue with that, so she didn't. Besides, when he rubbed her hands between his it felt good. too good.

"Do you want to talk about what's upsetting you?"

"I'm an aberration," Hazel said. "All of us are."

"An aberration?" Duncan's hands stilled but didn't release hers. "Why would you say that?"

"What would you call it?"

"A gift."

The waitress returned with their tray and Duncan did let go of her hands. It was then that Hazel noted the shop was about half full and while no one was openly watching them, several patrons were glancing in their direction. By that evening they were going to be the talk of every ballroom.

It was fortunate they were already courting.

"I'm actually somewhat jealous," Duncan said, spreading butter on a scone. "The things you must see."

Hazel pursed her lips. "It's not as though I get to choose my visions. Besides, it's not as though you're lacking in abilities. You tell falsehoods with remarkable ease."

"I don't know what you mean," Duncan said, and Hazel watched in fascination as he ate the scone in three bites. She sipped her tea.

"All those things you told Dr. Sahni about your friend in Scotland Yard."

Duncan grinned. "But I do have a friend in Scotland Yard."

"Yes, but he's not interested in our case."

"I never said he was. Not directly."

"Am I to hold up all of your statements for examination from now on?"

"Would that bother you?"

Hazel knew it would. They were to be partners afterall. "Yes."

"Then I promise to always be truthful and upfront with you."

"Even if it's something I won't like?"

"It wouldn't be much of a promise otherwise."

CHAPTER TWENTY-THREE

Madame M was in her glee.

"A house party," she said, fanning herself with a bright pink handkerchief. "At Lord and Lady Ashburn's."

"I just need to fit in with the other guests," Hazel said. "Nothing outrageous or fussy."

"The cream of society will be there," Adelia said, snapping open a scarlet fan and closing it again. She'd been happy to accompany Hazel when she'd gotten word of a planned visit to Madame M's.

Madame M took out a book of swatches and held them up to Hazel's face.

"We'll continue in the green family," she said. "Perhaps even some turquoise."

"Whatever you think is best," Hazel said. "So long as I can get two more day dresses and an evening gown."

Madame M muttered something and then went off into a back room with her assistants.

"How are you set up for fans and gloves?" Adelia asked, running her fingers along a rack of silk fabrics.

"I should probably pick up a few things." Hazel went to look at the accessories with Adelia.

"May I ask how you're finding your work with the Agency?" Adelia asked in a low voice.

"I fear I've not been much of an asset," Hazel said. "So far all I've managed to do is get invited to house parties."

"Which is more than I'd have managed." Though Adelia smiled, Hazel sensed there was a bitterness there.

Hazel picked up a lace fan and put it down again. "May I ask how you got involved in the Agency? Captain Lancaster recruited you?"

Adelia looked up from the fabrics she'd been examining. "He's the one who made the formal offer, but it was another Agency member who originally scouted me."

Hazel wasn't sure if it was her imagination, but she could have sworn there was a tightening around Adelia's lips as she spoke.

"How many Agency members are there?"

"I don't rightfully know, but I believe it's a select group."

"How strange to not know the others," Hazel said, examining a filigree brooch. She should pick it up for Lilith as a peace offering. Her sister still hadn't forgiven her for getting invited to the house party.

"The best way to protect each other is for us to know as few fellow agents as possible. Especially in the event that any of us were caught."

"That's a sinister thought," Hazel said, a coldness filling her insides at the thought of being held captive.

Adelia laid a hand on her elbow. "Duncan would never let anything happen to his partner. Of that you can be sure."

Hazel took a deep breath and picked up two fans. It

wasn't in her nature to revel in dark thoughts and she wasn't about to form the habit.

"Help me pick a fan?" She asked Adelia. "Preferably something that will go nicely with shades of green."

After agreeing on a black lace fan with silver accents, Adelia walked Hazel back out to the street.

"I won't see you until after the house party," Adelia said, giving Hazel a quick hug. "Best of luck."

Hazel watched Adelia walk back toward the theater and headed in the direction of her own home. Halfway there she had to pause and put on her mask as the air turned acrid.

For once that evening she had no outside engagements, just a small dinner at home with the Ellis' as their guests. It would be a tedious meal, but Mrs. Ellis did not stay out late and there would be less time needed to get ready since they were not going out.

As she entered the foyer, Hazel was looking forward to an afternoon of quiet reading.

"Your mother and sister are having tea in the drawing room," Penny told her as they crossed paths on the main staircase. "I've been told to direct you there upon your arrival home."

Realizing *Middlemarch* would have to wait, Hazel handed her reticule, jacket and bonnet over to Penny and went to find her mother.

"And where have you been this morning?" Lady Winchester asked as Hazel sat on the settee across from her. Lilith sat to the right of their mother.

"The dressmaker's," Hazel said, taking a cup of tea from the maid.

"Indeed?" Lady Winchester brightened. "And what did you order?"

"Two day dresses and an evening gown."

Her mother set down her teacup. "I only wish you'd told me. I could have come with you, given advice."

"It was a whim, really," Hazel said, raising her cup to her lips. She had no intention of bringing her mother shopping with her ever again. Adelia had a much better eye.

"Well I've barely had anything new all season," Lilith said. "Why should Hazel get three new dresses without having to consult with father once?"

"Because I've saved my allowance," Hazel said. "And have had it for a rainy day."

"For a house party, you mean?" Lilith frowned. "Why couldn't you have gotten me an invitation to Lady Ashburn's?"

"I've already told you, I barely managed to get invited myself."

"Mr. Walters must value your company," Lady Winchester said with a smug smile and Hazel wished she hadn't shared Duncan's involvement in the obtaining of her invitation. But she didn't know any other way to get her sister to leave her alone.

Lilith huffed, but turned her attention to a tray of tarts.

"I think I'll go upstairs," Hazel said, rising to her feet. "I'd like to rest before dinner."

"As you should," Lady Winchester said. "I'm sure Mr. Ellis will appreciate you looking your best."

"I'm certain he would," Lilith agreed. "But Hazel has

her eye on a bigger prize."

"Indeed," Lady Winchester raised an eyebrow. "And while Mr. Walters would be an excellent match, we must not count our chickens before they are hatched. It would be foolish to turn Mr. Ellis away at this juncture."

Hazel felt the blood rush to her face and knew her cheeks were turning pink. She had no intention of encouraging Mr. Ellis.

However, could she really say the same about Duncan? As she climbed the stairs she found that she was rather looking forward to being in his company at the house party.

But surely that was because they were working together and nothing else. She couldn't be falling for Duncan. He was bound to leave town again and she'd be left behind, pining.

That would be dreadfully embarrassing indeed.

Duncan hadn't realized a house party required so many trunks.

In addition to the family carriage, they'd had to rent a second one devoted to nothing but baggage. He liked to think that they were mainly belonging to the ladies, but his mother wasn't staying long and he'd seen Myers direct several cases marked with Duncan's initials.

"It was very kind of Lady Ashburn to invite us," Mrs. Walters said, standing next to Duncan in the doorway of the townhouse. "And under other circumstances I would have appreciated going all the more."

"I know you would rather be here with father," Duncan said. "And Flora."

"But if I stay, you cannot bring Lady Hazel in your carriage," Mrs. Walters said, touching her son on the arm. "And I know that would disappoint you. I'll return again tomorrow, a day away will do me a world of good."

"Thank you," Duncan said. "And I agree, you could use a distraction, even if just for a day."

"There's Lady Hazel now," his mother smiled and nodded as Hazel descended from a hired carriage. She wore a coat of bottle green with black buttons down the front. It was a plain, simple garment but the color did wonders for her hair and complexion.

"Good morning!" Hazel called as she descended. Her trunks had already been sent ahead and had been loaded into the second carriage.

Duncan stepped forward to meet her.

"Is that another concoction of Madam M?" He nodded at her outfit.

Hazel nodded. "She has decided that green is to be my color."

"I very much agree with her."

Hazel flashed a smile and dropped her voice. "I suppose it is more becoming than the trousers I wore to Mr. Banks' gaming room."

At the memory of Hazel's well clad legs, Duncan suddenly found it hard to swallow. "I think this is more appropriate for Lady Aston's drawing room."

"On that we can agree."

The footmen finished packing the second carriage and Hazel took Duncan's arm as he led her up the steps to his mother.

"Thank you, Mrs. Walters, for inviting me to ride in your carriage."

"It is you I should be thanking," Mrs. Walters said. "It will be nice to have company during the voyage."

"Once we get out of the city I'll be riding along side," Duncan said. "At least for the first hour or so."

He'd already explained to Hazel that he was hoping to arrive early and get some idea of where Cravenwood lay in relation to the Ashburn estate.

"Lady Hazel and I will have a lovely time," Mrs. Walters said, adjusting her gloves.

Duncan had the distinct impression that his mother was up to something. "Shall we go? I fear the fog is coming in."

Duncan offered an arm to hand his mother into the carriage. Once she was settled, he turned to offer Hazel the same service.

"Thank you," she said, taking the seat across from his mother. Duncan hesitated a moment before taking the seat next to Hazel as the driver closed the door behind them.

CHAPTER TWENTY-FOUR

Hazel had been looking forward to the journey to the Ashburn's country estate with a great deal of anxiety. Aside from one afternoon tea, she'd never exchanged more than a few sentences with Mrs. Walters.

At least the carriage ride would be short, only about a half day.

They reached an inn on the outskirts of London and descended from the steam carriages. From here the view of the city was obstructed by the red tinged fog from factories, many of which processed the items that would conduct aether energy like the engines used in the steam carriages and airships.

However, outside the larger cities, the air quality was much better, largely due to the absence of factories and the ban on the use of steam carriages and other machines that gave off aether fumes.

Since steam carriages weren't permitted outside the city, Duncan had hired a horse carriage to convey herself and his mother to the Ashburn estate and had a spare horse for himself.

Hazel approached the waiting horses with some trepidation. City dwellers rarely saw horses anymore, the city air being particularly difficult for the animals to process. Her own family had given up its country estate long ago and aside from the occasional summer visit to the lake district, she'd never had an opportunity to spend significant time around horses. She'd certainly never ridden one.

"They won't bite," Duncan said, coming to stand beside her. He reached out to touch the nearest horse, running his fingers through the reddish mane.

"I've never done that," Hazel admitted.

"Try it." Duncan reached for her gloved hand and guided it to the horse's head. She held her breath while she let her fingers run through the long, straight hair.

"I don't think she minds at all," Hazel said, keeping her voice low.

Duncan released her hand and took a step back. Hazel felt him watching her. "If you want to go riding, I'm sure I could make arrangements at the house party."

Hazel gave the horse a final pat. "Let's not get ahead of ourselves."

The horse drawn carriage was a completely different experience. The windows were so much bigger, and even opened, allowing for fresh air. The ride was a little bumpier, but the view more than made up for it.

Once they were outside the city, the landscape gradually turned from muddy brown to green. Single trees began to appear, followed by clusters, then fields of grass and flowers. Even the sky had opened up and was almost blue.

It always surprised Hazel how much color there was away from the aether air of the city.

Duncan traveled by horse alongside the carriage for the first hour. Mrs. Walters opened the carriage window and much of the journey was spent tossing comments back and forth between the three of them.

But as the hour drew to a close, Duncan tipped his hat and promised to greet them when they arrived at the Ashburn's. Hazel knew he was going ahead to suss out the premises, but she wished he could have stayed talking to them.

When he rode off, Mrs. Walters closed the window and for a few moments they sat in silence.

Hazel searched her brain for something to discuss, but her mind was drawing a blank. For someone who spent her time interviewing others for a living she was doing a terrible job of coming up with topics of conversation.

Finally, it was Mrs. Walters who broke the silence.

"I think my son has come to rely on you," Mrs. Walters said. "As my husband once did. You are an asset to the *Daily*."

"I hope to be," Hazel said, a feeling of relief bubbling up inside her. "I very much enjoy my work there."

"The newspaper was Charles' project," Mrs. Walters continued. "Duncan tries his best, but it's the shipping that's in his blood."

"I think he does well with it," Hazel said. "For all it's not where his interests lie."

Mrs. Walters nodded. "And if he should ever decide to sell it, he'll get a good price."

"Sell it?" Hazel felt her hands grow cold. "Why would he sell it?"

"The shipping business is expanding. Duncan can't

possibly keep up with all of his responsibilities. Not if he's ever to settle down and start a family. Of course, if he found a decent editor, someone he could rely on, then I think he'd be inclined to keep it."

"Of course." Hazel turned to look out the window at the passing greenery, hoping to get her emotions under control. But how could she, when there was talk of selling the *Daily*? The paper had become a second home to her.

A tingling sensation, like a feather tickling the inside of her temple, shifted her focus. She tried to ignore it, brushing a stray hair off her temple, but it intensified and with a tightening in her chest she knew it wasn't going away. This was the worst time to have a vision.

"Are you feeling all right, my dear?" Mrs. Walters leaned forward and took Hazel's hand. "Is it carriage sickness?"

She needed to take her pill, preferably away from Mrs. Walters. "I'm so sorry. Would it be possible to stop for a moment?"

Mrs. Walters tapped on the roof of the carriage and it came to a slow halt without the hissing and jolting she'd grown accustomed to with the steam carriages. Hazel didn't wait for the footman. She jumped down and hurried towards a group of trees.

Once she'd scooted behind cover, the vision overtook her completely.

She paced back and forth in a small study.

"I trust everything is taken care of?" She said to whoever came into the room behind her.

"We're completely on track."

Turning around she saw a man with sandy blond hair, just a little too long to be fashionable. He gave her a wide smile that didn't completely reach his eyes. "And might I add that the pay-out will be quite substantial? The largest yet."

"Indeed?" She felt the muscles in her face contract into a thin smile. "I'm glad you think so."

"You did bring in excellent stock…"

The small room disappeared and Hazel was once again in the copse of trees. Her hands were shaking and there were bits of leaves and twigs sticking to her gloves where she'd grabbed onto a tree trunk for support.

The vision itself didn't bother her. They were in the country, likely someone negotiating the sale of sheep or milking cows. She forced it out of her mind and searched through her reticule for her tablets. She stuck one under her tongue and forced deep breaths through her lungs. She must have forgotten to take her tablet that morning. It hadn't used to matter when she missed a dose here or there, but that no longer appeared to be the case.

When the shaking in her hands subsided to a mild tremor, Hazel made her way back to the carriage and allowed the footman to hand her in.

"Here," Mrs. Walters held out a green bottle as she settled back into her seat. "Have a drink of this."

Hazel took a tentative sip. It was brandy.

"Are you better now?"

"Yes, thank you. I'd forgotten how easy it is to get overcome by the heat in a carriage."

Mrs. Walters opened the window again and tapped on the roof. The carriage jerked into motion.

"How shall we pass the rest of the time?" Mrs. Walters asked with an easy smile. "Why don't you tell me about yourself? You have siblings?"

"A sister, Lilith."

"And is she younger?"

"No, older," Hazel said.

"Indeed?" Mrs. Walters glanced out the window. "And how old would that make you now?"

Hazel cleared her throat. "I'll be twenty-one in a month's time."

"A good age," Mrs. Walters said, but she didn't ask Hazel any more questions and they soon sighted the sandstone mansion that was the crowning jewel of the Ashburn estate rising in the distance.

Duncan had arrived an hour ahead of his mother and had taken a cursory ride over the property, but had needed to bring his horse in for a rest before getting too far. While waiting for the ladies, he had joined a rather dull game of billiards with Mr. Ellis and avoided a lengthy discussion of silver mining rights with Lord Ashburn by heading out to meet his mother's carriage.

As they pulled up in front of the Ashburn's house, Duncan stepped forward to help first his mother, then Hazel to descend. A brown-haired maid named Ginny came forward to show the ladies to their rooms and Duncan waved them off until dinner.

Unused to idleness, Duncan was contemplating how he might pass the afternoon when the next group of guests rode up to drive. Lord Fletcher jumped out of the carriage and handed his mother out.

"Duncan," Fletcher nodded at his friend. "Here already?"

"I arrived an hour ago," Duncan said.

"Suppose you rode in?" Fletcher said. "After sitting in a carriage for the better part of a day I could use some proper exercise."

"I could be persuaded to go for a ride," Duncan said, figuring he could borrow a horse until his own was fully recovered.

They headed to the stables and waited for their horses to be readied. While there, one of the stable boys directed them to stick to the paths on the right side of the house and not to go past the lake.

"Her ladyship has a surprise planned for the guests," the boy continued.

"Indeed?" Fletcher squinted at the retreating back of the stable boy. "I wonder what that's about."

"Probably some activity planned for the house party.

Fletcher shook his head. "More like the Ashburns can't afford to keep up their property and don't want anyone to see the disrepair. Why else were we not permitted to bring our own servants?"

"You think the Ashburns are in financial trouble?"

"Who isn't these days?" Fletcher said, leading his horse out of the stable. "Yourself excluded, of course."

Duncan followed his friend outside. He saw the conversation Lord Ashburn had tried to have with him about silver mining in a whole new light.

Perhaps Lord Ashburn needed investors. But who'd invest in metal during a time of peace when all the money was in brandy and corn? Duncan climbed onto his horse and easily caught up with his friend.

From what he could see as they rode, the Ashburn estate was in immaculate condition with manicured lawns and trails.

"Did you have any news before you left?" Duncan asked.

"I heard rumors of a few more ladies being shipped off to Cravenwood, but I haven't had time to confirm anything."

"Are the rumors so very secret that the families sending their daughters off have yet to be tipped off to the disappearances?"

"That is the hope," Fletcher said, his face wearing a rare serious expression. "Otherwise that would make them complicit."

CHAPTER TWENTY-FIVE

What had Duncan gotten up to? Hazel wondered as she let the maid, Ginny, help her dress.

"Would you like some curls, ma'am?" Ginny asked. "Or I can do braids?"

Her room was small, but comfortable, with pale blue walls and a small window overlooking the garden. It was also located near the servant's wing, which made sense, given she was a late addition to the party.

She had taken out a sea green dress that was one of Madam M's creations.

"Braids are fine," Hazel said, giving the nervous young maid a smile in the mirror. "You are doing an excellent job."

"Thank you, ma'am," she said, her brows drawn together in concentration. Hazel held her breath and tried not to flinch when a pin hit her scalp.

Nerves or not, Ginny did an excellent job on her hair, even if a few pins went astray in the process. Hazel stood up, smoothed her skirts and glanced at the clock.

"This won't be a late night," Hazel said, heading to the door. "I think it's just a quiet dinner."

At least, she very much hoped it was.

Hazel was the first one down to the drawing room. Like every other room, it was lavishly decorated with silk paper—this one all yellow and gold diamonds. She did what she always did when alone in a room and went to the stack of books that had been left on a small round table near a set of French doors.

She was turning through the pages of *Pilgrim's Progress* when she was joined by Lady Cora Cartwright.

Lady Cora was closer in age to Lilith and had made a spectacular match at the start of her second season, landing a husband with both money and a title. Since she spent much of her spare time devoted to the Ladies' League and their activities, Hazel had spent little time with her, though she'd never been anything other than polite to Hazel and her sister.

"Lady Hazel," she said with a small curtsy of acknowledgement that Hazel returned. "You look quite charming in that shade of green."

"Thank you," Hazel said. She could have added that Lady Cora looked a vision in a pink dress that would have clashed horridly with Hazel's hair but was perfect with Cora's cornsilk curls.

She didn't speak though, because Lady Cora always looked perfect and didn't need that reassurance from Hazel of all people.

"How's the selection?" Lady Cora asked, approaching the table and picking up the top book.

"I haven't looked through them all, but I've heard the library here is second to none."

They were still standing at the table when Lord Fletcher walked in with Rosamund on his arm. Of course Rosamund had gotten an invite. Her parents were good friends of the Ashburns.

Rosamund gave Hazel and Lady Cora a once over, her lips curving.

Rosamund smiling. That wasn't good. Though she was probably mentally comparing the two ladies and finding Hazel lacking.

Duncan arrived next with Lady Ashburn and several more guests. He was wearing black evening clothes, but Hazel found he looked so good in them that she wouldn't want him in any other color.

Not, she reminded herself, that she ought to have an opinion about Duncan's choice in clothing.

Upon seeing her, he smiled and made his way across the room. She knew he was doing it for show, but at that moment, Hazel didn't care. A warmth spread through her chest and she felt herself smiling back.

At least she was until he stopped beside her and the expression froze on his face as he took in the lady standing next to her. Remembering her manners, Hazel made the introductions.

"Lady Cora have you met Mr. Walters?"

"I have," Lady Cora said her eyes directed downward as she bowed. "Though it has been some years."

"Indeed, it has," Duncan said.

"Would you excuse me?" Lady Cora glanced across the room. "I believe Lady Ashburn is about to announce dinner."

Hazel turned to Duncan as Lady Cora moved across the room.

"What am I missing?" She asked.

"I don't understand your question," Duncan said. "Is that a new dress?"

"It is and stop trying to change the subject. Is there a history between you and Lady Cora?"

"History is a strong word." Duncan offered his arm to Hazel as other couples lined up for dinner. "We met during her first season. Nothing of note."

Hazel found she very much wanted clarification on that encounter, but as theirs was not a real courtship, she didn't feel she could ask.

At least not over dinner.

As they entered the dining room, Hazel noted the sheer number of guests at the house party. There were no less than a dozen couples and more were expected in the lead up to the grand ball in three days time.

Much to her delight, Hazel found herself seated next to Lord Fletcher during supper.

"May I say how pleased I am to see you at this house party?"

Hazel cocked an eyebrow. "You may say whatever you like. You always do."

Fletcher laughed out loud, causing a look from Duncan who Hazel noted was seated next to Rosamund.

"I believe congratulations are in order," Fletcher said as they were served the soup course. "On your recent work."

"My recent work?" Hazel repeated. She stopped in the middle of reaching for her water glass.

"At the *Daily*. I should have known you were more than up to the challenge."

"And what challenge would that be?"

"Why, interviewing the young princess. What else could I possibly be referring to?"

"Yes." Hazel picked up her water glass and took a sip. "What indeed?"

"Though, this is a departure from your previous work, is it not?"

Hazel laughed. "My lord, I didn't take you for one to read the ladies' columns."

Fletcher leaned in and dropped his voice. "I've been interested in your work for some time."

"Indeed?" She said, her breath catching. She had the distinct impression that Lord Fletcher wasn't referring to her columns. Which was a ridiculous thought. She caught Duncan watching her, a frown on his face. She would need to do a better job of schooling her features.

She picked up her soup spoon and turned back to Fletcher.

"My lord, how is your dear mama? I heard she had presented you with no less than fourteen eligible brides this season. Are we to hear wedding bells in your future?"

"Perish the thought," Fletcher said with a scowl. His mother was halfway down the table, seated across from Mrs. Walters. At the mention of his mother, Fletcher's attention was taken by Lady Ashburn's Great Aunt Edmunds who was seated to his left and Hazel noted that Duncan too had allowed himself to be drawn into conversation with Rosamund.

For once, Duncan had actually been looking forward to after dinner drinks. Normally he disliked sitting around with arrogant gentlemen, listening to them complain about gambling debts and women when he'd much rather be working.

But for tonight, there was the opportunity to avoid a certain encounter.

It had not occurred to him that Lady Cora Cartwright, the former Miss Cora Blackwood, would be on the guest list for this particular house party, though he should not be shocked. Of course she'd move in Lady Ashburn's circle.

It wasn't that he still held a torch for her, not in the least. Any affection he'd felt had dried up as soon as she'd made it clear his affection wasn't worth giving up a title for. It was more that he didn't want to be reminded of the feelings he'd had at that time. Feelings of being inadequate, of not belonging in the better social circles.

It was all silliness, of course. He'd had three years to come to terms with who he was and whether he was accepted in the best drawing rooms or not had no effect on how he felt about himself.

Still, he didn't like the reminder Lady Cora represented.

After half an hour of talking about the promising state of his silver mines, Lord Ashburn released the gentlemen.

When Duncan entered the drawing room, the first thing his eye was drawn to was Hazel, sitting with Lady Carmella. She looked desperately in need of rescuing.

"Mr. Walters!" Lady Ashburn called out. "Won't you join us for whist?"

She was at a table with Mr. Ellis and Great Aunt Edmunds who insisted on giving a full account of the family's history to anyone unfortunate enough to be seated next to her.

"Another time," Duncan said, scanning the room, but Hazel's companion showed no sign of letting her go.

"Are you looking for escape already?" Duncan turned to find his mother standing at his elbow, looking up at him.

"Not at all," Duncan said. "Just getting my bearings."

"It's quite a gathering," Mrs. Walters said. "Is it not?"

"Indeed," Duncan agreed, though something about the observation made him uneasy. They had a mission to accomplish and only three days to do it. He needed to find an opportunity to ask Lady Ashburn about a visit to Cravenwood.

"I very much enjoyed my carriage ride with Lady Hazel," his mother continued. "Such a charming, well-bred lady."

"I am glad you think so," Duncan couldn't help glancing back to where Hazel sat on the settee. Several of the young women were being prevailed upon to play the pianoforte, but so far she had begged off all invitations.

"Our journey wasn't completely without incident. We had one brief stop when Lady Hazel wasn't feeling quite the thing."

Duncan looked to his mother. "What do you mean?"

"She claimed carriage sickness," Mrs. Walters said, joining in the applause as Lady Rosamund finished a set.

"That's unfortunate."

"It is, isn't it? Though she recovered quickly and we

had the most interesting conversation. Did you know she's the same age as Flora?"

"I did."

Duncan kept his eyes on his mother's face as she watched Lady Carmella take a seat at the pianoforte.

"It's got me thinking that perhaps you are right."

Duncan raised an eyebrow. "In what way?"

"It's time to change Flora's treatment."

CHAPTER TWENTY-SIX

For the third time that evening, Hazel declined an invitation to play the pianoforte. Never having been musically inclined, she'd given up any pretense of practicing altogether when she'd started working at the *Daily*.

With no other ladies to prevail upon, the musical entertainment came to a close and everyone went back to their tea and cards.

Hazel watched while Duncan and Mrs. Walters engaged in a conversation and she was aware that their eyes occasionally stirred in her direction.

"Are you enjoying yourself, Lady Hazel?" Carmella asked.

"I am, thank you."

"Lady Ashburn was most insistent that you attend. Lord Ashburn was most anxious to further his acquaintance with Mr. Walters."

Hazel was hardly likely to forget the reason for her invitation.

"And Lady Ashburn has the best parties," Carmella continued, "I understand there's to be a rather substantial surprise during the ball."

"Indeed?" Hazel said, putting down her teacup. "What sort of surprise?"

"Whatever it is, it's bound to be elaborate," Rosamund said, taking the seat on Hazel's other side. "Last year they had fireworks."

"How delightful," Hazel said, and it wasn't a complete lie. She'd never seen fireworks as they'd been banned in the city for more than twenty years."

"Isn't it?" Rosamund said, then turned her attention to Carmella. "I believe your mother is wanting to speak to you."

"Really?" Carmella stood up immediately. "I wonder what she could want?"

As Carmella made her way to the whist tables, Hazel's sense of foreboding grew. Being alone with Rosamund was never good.

"I couldn't help but notice that you and Lady Cora were having quite a tete-a-tete earlier."

"We were merely looking at books together."

"Indeed. I suppose there's no point dredging up the past, is there?"

Yet, Hazel felt certain that's what Rosamund was about to do.

"But I do think you should be aware of the history between your suitor and Lady Cora. Or perhaps you already know?"

Hazel decided it was best to take the medicine all in one dose. Afterall, how bad could it be? "What history?"

"Why Mr. Walters and Lady Cora were very nearly engaged three years ago. In fact, it is generally believed that she's the reason he left town."

Hazel recalled their awkward meeting in the drawing room before dinner. Duncan had said there was nothing of note between himself and Lady Cora.

Evidently that wasn't the case.

Rosamund's lips formed a perfect pout of sympathy, but her eyes held a malicious gleam.

Hazel set her cup down on the side table.

"You'll excuse me, won't you?" Hazel asked, getting to her feet. "I found the drive more tiresome than I expected."

She turned and walked away before Rosamund could answer.

Of course it didn't matter that Duncan had been in love with Lady Cora. Hazel had no real claim on him or his emotions.

In fact if he were still in love with her, what did it matter?

As she reached the hallway, a footman stopped her.

"You be Lady Hazel?"

She nodded.

"This is for you, ma'am." With a bow, he held out a note. Hazel took it and continued to the hallway where her bedroom was located. She waited until she was inside before unfolding the paper. There were two words scrawled in the middle of the page.

Library. Midnight.

Duncan walked into the dark library and stumbled toward what he thought was the fireplace.

Instead his hands came up against a soft, velvet clad body.

"Duncan?" Hazel whispered. "Is that you?"

"It's me," he said, realizing that they must be standing barely inches apart.

"I can't find the lamp," Hazel said. "I was heading toward the fireplace—"

Just as the words were out of her mouth, the lamps blazed to light and Duncan saw a grinning Lord Fletcher standing next to the mantle.

"Well," Fletcher said, looking Duncan and Hazel up and down. "If I didn't know differently, Lady Hazel, I would say you are well and truly compromised now."

Duncan looked down and realized he was holding Hazel by the shoulders, her body pressed close to his. She was fully covered in a velvet green dressing gown, but still, it was a dressing gown.

He immediately released her and she stepped back. He noted the flush of pink in her cheeks as he did so.

"Fletcher, how kind of you to make your presence known."

Lord Fletcher flopped into an armchair. Despite having entered a dark room, he still managed to have a glass of whiskey in his hand.

"So you both got my summons then?"

Hazel smoothed her hands down her robe, something Duncan had come to note that she did whenever she was nervous. She looked at Fletcher with a frown.

"Your note?"

"Yes," Fletcher said. "We must be discrete."

Hazel looked at Duncan. "He's one of us?"

Duncan nodded.

She frowned but sat down in a chair in front of the empty fireplace. Duncan remained standing.

"Let's get this debriefing over with before someone realizes Hazel isn't in her room."

"As you wish," Fletcher said, sipping his drink. "And while you're standing Duncan, you'll want to lock the library door. We can ill afford to be caught in here, the three of us together."

Duncan checked the door and took a seat next to Hazel. "You called this meeting, what did you wish to discuss?"

"I have it on good authority that there will be a picnic this Sunday," Fletcher asked. "After church of course."

"I assume this will have something to do with Cravenwood?" Duncan said.

Fletcher sipped his drink. "Peripherally. Several of the girls attend church and will be in attendance."

"You think that will provide an in?" Duncan asked.

"For Hazel. I feel if she takes an interest in the girls, maybe talks to a few of them at the picnic, perhaps she'll have a reason to get into Cravenwood during visiting hours."

Hazel sat up straighter. "And what do you expect me to find there?"

"Hopefully nothing," Fletcher said. "But let's get a foot in the door first."

Duncan stood up, assuming their midnight meeting was over, but Hazel remained seated. She was watching Fletcher.

"May I ask a question?"

Fletcher swept his arm in an inviting gesture. "Of

course."

"Are you in charge of the Agency?"

"In charge? No. I merely coordinate the assignments."

While Hazel appeared to think about his answer, Duncan moved to stand behind her chair. "You should get back to your room."

"Perhaps," Hazel said. "But I have a few more questions."

He realized she hadn't looked his way since Fletcher had turned the lights on. Perhaps he'd embarrassed her by holding her the way he had.

"Do you have any agents stationed at the docks?" Hazel continued. "Where the black market shipments come in?"

Fletcher abandoned his drink and leaned forward in his chair. "And what do you know about the black market?"

There was a gleam in Fletcher's eye and Duncan felt a jolt. He didn't like the way his friend was looking at Hazel.

"I have my sources."

"Well so do I, and I can assure you nothing of interest has come through the London docks in weeks."

"Well, that's a relief." Hazel stood up. "I'll head back to my room."

"I can escort you." Duncan stepped out from behind his chair, but Hazel was already at the door.

"Best not," she said, grabbing a random book off a shelf. "If anyone sees me I'll just say I was looking for something to read."

She was out the door before Duncan could argue.

CHAPTER TWENTY-SEVEN

Hazel stared at herself in the mirror the next morning. Her skin was pale, her eyes dark. Evidence of a particularly sleepless night.

She picked up the small tin container with the hummingbird engraved in enamel. She quickly took her pill.

A light tap on the door had Hazel hurriedly dropping the pillbox back into her reticule.

"Good morning," Ginny said, coming through the door with a tray. "I heard you didn't make it down to breakfast."

"Thank you, Ginny," Hazel said. "Just leave it on the desk."

"Yes, my lady." Ginny set down the tray. "Are you ready to dress?"

Hazel figured she had under an hour to be downstairs in time to leave for church. It was time to put on her corset, pull up her stockings, and face the day.

"Yes Ginny, thank you."

As the activities for the afternoon included the church picnic, Hazel wore one of her older dresses in a shade of pale blue and a heavy gray coat with a matching bonnet.

The weather was unseasonably warm, but it was still not quite spring.

She was just in time to join the others in the foyer. As they set out, she fell into a group that included Carmella and Rosamund as well as Lord Fletcher and Mr. Ellis, who had apparently arrived the evening before.

The sky was overcast, which matched her mood.

Duncan walked several feet ahead with his mother, his tall, broad frame easily visible despite the couples between them.

"You aren't walking with Mr. Walters this morning?" Rosamund asked. She was on the arm of Lord Fletcher while Mr. Ellis escorted both Hazel and Carmella, the latter of whom's husband had not risen in time to attend church.

"No," Hazel said. "His mother is heading back to London after this morning's service."

"How nice it must be for her to see him," Rosamund called. "Particularly as he's been gone so long."

And Hazel now knew why he'd left town. Try as she might, her eye drifted over to where Lady Cora walked with Lord Cartwright. She was dressed impeccably in a deep shade of mauve that contrasted beautifully with her coloring.

Her husband was a nice enough looking gentleman who was very nearly as fair as his wife, though he was somewhat thick around the middle. Certainly no one to compare with Duncan.

And where had that thought come from? She shouldn't be comparing any man to Duncan.

Hazel realized that while she'd been lost in thoughts

of Duncan and Lord and Lady Cartwright she'd not been paying attention to the beautiful tree lined avenue they were walking down. It would be something to behold in the spring when the leaves were in full bloom. She'd also missed the story Lord Ellis had been telling and now he was waiting for a reply.

"Would you not agree, Lady Hazel?"

"Of course," Hazel said, though she could not say to what she was agreeing.

The church rose up before them, a quaint stone building with a small cemetery on one side and lawn on the other where Hazel assumed the picnic would be held.

As they approached, the bell chimed and Hazel was relieved that she no longer had to pretend to listen to Mr. Ellis.

The inside of the church was dark and smelled strongly of candle wax. Mr. Ellis led Hazel and Carmella past the rows of villagers to the pews near the front. Hazel found herself seated behind Lord Fletcher, his mother, and Rosamund. Duncan had taken a seat across the aisle.

Not that she'd been looking for him.

She allowed her eyes to skim around as the vicar entered from the vestibule and began the service. It didn't take long to identify what she assumed had to be the girls from Cravenwood. There was a row of them, all in white dresses, all staring straight ahead. A severe-faced woman dressed in dark gray sat at the end of the row.

Aside from the obvious fact that the girls appeared heavily medicated, Hazel scanned their faces, surprised when her gaze rested on a familiar face.

Duncan wasn't sure, but he thought Hazel was un-happy with him.

He needed to get her alone so he could apologize for the way he'd been holding her in the library the previous evening. Obviously his actions had been far too forward.

She was a lady afterall.

Once the service ended, he escorted his mother to the carriage that would bring her back to London.

"You needn't have escorted me," his mother said as he handed her into the carriage. "Not when I'm sure you'd rather be at the picnic."

"I'll be away for mere moments," Duncan said. "And I'm sure I'll hardly be missed."

"I don't know about that. I did see Lady Hazel glance in your direction several times this morning."

They came to a stop in front of the carriage, Duncan's lips quirked. "A well bred Lady such as Lady Hazel would never do such a thing during a Sunday service."

"Well then she really must be quite smitten with you." His mother laughed as she took his offered hand and climbed into the carriage. "I will see you back in Lon-don."

"Safe travels." Duncan waved his mother off and turned to head back to the picnic, his mind on his moth-er's teasing.

Of course his mother would think Hazel had feelings for him. His mother thought every woman had feelings for him.

The picnic was in full swing as he approached the field. He could see Hazel just ahead, talking to a young lady dressed in white with a light gray cloak. One of the Cravenwood girls if he wasn't much mistaken. A woman in black hovered closely at her side. He was about to head over to speak with her when he was cut off by Lady Cora.

"Mr. Walters," she said, dropping a curtsy. "I wondered if we could speak?"

"I don't know what we could possibly have to speak of," Duncan said, he could see that Hazel had looked in his direction and was moving on.

"I wanted you to know how sorry I am about what happened to us."

Duncan turned his attention to the woman in front of him. Cora was every bit as beautiful as he'd remembered. The purple jacket and matching bonnet perfectly highlighted her porcelain skin and blonde hair.

But other than an appreciation for her looks, Duncan felt nothing.

"There's nothing to be sorry for."

"It's kind of you to say. " Cora hesitated. Over her shoulder he watched as Hazel approached Lady Ashburn. He watched their conversation and saw Lady Ashburn give Hazel a once over before nodding at something Hazel said.

"I don't want there to be hard feelings between us," Cora continued.

"As I said, don't waste another thought on it," Duncan said, watching as Lady Ashburn moved onto another group of guests. "If you'll excuse me."

Duncan didn't wait for Cora's reply. He hurried across the lawn meeting Hazel as she went to the table laid out with sandwiches. A footman handed out hot cider to fight the cold.

"What did I miss?" Duncan asked as he handed Hazel a small plate and picked one up for himself.

"One of the ladies at Cravenwood is an acquaintance, Lady Felicity." She didn't look at him while she spoke, instead focusing on choosing between strawberry and blackberry preserves for her scone. "I asked Lady Ashburn if she thought it would be possible to visit."

"And?" Duncan piled sandwiches onto his plate.

"And she told me there were visiting hours the day after tomorrow, in the afternoon."

"Excellent work," Duncan said but Hazel merely gave him a stiff nod and headed to an empty table under a nearby tree. He balanced two cups of cider with his plate and followed her.

"You needn't dance attendance upon me," Hazel said when Duncan took his seat and settled a cup in front of her. "I don't mind being on my own. It gives me a chance to observe."

"I wanted to apologize. If you'll let me. I know it was terribly inappropriate of me to hold you like I did last night in the library."

Hazel looked up from her untouched plate. "You want to apologize for touching me?"

"Of course, what else?"

"Indeed." Hazel pushed her chair out and stood up.

"Have I upset you?"

"Of course not," Hazel snapped the words. "If you'll excuse me."

Duncan watched her walk away, wondering how it was possible for an apology to make everything so much worse.

CHAPTER TWENTY-EIGHT

Hazel dressed in her plainest ensemble for the visit to Cravenwood. She chose the gray skirted dress and matching jacket because she wanted to fit into the institute with relative ease.

She took her reticule, which included her journal and a fountain pen and fixed the bow on her gray bonnet before heading down the stairs.

The houseguests were spending the afternoon playing croquet and other games on the lawn in front of the Ashburn estate. The previous evening had been spent quietly at cards and musical entertainments as everyone preserved their energy for tonight's ball.

She hadn't spoken directly to Duncan since she'd left the picnic two days ago. It wasn't her intention to never speak to him again, but she was still feeling raw. He'd actually apologized for touching her. As though that was something he regretted.

Hazel was pulling on her gloves as she approached the steps leading down to the foyer and was surprised to find Duncan waiting there.

"Why are you here?"

He quirked a brow. "I'm accompanying you to Cravenwood."

Hazel frowned. "I don't need you to accompany me. I know the way."

"I don't doubt it," Duncan said, heading to the front door. "But as you've been avoiding me, this seems to be the only chance I'm likely to get to speak to you."

Hazel followed him outside and down the front steps.

"I haven't been avoiding you."

Duncan came to a stop, holding his arm out. Knowing they were in full view of the croquet match, and not wanting to cause a scene, Hazel placed her hand on his elbow.

"You didn't let me lead you into dinner last night."

Hazel shrugged. "Mr. Ellis got there first."

"Indeed," Duncan said. "Given how he was hovering about your person it would have been quite difficult for him not to be there first."

They reached the end of the lawns and walked through the large entry gates.

"He was not hovering," Hazel said.

"Of course he was and given you were avoiding me is it any wonder that he was?"

Hazel stared straight ahead. The road was covered in a light frost and the sun was shining in a way Hazel realized it only could outside of London.

"I wasn't avoiding you. It isn't necessary for us to spend all of our time together. Besides, I thought you might enjoy the opportunity to mingle with the other guests."

"What other guests? Do you mean Fletcher? There's

nothing we'd talk about that you couldn't hear."

"I wasn't referring to Lord Fletcher."

"Then who?"

Hazel's throat felt dry. Likely from the dust on the road. "I thought perhaps you might want to get reacquainted with Lady Cora."

Duncan slowed his pace and since Hazel's arm was through his, she had to slow as well. "Why would you think that?"

"Certainly not because of anything you told me. You play your cards remarkably close. It was Lady Rosamund who informed me of your attachment."

Now Duncan fully stopped. "What exactly were you told?"

"The truth; that you'd offered for Lady Cora three years ago and when you were turned down you left town to mend your broken heart."

"That's a truth," Duncan agreed, "though it isn't mine."

"Since you didn't share the information yourself, what was I supposed to think?"

Duncan's eyes narrowed and Hazel realized she was about to see him get well and truly angry. She would have taken a step back but he still held her arm.

"Did it not occur to you to ask me about it yourself?"

"The last time we spoke, you apologized for touching me. You made it more than clear that being close to me isn't something you enjoyed."

"Indeed?" Duncan's voice had grown so quiet that if they hadn't been all alone on the country road Hazel wasn't sure she'd have been able to hear him.

She swallowed hard. "Well why else apologize?"

"Because I was worried I'd offended you," Duncan said. He reached out and took her other arm so they were facing each other completely. "Perhaps I was mistaken."

The kiss happened so quickly, for a moment Hazel wasn't certain she hadn't imagined it. One moment his lips were on hers, the next they were once again walking down the country lane like a proper lady and gentleman.

Except her lips were warm and tingling.

They walked in silence for a few moments until Hazel dared to glance his way. He looked straight ahead, as though nothing were amiss. Whereas her insides felt as though they'd melted together.

But then, perhaps he often kissed ladies, whereas for Hazel it was not at all a common occurrence.

They turned right onto a tree-lined drive and Cravenwood rose before them, a converted country estate with white siding and navy trim. There was a lawn out front where a few ladies strolled on the arm of their nurses.

As they passed one girl with a faraway look in her eyes, Hazel couldn't help the shiver that spread down her spine.

"Are you all right?" Duncan asked, his voice soft with concern.

Hazel nodded as they walked up to the main entrance. She pulled her arm away from Duncan's and rang the bell.

They stood outside long enough that Duncan was about to ring the bell again when the door opened. A middle-aged woman dressed in black opened the door.

"May I help you?"

"Hello," Hazel said. "I believe Lady Ashburn left word that I'd be visiting. I'm Lady Hazel Winchester."

"Indeed?" The nurse looked her up and down. "One moment."

The door closed again and Hazel glanced at Duncan. He shrugged and took a step back, eyeing the lower windows.

"We're not breaking in," Hazel said.

"Just taking stock."

The door opened again and the nurse looked from Hazel to the piece of paper. "You're here to see Lady Felicity then?"

"I am."

The nurse turned her attention to Duncan, her thick brows meeting over her nose as she frowned. "Your gentleman will have to wait here."

"Of course," Hazel said before Duncan could object. "He doesn't mind."

"Doesn't he?" Duncan muttered, but Hazel was already following the nurse into a small dark foyer that smelled strongly of vinegar, which she assumed was used for cleaning when the smell only intensified as they walked into the main hallway.

Without a word, the nurse headed up the staircase, up two flights, and down a wood paneled hallway lined with identical doors. Hazel noted there were small name plaques outside each door with floral embellishments. They stood out as the only cheerful touch in the otherwise dreary hall.

They passed an open door with a lily plaque outside. A pretty dark haired girl stepped out and looked at Hazel.

"Hello," she said, a vague smile on her face. There was something familiar about the girl.

The nurse stopped and took the girl by the arm. "Back inside, Lilianne."

At the mention of her name Hazel realized how she knew the girl. She was Lord Dennison's sister.

"Forgive the interruption," the nurse said, closing the door firmly behind Lilianne. "Here's the room we're looking for."

The plaque outside this door was a clutch of violets, which was fitting, since Lady Felicity had the most lovely violet-gray eyes.

The nurse opened the door and Hazel followed her inside a small, bare room where a young lady with soft brown hair sat on a narrow bed. A block of sunlight streamed in through the one small window, making a cross on the floor where the panes met. It did little to add warmth to the bare room.

"Felicity?" Hazel approached the bed but the girl didn't acknowledge her.

"I'll be back, Dr. Cadavy is about to start his rounds," the nurse said, closing the door behind them.

Once they were alone, Hazel went to sit on the bed, next to Felicity.

"Do you remember me?" Hazel asked. "We had our come out together."

Felicity bit her thumb nail, her head bent and her hair hiding her face. Hazel felt a pang of sadness. Felicity had always been so well put together. So lovely.

"The queen was quite taken with you," Hazel continued, finding the silence in the room unbearable. "Do you remember now?"

Felicity looked up, her eyes focussing on something past Hazel. "Don't let them take us."

"Take you where?" Hazel asked, but at that moment the door opened and a fair haired man in his mid-thirties came in, followed by the nurse.

Hazel's breath caught in her throat. She'd seen this man two days ago when she'd had the vision on her way to Lady Ashburn's.

"You must be Felicity's friend," the man said with a kindly smile. "I'm Dr. Cadavy."

Hazel forced herself to nod and smile.

"We'll need to give Lady Felicity her medication. Perhaps you could wait outside? It won't take long."

"Of course." Hazel stood up and was glad her legs were steady under her. As she walked to the door, the nurse held up a bottle and sprayed something into the air.

"My apologies," the nurse said. "I was giving the bottle a test."

Hazel was about to tell her it was fine, when a metallic taste filled her mouth and she coughed.

"Excuse me," she hurried out of the room just as the tingling started in her forehead. Hazel ran down the stairs, nearly slipping in her haste as she reached the dark foyer and threw open the main door.

The tingling intensified. She'd never had an episode come so quickly.

The trees, she needed to hide in amongst the trees.

She barely registered Duncan's presence as he chased

after her.

"What's wrong?"

Hazel was afraid to answer. Her vision was already blurring and the taste of metal was so overpowering it affected her other senses.

She reached a wooded area behind the main Cravenwood building just as she lost her vision completely.

"I don't want to be here." She looked around at the little room with it's bare walls.

The doctor came to stand in front of her, a smile on his face but she didn't trust him. Not anymore.

"This is for your own good," he said. *"We all want what's best for you."*

The sunlight shone through the one small window, the panes casting cross shapes onto the bare floorboards. She wanted to stand in the sun.

"Don't worry," the man continued. *"If all goes well, you'll leave soon enough. Now take your medicine."*

She backed away but her shoulders hit the wall behind her. She didn't want to take the medicine. It tasted like tin and no matter how much water she drank she couldn't make it go away.

"Nurse," the doctor called out. *"You're needed in the violet room."*

A stern faced woman with jet black hair appeared...

CHAPTER TWENTY-NINE

Duncan caught up with Hazel just as the vision overtook her. She stood still, looking into the distance at something that wasn't there.

The vision lasted only moments, but as it finished she began to crumple toward the ground as though her legs were about to give out. Duncan grabbed her before she could fall, one arm catching her firmly around the waist. She was shaking all over as he pulled her against his chest, hoping his warmth would help.

"It's all right," he said, rubbing his free hand on her upper arm. "You're safe."

"I'm n-not," Hazel said, her teeth chattering as she tried to speak. "I'm not ok."

A rustling sound had Duncan glancing over his shoulder. It was probably nothing, just a small animal, but he was all too aware that they were only feet away from the back of Cravenwood and someone could stumble upon them at any time.

Knowing he needed to get Hazel away, Duncan half carried her further into the woods, finding a path that led to the ruins of a folly, overlooking the lake behind the

Ashburn estate. He set her down on a stone bench and sat next to her, keeping his arm around her. Her bonnet had been lost somewhere along the way and several strands of hair had escaped from the braided bun at the nape of her neck.

He moved close so her head rested her head against his shoulder. "You're safe now."

"I don't think I'll ever be safe again," she shivered.

"Can you talk about it?"

She took a deep breath, her eyes focused on the lake and for a moment Duncan wondered if she'd even heard him. Her skin was so pale as to have a faint bluish tinge.

"I saw Felicity," she said, her voice almost a whisper. "She's so afraid. She said they're going to take her away."

"She said that?"

Hazel nodded. "And then that horrid doctor came in and the nurse sprayed something in the air and there was a tinny taste to it and I swear it triggered the vision I had."

Duncan leaned in close, there was a faint smell of aether coming from her hair.

"I don't think Dr. Cadavy is trying to treat the visions, I think he's trying to find ways to bring them on."

"Then someone must have tipped him off about you," Duncan said, suddenly feeling like ants were crawling over his skin. "And I'm going to find out who it is."

"We have to get the girls out first," Hazel said. "They're the priority."

"You're the priority," Duncan muttered, but he could feel she was upset. They were going to have to talk to

Fletcher when they got back. They needed back-up and the sooner the better.

"I think I'm ok now," Hazel said, sitting up straight. She smoothed her hands over the front of her dress. A strand of hair caught in the gentle breeze and Duncan reached out, replacing it behind her ear. His fingers lingered on the smooth skin of her neck and he couldn't help himself. Her lips were so pink and inviting.

He pulled her toward him, a little sigh escaping her lips as they parted for his kiss. He let his hand move up her neck to touch the hair at the back of her head as his lips played over hers, tasting her. It was so much more satisfying than the peck on the lips they'd shared on the road earlier.

Her hand rested against his chest, grabbing onto the fabric of his shirt as he deepened the kiss. He'd only intended it to be a quick touch of the lips, but somehow he'd lost himself in her completely.

When he finally pulled away they were both breathing hard and Hazel had a dazed look in her eyes.

"I shouldn't have done that," Duncan started but Hazel rested a finger on his lips.

"I'm not letting you apologize again." She stood up and Duncan was relieved to see that some of her natural color had come back, whether from the fresh air or from the kiss he didn't know.

She turned about, looking at the ground. "Where's my bonnet?"

"I'm afraid we lost it back in the woods," Duncan said.

Hazel frowned. "We need to find it."

"I'll get you a new one."

"I can't return without it. What will people think?"

Duncan laughed. "Are you worried about your reputation?"

"Perhaps I'm worried about yours." She crouched down to look under the bench.

"Then I suppose we ought to marry then."

"Pardon?" Hazel looked up, her eyes round. "You can't be serious."

Duncan reflected for the barest of moments. He could easily laugh it off as a joke. But he didn't want to.

"Why not? We're courting after all."

"That wasn't the plan."

Duncan shrugged. He reached down, offering Hazel a hand to get back on her feet. "Plans change."

"I don't think-"

"Quite right." Duncan offered her his arm. "This isn't the time. We need to get back and speak with Fletcher."

Hazel opened her mouth to argue, but Duncan was distracted by something happening over her shoulder. There was construction happening on the far side of the lake.

"That's quite a wharf," Duncan said, squinting against the sun for a clearer look.

"Perhaps it has something to do with this evening's firework display."

"Perhaps," Duncan agreed, leading Hazel away from the lake and back toward the house. "Let's go have a chat with our friend Fletcher."

⚙○

Hazel had been fortunate to sneak into the Ashburn house through a side entrance used by the staff, thus saving herself the embarrassment of being seen arriving back in such disarray.

Duncan had gone looking for Fletcher and as she couldn't be seen meeting up with two unmarried men, Hazel stayed in her room to prepare for the ball that evening.

It also gave her time to recover from his proposal.

Surely he hadn't really meant they should marry? He was likely feeling guilty after the kiss they shared.And for carrying her through the woods.

Hazel felt her face flame as she remembered the way she'd held onto Duncan.

Fortunately, Ginny arrived and all thoughts shifted to the ball. The maid was beyond thrilled with the idea of having extra time to work on her hair.

"We'll do curls this time," Ginny said. "You've got such a pretty dress, it would be a shame not to."

The emerald green satin, courtesy of Madame M, was already laid out and Hazel had to agree, it was a stunning garment. The nicest she'd ever worn.

Not that she was interested in the ball. She was hoping the dancing would give her time to confer with Duncan and Fletcher. Hopefully they'd already called for reinforcements.

She waited patiently while Ginny completed her curls.

"What do you think of these for your hair, my lady?" Ginny held out a clutch of white lilies.

Hazel opened her mouth to say they were lovely, but

nothing came out. Her brain was working furiously as she remembered seeing the lilies outside Lilianne's door. Then she remembered the conversation she'd overheard between Mr. Banks and Lord Dennison.

The men you owe need to be paid and I'm afraid they're going to need something more than your word. Perhaps a lovely lily?

"My lady?"

Hazel realized Ginny was waiting for her answer. She forced a smile. "Yes, they're lovely. Let's get dressed, shall we?"

CHAPTER THIRTY

Duncan stood in the Ashburn ballroom, or what he assumed was the Ashburn ballroom. It was so covered in garlands of pink and white flowers and gold dipped candles that he couldn't be sure.

Several locals who'd had the poor taste to show up on time, wandered the room in their best clothes, wide eyed expressions of wonder on their faces.

"Ah to be so young and naive." Fletcher stopped next to Duncan, grinning at two white-clad young debutants who walked past them.

"Were you able to get a message out?" Duncan asked as they were once again alone.

Fletcher nodded. "I did, though it would be much better if we had an accurate time frame."

"We're working on it."

The house party guests slowly trickled in. Duncan saw Lady Cora enter with her husband on her arm. She was decked out in blue silk that Duncan knew would match her eyes exactly.

"She's still quite something, don't you think?" Fletcher asked.

"She is," Duncan agreed, because it was the truth, but he didn't feel any more towards her than he did any other attractive young lady.

With one possible exception.

Hazel walked into the ballroom in a gown of deep green silk. She stood out like a rare jewel and Duncan could see that Ellis had already spotted her.

Fortunately, she'd already spotted himself and Fletcher and was heading their way.

"We need to talk," she said. She'd taken out her fan and was waving it in such a way that the bottom half of her face was covered.

"We can't all go off together," Fletcher said, nodding as Lady Rosamund and Lady Carmella walked past. "The two of you confer and I'll catch up with at least one of you later."

Duncan offered Hazel his arm and they walked across the ballroom toward the balcony. He led her to the opposite end of the terrace. From here there was a clear view of the lake where the sun was only just starting to set.

"Fletcher has already sent to London for more agents," Duncan said when he was certain no one could hear them. "There's nothing to worry about."

"They're shipping the girls abroad, Hazel said, her voice cracking as she spoke. "It's a black market business and Mr. Banks is involved."

Duncan stilled. "How do you know this?"

"The night I broke into Mr. Banks' office I went through his books. It was clear he was up to some under-the-table business, but there was a page dedicated to flowers."

"Flowers?" Duncan repeated. "Why would anyone bother hiding flower shipments?"

"They wouldn't, because it isn't actually flowers. It's code for the girls' names."

Hazel went on to explain the plaques outside each room at Cravenwood and the veiled reference to Dennison's sister.

Duncan felt a sick feeling in his stomach but forced a smile as he waited for another couple to walk by them.

"Assuming someone is taking ladies from Cravenwood, to what possible purpose could they want?"

"Maybe they've reached the same conclusion as Dr. Sahni about our visions?" Hazel's hand twitched and she nearly dropped her fan. "Dr. Cadavy has obviously found a way to trigger them. Maybe he thinks the girls' visions will be of use."

"It will be all right," Duncan said. "We'll take care of it."

"What if we're too late?" Hazel asked. "We don't know when they're leaving or where they're going."

"That's why we're bringing in help." Duncan rested a hand on her shoulder. He could tell she was shaken. In truth, so was he. "You've done so well figuring all this out."

"I'll feel better about it once the girls are safe."

"Lady Hazel?" Carmella approached them on the terrace. "I've been looking all over for you. Lady Ashburn would like a word with you. Something to do with an article she'd like you to work on."

Duncan released her arm. "You go ahead. I'll speak with Fletcher."

She nodded and he could see her expression had softened. She trusted him.

If only he trusted himself.

A footman led Hazel to the yellow and gold drawing room overlooking the front lawn.

Hazel noted that their hostess looked impeccable in a gown of ruby silk that contrasted magnificently with the black hair piled high on top of her head.

"You wished to speak with me, my lady?" Hazel asked as the footman closed the door behind her.

"Do come in," Lady Ashburn sat on a yellow gold settee. "We have much to discuss."

Hazel took the seat across from her. She had the distinct impression she'd done something to upset her host.

"Is there anything wrong?" She asked. "I hope you know how much I appreciate the opportunity to attend your house party."

"And I've come to appreciate your presence," Lady Ashburn said, though her face showed no emotion. "My husband thought your presence would be worthwhile in attracting Mr. Walters, but I've come to the conclusion you're much more valuable than that."

Hazel frowned. "Would you like me to write an article about your house party? I'm sure Mr. Walters would be happy to run it."

Rather than answering, Lady Ashburn stood up and approached the mantle, picking up a silver knickknack.

"Always thinking about work." Lady Ashburn laughed, it was a high, brittle sound. "And who would have thought it, a girl like you, so poised, so confident. Not like other young ladies. But you've got a secret, don't you?"

A cold feeling came over Hazel, twisting her insides. Something was wrong. "I think perhaps I should go back to the ball. Mr. Walters—"

"Will be just fine." Lady Ashburn said in a soft cooing voice. "At least, he will in time."

Hazel backed up to the door but Lady Ashburn beat her to it. She held up the object she'd taken from the mantle and pushed down on a lever. The air filled with a metallic mist. Hazel's head began to swim.

"The one thing I've learned from all this, my lady, is that no young woman is indispensable. Not really."

Her vision blurred and Hazel reached out, grabbing for anything to anchor her before the vision completely overtook her.

CHAPTER THIRTY-ONE

"What on earth would anyone want with those girls specifically?" Fletcher frowned. For once he'd completely dispensed with the slightly amused mask he wore in public as he and Duncan stood in a corner of the card room. "I've heard of abducting well bred young women to sell overseas, but girls from an asylum? They'd make terrible companions."

"I don't think they're being abducted because they're girls," Duncan said, keeping his voice low. They took champagne glasses off the tray of a passing waiter but Duncan didn't touch his.

"Why am I getting the impression that there's more you need to tell me?"

As concisely as possible, Duncan explained Dr. Sahni's theories to Fletcher. When he finished his friend was frowning even harder.

"Visions that let you see inside someone else's head? The doctor is clearly as mad as her patients."

"Be that as it may, there's every reason to believe that someone abducting these girls believes her theories. For what it's worth, so do I."

"You're serious?"

"I have my reasons."

Never one to hold a filled glass for long, Fletcher drained his champagne flute. "I suppose that changes things. Fortunately, we have reinforcements coming. Agents should be on the way by morning."

"You don't think we need to act sooner?"

"How are they going to move these girls from Cravenwood? Did you see a line of carriages when you were there today?"

"No, I didn't," Duncan said. "I also didn't see a proper carriage house."

"Then I think we've still got some time."

"That's something," Duncan said, feeling calmer. There was little the three of them could do without more help.

"Attention please," Lord Ashburn's voice could be heard coming from the ballroom. "I'd like to direct everyone out to the terrace to see the surprise we've brought for you."

"We'd best go out," Fletcher said. "Wouldn't do to stand out in the crowd."

Duncan followed the crowd out to the terrace. He and Fletcher were tall enough not to need to push their way to the front of the crowd to get a good view. In the end, it didn't matter. There was absolutely no way to miss the gigantic balloons of the airship hanging over the lake. As the guests watched, gold and silver fireworks streamed from the bow of the ship.

"Lady Ashburn has certainly outdone herself," Lady Carmella said. She and Lady Rosamund stood nearby, the fireworks lighting their faces. "I heard she paid to have the ship stop over on her lake, just for this display."

Fletcher turned to Duncan, a wary look on his face.

"I think I might have been wrong when I said we had more time."

As the sky continued to light up around them, Duncan looked around the terrace, a terrifying thought creeping into his head.

"Where's Hazel?"

He looked out through the windows in the wheelhouse as the sky lit with sparks of silver and gold. Not much longer now. They'd get their payoff and the resistance would get their weapon and he'd return to Ireland, never having to set foot on English soil again...

Hazel opened her eyes, blinking several times. The darkness didn't abate.

The floor beneath her swayed gently and she realized with a creeping feeling that she was aboard a ship—likely the airship she'd seen in her vision.

She sat up, using her hands to feel around. There was a coarse blanket beneath her. She had no idea how long she'd been out, but didn't think it was that long. Her body was sore, but not as sore as it would have been if she'd been resting on that floor for hours. Hazel reached her hands out a little further to her right and touched muslin. A girl. She did the same to her left. Another girl. They must be laid out in a row.

Hazel crept forward on her hands and knees. At the

end of the blanket she touched a smooth floor. Reasoning that if there were a guard nearby, she'd see a light, Hazel let out a low whistle. The sound echoed back to her.

The cargo bay. That made sense because that's what she and the other girls were.

Not wanting to risk hurting anyone by accidentally stepping on them, Hazel moved around on her hands and knees until she reached a wall. Running her hand along the smooth surface, she took a few steps until she stubbed her slippered toes off a step. Thank heavens, she'd found the staircase. Her relief was short lived as she felt a rumble beneath her feet and her stomach sank. They were preparing to take off.

"Perhaps you should stay back," Fletcher said to Duncan as they watched the airship from the edge of the lake. "We don't know for certain she's on board. No need for both of us to take a risk."

"I'm going," Duncan said. "Besides, if she is on board with the other girls, you're going to need help."

"It was worth a try," Fletcher said, heading toward a small rowboat that had been dragged up on shore.

"You can always stay back," Duncan said, picking up the oars.

"And let you have all the fun? Never."

"Then you push us off, I'll row."

Duncan made good time across the lake. By the light of a mostly full moon he could see Fletcher's curious expression as he looked the airship up and down as they came upon it. His eyes rested on the bust of a winged woman on its bow.

"She's quite a beauty."

Duncan squinted at the figurehead. "That's the *Triumph*."

"Isn't that a navy ship?"

"She was recently decommissioned. Now she's available for rental to the highest bidder."

"You've been aboard?" Fletcher asked.

"Once."

"Once will have to be enough. You ready to climb?"

Duncan looked up at the boat towering above them. "We're going to scale the side of a ship?"

A rumbling sound filled the air. The ship was preparing to take off.

"Start climbing," Fletcher shouted over the noise and pointed at the anchor rope. Since Duncan was closer, he grabbed on and started hauling himself up. He didn't get more than a few feet when he felt the rope drag him and realized the anchor was being pulled up as part of take off preparations. He held on tight, glancing down to see Fletcher a few feet below him.

The moonlight couldn't hide the gray tinge to Fletcher's complexion.

"Are you afraid of heights?" Duncan shouted.

"Of course not!" Fletcher shouted back, but Duncan noted his friend kept his gaze straight up.

As the rope jerked, Duncan came level with the figurehead. He grabbed onto the torso and swung a leg around until he was on top. He looked to Fletcher and saw the frozen look of terror on his face.

Duncan leaned over, holding out his hand.

"I don't need help," Fletcher said, continuing to look ahead. He hesitated only a moment before launching himself forward and grabbing onto the wooden bust, his legs swinging out over the water until he managed to drag himself up next to Duncan. They climbed up over the figurehead, landing on the deck just as the ship rose out of the water.

"If we could avoid telling the ladies that I flailed around like a ragdoll, that would be most appreciated."

Duncan rolled his shoulder. "I don't believe I can promise that."

Fletcher ignored him, looking around the deck. "Which way?"

"I think we should go to the cargo area and work our way up."

CHAPTER THIRTY-TWO

Hazel made it to the top of the stairs with only the occasional stubbed toe. She pulled the handle, but the door didn't budge. She should have expected it to be locked, but she'd hoped since all the other girls seemed unconscious that perhaps no one would bother.

She took off her evening gloves, feeling the lock with her fingers. Perhaps she could force it with a hairpin.

A bump sounded on the other side of the door and Hazel froze, her heart hammering in her chest. She was already starting to back up when the door swung open and light flooded the doorway.

Having been in the dark so long, she couldn't fully make out the facial features of the two figures standing before her.

"Hazel?" She processed Duncan's voice at the same time she found herself pulled against a powerful chest, strong arms closing around her. "Are you all right?"

"Yes, I think so." Her voice was muffled by his neckcloth.

"Is it too much to hope you're alone down there?" Fletcher asked. Hazel had managed to take a step back, though Duncan hadn't completely released her, his arm still about her shoulders.

"No, I was in a row between two others but I can't tell how many of us are down there. It's pitch black."

Duncan's hand squeezed her shoulder and based on the hard set of his jaw she wasn't sure if the action was for her benefit or his own.

"Any others awake?" Fletcher continued.

"I don't think so. I assume they're all on Persephamine. I've heard that a strong enough dose will cause unconsciousness for several hours."

"Probably best that they sleep through this if they can." Fletcher ran a hand through his hair. Hazel had never seen him shaken. It made her stomach clench.

"Do you know who did this to you?" Duncan asked.

"Oh yes," Hazel narrowed her eyes. "And she won't be getting away with it."

"She?" Fletcher looked to Duncan. "Wasn't it the doctor?"

"Not on his own. Lady Ashburn is assisting him."

For a moment there was silence.

"Truly?" Fletcher finally spoke. They moved out into the hallway, under a gaslamp and Duncan released Hazel from his hold but still stood close by. "What could be her possible motivation?"

"Whatever it is, she'll pay," Duncan said. "That's for certain."

"It has to be money," Hazel said, looking up at Duncan. "Apparently this shipment is worth a lot."

"Shipment? Do you know where the ship is going?"

Hazel nodded. "Ireland."

"How do you know that?" Fletcher raised an eyebrow.

"I'm not sure you want to know," Hazel said.

"What would motivate Lady Ashburn to aid in the abduction of ladies?" Fletcher shook his head.

"What if they aren't as well off as they let on?" Duncan asked. "Lord Ashburn's family made their fortune in silver mining."

"Of course," Fletcher said, a gleam in his eye. "And the price of silver has dropped considerably since the navy stopped commissioning new aether engines."

"We can figure out motives later," Hazel said. "Right now we've got to figure out how to land this ship."

"She's not wrong," Fletcher said. "We need a plan."

"We'll have to enter the wheelhouse," Duncan said. "And force them to land."

"How?" Fletcher held out his hands. "We're going to charge in there weaponless?"

Hazel pressed two fingers against her temple. "I think we should start in the engine room."

"Where's that?" Fletcher asked, but Hazel was already heading down the hall.

"Do you know where you're going?" Fletcher called after her.

"This is the *Triumph*, isn't it?" Hazel called over her shoulder. "I did a tour of it for the *Daily*."

"Good thing you did," Fletcher said. "I've never paid attention beyond where the bar is."

Hazel tripped over the edge of her skirt. She grabbed the material about halfway down and pulled the fabric up a few inches off the floor.

"I wish I could have dressed as a boy," she muttered to herself as the door she'd been looking for came in sight. She led them into the communications room.

"This is incredible." Duncan looked up at the copper tubes that ran from floor to ceiling. "Is this an intra-ship communications system?"

"Yes," Fletcher said, clapping him on the back. "And you can drool over it later."

"There's also the ability to send and receive messages from external sources as well," Hazel said. "This is the hub for the entire ship."

"I'll work on a message," Fletcher said, "but we still need to find a way to force the ship to land."

"That's what this room is for." Hazel went to the door with a wheel at its center. She turned it clockwise before the door opened into a room covered in gold. She blinked hard as the light overwhelmed her eyes.

"This was on the tour?" Duncan followed her in, also squinting as his eyes adjusted.

"More or less." Hazel walked around the room, bunching her skirt to one side so her right hand was free. She ran it along the railing until she came to a stop at a series of levers.

"I don't think it's possible to run the ship from the engine room," Fletcher pointed out from the open doorway.

"No, but it might be possible to force a landing. And that's what we want, isn't it?"

"You can do that?" Fletcher asked.

"I think so."

Duncan looked up at the high ceiling, then back at Hazel. "Why is no one in here?"

"Captain Lancaster said there wasn't much to do on a short trek."

"What are you thinking?"

"The vents. If they malfunction, the engine will overheat and the ship will have to land."

"Or blow up," Fletcher said, coming to stand next to Hazel and examining the levers. "It's a good plan though."

"Actually, it was Captain Lancaster who explained it to me."

"Of course it was," Duncan said. "Are we certain this is the best option?"

Fletcher shrugged. "We're running out of time. At this point we can only assume the pilots would rather land the ship than die."

"I hope you're right," Duncan said.

Fletcher looked to Hazel. "Let's start opening vents."

CHAPTER THIRTY-THREE

Based on the acrid smell that filled the engine room, Duncan thought they'd likely pulled the correct levers.

"Now we have to make sure the boys in the wheelhouse know what's going on down here," Duncan said, closing the engine room door as they spilled into the communication room.

"Do you think the two of you could handle it?" Fletcher asked, tapping his knuckle against one of the copper tubes. "I'm going to use the coms system to get a message to surrounding areas."

"I could do it," Hazel said. "Lizzie at the office taught me to use the telegraph machine."

But Duncan shook his head. "You aren't being left alone. Not again."

"Not to mention there's every reason to believe once the bell goes off in the engine room, someone from above deck is going to try to check it out," Fletcher said. "And self-defense isn't part of your training."

"Not yet," Hazel said.

"Not ever," Duncan muttered.

"Be careful," Hazel said as she followed Duncan. She

caught Fletcher's wink before the door closed behind them.

"Aren't you worried about him?" Hazel asked as she followed Duncan down the hall.

"Fletcher knows what he's doing," Duncan said, taking her by the arm so that she walked at his side, matching his pace. His grip was firm, but not at all uncomfortable.

"Are we going to the bridge?" Hazel asked, picking her skirts up with her free hand again.

"Yes."

"Do you know the way?"

Duncan stopped under a gaslamp and turned to her. "I've been on board before as well."

"Really? Was it for a tour?"

He rested a finger on her lips. "It's a story for another time."

Duncan removed his finger, leaving her lips feeling oddly bereft but Hazel had no time to ponder her feelings. There'd be time when they got this ship landed.

They continued up a staircase and came out on a level with a viewing deck that had windows all along one wall. There were no lamps, but the moonlight streaming in lit the space enough for them to see their way along.

Duncan moved slowly, his back to the wall.

"There's no guard about," Hazel said. "I suppose a cargo of unconscious ladies is hardly a threat."

"I suppose." Duncan continued to inch his way forward. "Access to the wheelhouse is on this level."

"What's your plan?" Hazel asked, waiting while Duncan checked the hallway before holding the door open for her to follow. "We could set up a diversion of some sort, perhaps with a gaslamp and some—"

"Hazel?" Duncan cut her off. "There's no time. I'm going to go in and knock'em out."

"Knock'em out?" Hazel repeated.

"Surprise attack."

Her brows drew together in a frown as she observed Duncan's broad shoulders. She supposed he certainly had the build to knock a few men out, but she certainly didn't. "I don't think I know how to do that."

"You won't be. This is my specialty."

They reached a short staircase that led to a closed door. "That's the bridge?"

Duncan nodded.

"How many do you suppose are in there?"

"I'll guess four," Duncan said. "That's the minimum needed to fly the ship and set off the fireworks."

"Fireworks?"

"It happened while you were unconscious. It was Lady Ashburn's surprise."

"I'd beg to differ with that observation." Hazel thought back to the women in the cargo hold.

Duncan paused, pulling her into an alcove. He placed her so that she was behind him, her back to the wall. "Do you hear that?"

Hazel strained her ears. She could hear a bell. It was chiming every few seconds.

"I think it's safe to say they're aware of what's going on in the engine room."

Duncan put a finger to his lips and she heard the ringing get momentarily louder, then the sound of a door closing and footsteps. Someone had left the bridge.

As the steps got closer, Duncan put his foot out, causing the man to trip. Then Duncan jabbed his elbow into the man's upper back and with his fist gave him a swift jab to the left temple, causing him to sprawl on the floor, unconscious.

Hazel poked the incapacitated man with the toe of her slipper while Duncan crouched down, going through his pockets. The man didn't move.

"I would like to learn how to do that," she said.

"We'll discuss it," Duncan said, standing up with a pistol. "There's a closet just there. Help me move him."

Hazel took the feet and they dragged him across the hall and into a darkened closet.

"What if he wakes up?" Hazel asked.

"Give me your gloves," Duncan said.

Hazel pulled her elbow length gloves out of her sash and handed them over. Using her gloves and his cravat, Duncan had the man gagged and tied up in minutes. Considering the only light he had was from the hallway, Hazel was impressed.

"I'd like to learn how to do that too," she said.

"Later." He took her hand. "We've got to go."

The wheelhouse was the one area Hazel hadn't gotten a chance to visit on her tour. Duncan kept one hand on her upper arm to guide her up the stairs with him, and used the hand holding the pistol to open the door. Hazel saw windows that looked out on the blackest night. Three men manned the operations, the centerpiece of the space was a massive wood and brass wheel that steered the ship.

Counting the man they'd caught in the hall, there were four in total. Duncan had been correct.

The sound of a bell going off, combined with the chatter between the men as they tried to figure out why the bell was going off had covered the sound of their entry.

Duncan raised the hand holding the pistol straight in front of him and kept the hand holding Hazel's slightly behind him so that she had to shift to see around him.

Before Duncan could act, a barrel chested man sitting in front of the wheel glanced up and saw a reflection in the glass of the window.

"Who're you?" He turned around and stood up, nearly knocking over the stool as he held out his own pistol.

"The man who's here to tell you to land this ship."

The bell went off again and a blond haired man to the right kicked at the wall panel. "I can't figure it out, Cas."

"We're still losing altitude," the man to the left said. He was short and stout with a squat nose.

"Your ventilation system is broken," Duncan said to Cas, the barrel chested man. "So if you want to save this cargo, you'll need to turn back and land this ship."

"How did you get on board?" Cas asked, his face wreathed in suspicion.

"I was invited," Duncan said. "By Lady Ashburn."

The men looked at each other and Hazel held her breath to see if they bought his story.

"Why would she bring you around and not tell us?"

"Quality control," Duncan said. "And a good thing too. I don't believe her ladyship would want you to do anything to harm her cargo."

"What do you know about the cargo?" Cas' thick brows knitted together. "Why did you bring one up here?"

"I don't trust him," the blond said to Cas.

Hazel thought for a split second, then let go of Duncan's hand, taking a step back.

She burst into tears.

"What's wrong with her now?" Cas sounded frustrated.

"I woke up in the cargo hold," Hazel sniffed and pointed a shaking finger at Duncan. "And he was there with a pistol."

Though he kept an outward calm, Hazel could tell by the look in his eyes that Duncan wasn't pleased.

She'd gone off script.

"Good thinking, bringing her up here," the blond man said. "Wouldn't want her waking up the others."

"Right," Duncan said, his eyes never leaving Hazel. The bell chimed again. "But right now we need to land. As soon as possible."

"Are we close enough to go back?" Cas asked and the man on the left, the quiet one with greasy hair, looked at the map again.

"We should just make it so long as we continue to lose altitude at a consistent rate."

CHAPTER THIRTY-FOUR

Duncan tried to keep Hazel in his line of sight as they walked back down the hallway, Cas at his side, Hazel in front of him. Or, more accurately, Hazel in front of his pistol.

What was she playing at?

On the one hand, she'd found a way to keep his cover. On the other, she'd thrown herself right in the middle of a dangerous situation. Even now Cas' eye was roving over her figure in a way that made Duncan want to hit him between his two eyes.

They'd managed to land the ship, which completed part one of the mission. Now they needed to come up with a plan for getting out of there. With all the women.

As they passed the closet where Duncan had pulled the unconscious body of the man whose pistol he'd taken, Duncan thought he heard a shuffling noise, but he kept his eyes ahead and they were soon nearing the door leading down to the cargo area.

"Wonder where Todd went," Cas muttered to himself as they arrived at the door. Hazel glanced briefly in Duncan's direction. "It's not like him to run off."

"Probably got sidetracked," Duncan muttered.

But Cas had moved on, examining the broken lock on the door to the cargo area.

"Her ladyship never gave you a key?" Cas squinted, looking Duncan over again.

"She must have forgotten."

Cas squinted. "Or maybe you aren't who you say you are."

Realizing his cover was blown, Duncan shifted so that he was pointing his weapon at Cas.

"Hands up."

Cas smirked but slowly raised his hands. "If you're trying to steal the cargo, you'll be sorry. You have no idea who you're crossing."

"Actually, I think I do."

The floor under their feet shifted as the ship finished its descent and rocked in the water. Hazel fell forward, but before she could catch herself, Cas reached out, grabbing her, pulling out a knife and holding it at Hazel's neck.

"Drop the pistol unless you want to see me cut her pretty throat."

Certain his heart was about to beat out of his chest, Duncan bent forward, placing the pistol on the floor.

"Kick it this way."

Duncan caught a movement over Cas' right shoulder. His attention went back to Hazel. She remained still and Duncan knew she was trying to be strong, but her eyes gave her away.

He took a steadying breath. Hazel needed reassurance and he'd never been so scared of anything in his life.

Duncan kicked the pistol slightly to the right. It slid

past Cas.

"That wasn't well done of you." Cas frowned but he kept his eyes on Duncan, the knife steady at Hazel's neck.

"Must be nerves," Duncan said. "This is a bit outside my usual evening fare."

"Should've pegged you right away. Dressed like you are. You're no common criminal."

"No," Duncan agreed, "I'm not."

The sound of a shot being fired echoed in the corridor and Cas dropped to the floor, the knife clattering next to him.

Duncan went straight for Hazel, one arm pulling her to him while the other went to trace her neck,

"Are you all right?"

"I'm fine," her voice was slightly muffled and he realised she was pressed into his chest. He eased his hold a little.

Cas rolled on the floor a few feet away, howling while Fletcher stepped around him, pistol in hand.

"That was a lucky shot," Hazel said as Fletcher stopped in front of them.

"Nothing lucky about it," Fletcher said, puffing up. "I'm an excellent shot."

"And I'm grateful," Hazel said. "Now what are we going to do about the girls in the cargo hold?"

In the end, the plan was simple. Hazel went back to her spot on the floor and pretended to be unconscious while the cargo door opened and she heard several people enter.

"There'd better be a good explanation for this," Hazel heard Lady Ashburn's voice and the sound of footsteps echoing off the walls. They came to a stop momentarily and Hazel was sure she could feel Lady Ashburn's gaze boring into her. She forced herself to stay perfectly still, not even breathing.

"Probably a mechanical issue," Dr. Cadavy spoke next and Hazel felt as if her skin were crawling. "They'll be back up in no time."

Finally the voices faded as Lady Ashburn and Dr. Cadavey climbed the stairs. Hazel remained still until she heard the door at the top of the stairs close. She sat up and a light came on a moment later. It didn't take long for Hazel's eyes to adjust. Duncan and Fletcher came out from behind crates and hurried up the stairs, each carrying a chair they'd taken from the mess hall. They blocked the door as best they could and Hazel joined them.

"I don't think we'll have to wait long," Fletcher said. "My message should have gotten to all the magistrates within a ten mile radius."

"What if Lady Ashburn returns first?" Hazel asked.

Fletcher held up the pistol. "Then I'll be ready for her."

"Shhh." Duncan looked out the cargo hold. "Do you hear that?"

Hazel strained her eyes to see out the hold, but it was too dark. "What if it's more of Lady Ashburn's henchmen?"

"Only one way to find out." Fletcher turned the knob on the lantern, leaving them in darkness except for the moonlight coming in through the opening in the cargo hold.

As though the lack of light were heightening her other senses, Hazel heard footsteps on the gangplank. Soon there was a light shining from a series of lanterns.

"What's this then?" A shocked voice called out as an arc of light lit up the bodies of the women on the floor.

"Who's there?" Fletcher called.

"Lord Haliday," the haughty voice called back. "Magistrate."

The sound of several more sets of footsteps could be heard, more of Lord Haliday's men. Hazel knew soon the light from more lanterns would be upon them.

"All right Hazel," Fletcher said in a low voice. "You know what to do."

She took a deep breath and flew down the stairs, ripping the hem of her skirt as she nearly stumbled on the bottom step.

"My Lord," she said, coming to a stop in front of the magistrate. "Thank goodness you are here to rescue us."

"Rescue you?" Lord Haliday looked Hazel up and down. Then he took in the forms of the dozen women lying on the floor around him and all the color drained from his face. The men at his back looked at each other, then at Hazel.

"You've just stopped a kidnapping," Fletcher's voice joined them right before he entered the circle of the lantern's light. "My congratulations, my lord."

"Lord Fletcher?" Lord Haliday's bushy gray brows drew together. "Is that you?"

Hazel wondered where Duncan was. Probably waiting in the background, just in case things with Lord Haliday took a turn.

"Indeed, and it appears I'm just in time to witness your heroics."

"Heroics?" Lord Haliday waved his hands ineffectually. "Just doing my duty."

"And so modest." Fletcher looked around at the dozen or so women still resting in the cargo area and then at the men at Lord Haliday's back. "We'll need to find a place for the ladies to recover but first there are some people you'll need to take into custody."

"You know who's responsible for this?" Lord Haliday straightened.

"Lady Ashburn," Hazel said. "And Dr. Cadavy. They're on the bridge."

"Are you certain?" Lord Haliday frowned. "Lady Ashburn is a peer."

"As is Lady Hazel," Lord Fletcher said. "And most of the ladies here."

Lord Haliday shone the light around the cargo hold again, taking in the careful line of ladies on the floor.

"I'll get more men."

CHAPTER THIRTY-FIVE

Duncan spotted Meri sitting near the fire in the card room at Burke's Club. He tipped his glass at Duncan as he sat down.

"Nice work," Meri said. "I heard you're up for a knighthood."

"I think that's an exaggeration."

A footman came by and Duncan ordered a brandy. He'd come to see his friend after learning Meri had been in the room during the interrogations of the Ashburns.

"It appears Lord Ashburn knew nothing of the plan," Meri said after the footman delivered the drink. "Or at least nothing of any real significance."

"How is that possible?" Duncan asked. "They were married."

"He suspected she had a plan to help the mine because there was a steady stream of money coming in, but he assumed she was seeking out investors, not selling ladies."

Duncan shook his head. "How is the questioning of Lady Ashburn going?"

Meri grimaced. "Good and bad. She's been most forthcoming with what she knows, but the information she has isn't as fruitful as we'd like. She knew the buyer for the women was in Ireland, but not what his plan was for them."

"Hazel believes the buyer wanted them for their abilities."

"And do you believe that?" Meri asked, sipping his gin. "Ladies who can see inside other people's heads? It seems impossible."

"You were speaking to Fletcher then?"

Meri nodded. "I have to say, he seemed more than a little convinced by your theory."

"It isn't a theory, I've seen the evidence with my own eyes."

"Then I won't question you again."

Duncan tipped his glass toward his friend. "What about Dr. Cadavy? Has he been found?" The doctor had thrown himself overboard rather than face arrest.

"No," Meri shook his head. "The plan is to drag the lake."

"Do you think the Amer-Irish are behind it?"

"It fits their style. Several players, none of them knowing too much."

"It was a close call though," Duncan said, remembering how he'd almost lost Hazel. "I wouldn't want to repeat it."

"You shouldn't have to," Meri said, finishing his drink. "That's why I'm hoping to take my leave in Ireland. Ferret out this uprising once and for all."

"You'll go with Adelia?" Duncan asked.

Meri nodded. "Her company is doing a tour and it will provide an excellent cover."

"Good luck," Duncan said, sipping his brandy. "I'll be glad to have some peace for a while. It will give me time to see my mother and sister."

"And your father?"

"No change."

"I'm sorry to hear it."

"Thank you." Duncan stared into the fire.

"How's business?"

"By all accounts we're booming," Duncan said. "The shipping has increased by almost twenty percent."

"And the paper?"

Duncan frowned. "*The Daily* continues to thrive despite my efforts as publisher."

Meri cleared his throat. "There's one other thing you'll need to address."

"What's that?"

"Lady Hazel."

"Our courtship you mean?"

Meri leaned forward, dropping his voice. "It seems that Lady Rosamund has noted repeatedly that Lady Hazel spent a great deal of time alone in your company at the house party."

"That woman is a viper."

"Then there's the excursion on *The Triumph*," Meri continued. "Her attempted kidnapping has been in all the papers and you were present there as well."

"That was hardly her fault."

"Still, her reputation is a little worse for wear."

"Just hers?"

A smile tugged at Meri's lips. "Presumably yours as well, though I imagine, like most gentlemen, you can survive the hit."

"Undoubtedly, but I don't like to leave Hazel in such straits. Not after everything she did to help us."

"You could always propose," Meri said. "After all, what more could you want in a partner?"

"Perhaps," Duncan said. "But what can I offer her? I am fairly certain that all she wants is the freedom to work at the paper."

Meri grinned. "I think you've got your answer."

Duncan took his leave of Meri and walked back home. It was a cloudy day, but the fog wasn't thick enough that he felt he needed a mask, not when he only had a few blocks until he was home.

His thoughts wandered to Hazel. They hadn't spoken since arriving back in London, three days ago. Which meant they hadn't been able to follow up on the conversation they'd had while overlooking the lake. He'd meant it when he'd said he wanted to marry her. She was intelligent, she made him laugh and of course she was beautiful.

But more than that, he was better when he was with her. She complimented him in ways he'd never thought a woman could.

He just needed to convince Hazel marriage was best for her as well.

Arriving at his house, Duncan climbed the steps and walked into the hallway to find the house in upheaval with servants running back and forth. Even Briggs was hurrying up the main staircase.

"What's going on?" Duncan asked as a maid rushed

past.

"Begging your pardon sir." She crouched into a hurried curtsy. "It's your father."

Duncan didn't wait for an explanation. He ran up the stairs, taking them two at a time and didn't slow until he reached the corridor with his father's room. He heard muffled voices inside but he saw Flora standing in the hallway. Her eyes were wide, but clear.

"What is it?" Duncan asked, bracing himself as he touched his sister's arm.

"It's father. He's awake."

Duncan went to the door of the room, taking in the scene before him. His mother kneeling next to the bed, tears in her eyes, Dr. Sahni standing across from her, on the other side of the bed, making notes. He knew his mother had planned to consult with the doctor, but he hadn't expected to see her here with his father.

And there, in the middle of the bed was his father, eyes blinking slowly.

Duncan went to stand at the foot of the bed.

"Father?" His voice cracked on the word.

Charles' lips moved, but nothing came out.

"Come closer," Dr. Sahni said, stepping back. "He hasn't spoken in so long, his voice is hoarse."

Duncan hesitated only a moment before going to the bed and dropping to his knees like his mother had done.

His father's eyes followed his movement and Duncan saw he was trying to speak again. He moved in close, hoping to hear something.

"It's... it's... good... to see you."

The sound of Penny moving around her room woke Hazel from a deep sleep. She forced her eyes open, noticing the sunlight streaming in at an odd angle for morning.

"What time is it?" Hazel asked, sitting up.

"Just gone noon," Penny said.

Hazel threw back the covers. "Why didn't you wake me?"

"You were nearly kidnapped," Penny said. "And you've spent the past two days being interviewed by officers of the Crown. Pardon me for thinking you could use a lie in."

"I planned to go back to the office today," Hazel said, getting to her feet. "I have a story to write."

"I think you are the story." Penny nodded at a stack of papers on the dressing table. "Those are interview requests."

"For me?"

"Well they certainly aren't for me."

Hazel grabbed the papers and leafed through them. The notes came from as far away as Cardiff.

"Why would anyone want to interview me?"

"Why indeed?" Penny took a day dress out of the wardrobe and laid it out. Hazel noticed it was one of Madam M's creations and not her usual gray dress for the office. "You were only in the middle of the most interesting event since the end of the war."

Hazel wrinkled her nose. "I don't really care for being the story."

"You'd best adjust to it."

Hazel dropped the papers back on her dressing table. "I think I'd rather keep my head down and go back to work."

"That will have to wait until tomorrow," Penny said. "Your mother has requested your presence in the drawing room this afternoon. It's her usual day for visitors."

"And she wants to show me off?"

"It's quite the turnaround, isn't it?"

Hazel pursed her lips. "I'd best get dressed."

She let Penny fix her hair into a braided crown but refused to let her pin in any of the many flowers that had been sent to her in the last two days.

"I don't want to be too fussy," she said, standing up and looking at herself in the mirror. She looked tired despite the sleep, but the green day dress brought out her eyes and gave her a healthier glow than she felt.

Lady Winchester and Lilith were already in the drawing room when Hazel came down the stairs, but fortunately she'd arrived before any of the afternoon guests.

"What are we to do?" Lady Winchester was pacing. "We can't just ignore the rumors."

"What rumors?" Hazel asked. She noticed the trays already laid out with cakes and sandwiches and her stomach rumbled—a reminder she'd yet to eat. She picked up a plate and piled on a slice of sponge cake and two sandwiches which she planned to eat before any guests arrived. She perched on one of the sofas.

"The rumors about you and Mr. Walters," Lilith said.

"Pardon?" Hazel said around a mouthful of cake.

"Your behavior has not gone unnoticed," Lady Winchester pulled on the edges of her gloves as she paced.

"You were alone with two gentlemen for several hours."

"They came to my rescue," Hazel said. "Otherwise who knows what would have happened to us?"

"Likely sold off to rich men throughout Europe," Lilith said, coming to sit next to her on the sofa. "We'd never have seen you again."

The sponge cake weighed heavily in Hazel's stomach and she set her plate down on the coffee table. She'd had a brief conversation with Duncan and Lord Fletcher while on the boat and, to preserve the anonymity of the Agency, had agreed on a cover story. Hazel would tell everyone she'd been rescued by Duncan and Fletcher after they'd noticed she'd gone missing. Which was the truth. They'd opted to leave out the motivation for the kidnapping, not wanting it to get around that the ladies who were abducted all suffered from aether fever visions.

For which Hazel was immensely grateful.

"Surely I can't be held responsible for being rescued?" Hazel asked. "Shouldn't we be grateful?"

Her mother pursed her lips and stopped pacing. "If only you were engaged to Mr. Walters instead of merely courting him."

Hazel's stomach flipped and she was glad she hadn't gotten a chance to eat much yet.

"Mr. Walters has already done me a great service. We will not be pressing him to propose."

Lady Winchester dropped into one of the wingback chairs, giving Hazel a pleading look. "Of course I'm grateful for your safe return—we're all grateful—but it has put you in a difficult situation, Hazel. I'm certain Mr. Walters will make an offer without your father getting involved, and when he does you must say yes."

"Surely it isn't necessary?" Hazel wondered how her mother and sister would react if they knew he'd already proposed. She was glad they didn't know. Duncan hadn't meant it, not really. And she wasn't the sort of lady to force a man's hand.

Besides, she didn't want to give up her freedom.

Though when she thought of choosing between Duncan and the paper she found that her heart constricted a little. It wasn't as easy a decision as she'd thought.

What decision? Hazel gave herself a mental shake. Duncan hadn't properly proposed and he wasn't likely to.

CHAPTER THIRTY-SIX

Duncan paced back and forth in Lord Winchester's study. He'd just had a most enlightening conversation with the man and now awaited Hazel's arrival.

She walked into the room, closing the door behind her. Duncan stood up and waited for her to take a seat in the chair across from him.

He noted that she did not smile.

"You're looking well," he said, sitting back down on the settee. He hated the stilted way his voice sounded, as though he was greeting a stranger.

"As do you," Hazel said. He noticed that Hazel looked toward the window or at the bookshelves, but not at him.

He searched for something to say, something that would put them both at ease, but it was Hazel who broke the silence.

"I know why you're here," she said.

"Do you?" Duncan asked.

She folded her hands in her lap. "Our excursion has had some unintended consequences."

"Yes," Duncan agreed. "I've heard the rumors."

"They're ridiculous. There's no reason for you to offer

for me."

"Of course there isn't," Duncan said and Hazel finally looked his way. He watched her face, seeing surprise and a touch of disappointment that she covered immediately. His heart lifted.

"You aren't here to propose then?"

Duncan stood up. He needed to move.

"You can be a very vexing woman."

"I know," Hazel agreed.

"What I actually came here to do was to ask your opinion on something to do with the paper."

"Really?" She straightened up in her chair. "What did you want to discuss?"

"The editor's position."

Hazel frowned. "That's your job."

"I think you know I only ever planned to take over temporarily," Duncan said. "Just until I could find a replacement for my father."

"You're leaving then?" Hazel looked down at her hands. "Going back out to sea?"

Duncan never thought he'd be excited to see sadness cross Hazel's features. Would she really miss him if he left?

"No one could ever replace your father," Hazel said, still not looking up at him.

"But you haven't heard who I have in mind."

"You have a list?"

"No, not a list. Just one name."

"And whose name is that?"

Duncan walked back to his seat and settled across from her. "Hazel."

"Yes?" She finally looked up, a pained expression in her eyes and his heart thudded painfully in his chest.

"The name on my list is yours."

She blinked. Twice. Her eyes grew wide.

"You can't be serious."

"Why not? You are the most qualified person I can think of."

"But... I'm a woman."

"I had noticed."

She stood up, pacing. "Women don't run newspapers."

"Until now."

She shook her head. "My mother will have a fit."

"Probably."

"What will people say? It'll be such a scandal."

"Scandals sell papers."

"Perhaps, but my mother will never allow it. Not while I'm living under her roof."

"Well, we could address that as well."

She took a step back, startled. "You did come here to propose."

"No, I proposed to you that day at the lake," Duncan said. "Now I'm waiting for your answer."

"You were serious?"

"Why on earth wouldn't I be?"

Hazel thought for a moment. "Is it to save my reputation?"

"You must know I don't care what the *ton* thinks."

Duncan watched Hazel sit down again, this time next to him on the settee. Her brows drawn together in a frown.

"Is marrying me such a terrible thought?" He asked.

Hazel bit the inside of her cheek. "To be clear, you're proposing marriage so that I will remain at work."

Duncan took her hand. "It's one reason."

"There are others?" Hazel asked.

"Many." Duncan reached into his pocket with his free hand and pulled out a ring box. "Now, what's your answer?"

Madam M had outdone herself.

Not only had she repaired the emerald green dress that she'd worn to the Ashburn ball, she'd done it in less than a week.

"I'd like to meet this Madame M." Penny stood back, admiring the dress. "And she's absolutely right about keeping you in greens. It sets off your eyes."

"Almost makes the red hair tolerable," Hazel said, picking up her fan. The emerald stone in her engagement ring caught the light from the gas lamp in her room and she admired it once again.

Apparently Madame M wasn't the only one who thought green suited her.

The most remarkable thing was that Duncan had bought the ring the same night she'd been spying in King's Pawn Shop.

He claimed to have gotten it on a whim.

"I suppose I should get downstairs before my mother comes up here and drags me down," Hazel said, giving herself time for one last look in the mirror.

"There's every possibility of that happening."

Hazel went down the stairs into the foyer and found

that Duncan was the only one there. He stood in his black evening jacket and crisp white shirt. Hazel felt a squeezing in her chest. All that was hers.

"And here I was thinking we were in for another boring evening," Duncan said with a grin. "You look beautiful."

Hazel felt her face grow hot and knew she was blushing. She cleared her throat. "It's the dress."

"I think it's a lot more than the dress—" Duncan started but he was cut off as they were joined by their mothers.

"The ballroom is absolutely divine," Mrs. Walters said. "Duncan, you must go look."

"Guests will be arriving any moment, Mama," Duncan said. "I think I should stay here."

"Your sister Flora did an excellent job on the flowers," Lady Winchester said. "She's a charming young lady."

"Speaking of which, where is she?" Duncan asked. As though hearing her name, Flora came out of the ballroom, followed by Lilith.

"We were just making certain that everything was exactly as it should be," Flora said. She wore a dress of lemon yellow that contrasted beautifully with her dark hair. But the most notable change, at least as far as Hazel was concerned, was how alert and aware she was.

Evidently, since she'd become a patient of Dr. Sahni, her old personality had come back.

"And is it all as it should be?" Duncan asked.

"Of course," Lilith said, though there was a crease between her brows. "Where's Papa?"

"I imagine he's in the study," Hazel said. "Let me go

get him."

Hazel hurried up the stairs, grateful to get one more moment of peace all to herself before she walked into the ballroom to announce the decision that would forever change her life.

She tapped on the study door and peeked inside. "Papa? It's time to join us downstairs."

"Oh? Is it indeed?" Her father stood up, leaving the book he'd been poring over on the desk.

"Don't forget to straighten your cravat," Hazel said.

"I can hardly believe it's time for your engagement ball," Lord Winchester said, joining Hazel in the doorway.

"Mama would argue that it's long overdue."

Her father sighed. "I have been spoiled having you here for so many years. You've been an intelligent, charming companion and you've always kept me on my feet."

Hazel felt her chest constrict. Was she actually considering walking away from her father's house?

"But when your Mr. Walters told me of his intention to let you keep working at the paper, I knew he was the one."

"You spoke of that?" Hazel frowned.

"It was part of the marriage contract," her father took off his spectacles and cleaned them on the end of his waistcoat. "He didn't want there to be any misunderstanding on my part."

Hazel took her father's arm and allowed him to lead her back down the stairs.

"And you were in agreement?"

Lord Winchester stopped on the landing and looked

at her. "Of course. I couldn't have possibly let you go for anything less."

Duncan watched while Hazel made her rounds in the ballroom. After having greeted everyone at the door, they'd been permitted to separate and greet their friends in the ballroom before the dancing commenced.

He spied Lord Fletcher and was pleasantly surprised to find him on his own. Though, as usual he already had a drink in his hand.

"Congratulations on your most recent acquisition," Fletcher said, raising his glass.

"Thank you," Duncan said. "I think she'll make an excellent editor."

"That too."

Watching his friend, Duncan noted a tenseness in his features despite the attempts at an easy-going smile.

"Everything well with the Agency?" Duncan asked, dropping his voice.

"Why do you ask?"

Duncan glanced around the ballroom. He still had a few minutes before the dancing started.

"What else would be stressing you out?"

"I had a meeting with Meri," Fletcher said. "His leave has been revoked. He can no longer accompany Miss Dumont on her tour of Ireland."

"What does that mean for the mission?"

Fletcher finished his drink and set the glass down on the tray of a passing waiter.

"Well, since I have no immediate plans, it means I get

to go to Ireland."

"With Adelia?"

"As her companion, yes."

Duncan cleared his throat. "When do you leave?"

"Within the week."

"She's a charming lady."

Fletcher raised an eyebrow. "I'm glad that's been your experience."

"It hasn't been yours?"

Before Fletcher could answer, a footman came over to tell Duncan it was time to start the dancing. He went in search of Hazel and found her across the room, speaking with her friends Lady Beth and Miss Eloise.

"I believe we are expected on the dance floor," Duncan told her.

She nodded and took his hand, allowing him to lead the way. When they didn't line up for a country dance, she frowned at him.

"What's the first dance?"

Duncan grinned. "A waltz."

She did not return his smile. "We're to open the dancing with a waltz?"

"Relax," he said as the music started. "I've got you."

She rested her hand on his shoulder as the string quartet began to play its first chords. "You're asking me to place an awful lot of trust in you."

"I think it's only fair. Considering I've put so much into you."

Her face broke into a smile as their feet started to move. "Fair enough, Mr. Walters. Fair enough."

Acknowledgements

I am very grateful to Kelley Power and Lauralana Dunne for beta reading this work at various stages and giving wonderfully constructive feedback. Also thanks to my editor on this project AJ Ryan for being much more careful with names and commas than I ever could be.

Thanks to Matthew LeDrew for layout and technical support and to Ellen Curtis for cover design.

As always I'd like to think my awesome husband Mike for being my last line of defense copy editor and generally supportive partner.

Also from Amanda Labonté

HEED THE CALL

After a heated fight at sea between twins Ben and Alex, Ben vanishes from their boat without a sound or even a ripple in the water. Unwavering in his dedication to find his brother, Alex begins the adventure of a lifetime armed only with the help of a local girl named Meg and his own mysterious musical abilities… the key to which, and to the mysteries that surround him, may be tied to the alluring song of the dangerous girl he finds among the ocean's frothing waves.

#1 OCCULT BESTSELLER!

College freshmen Liesel Andrews spends her days studying pre-med and her nights stitching up werewolf bites.

Buy the book that Ali House raves "gives the pre-existing mythology of vampires some new blood!"

Photo by Joy K. Gallant

ABOUT THE AUTHOR

Amanda Labonté is a bestselling author living in St. John's, Newfoundland, where she gets much of the inspiration for the characters and places about which she writes. Though she knew she wanted to be a writer since the eighth grade, it was many years before she finally walked into a creative writing class and found a new home.

Amanda is the co-owner of an educational business and a mother of two, and as such she spends much of her day with kids of all ages. They give her some of the best reading recommendations.

She has written six novels: *Call of the Sea, Drawn to the Tides, Return to the Depths, Supernatural Causes* Volumes 1 & 2, and, *Lady of Vision*, all of which are available through Engen Books.